# THE
# GOOD
# NEIGHBOUR

## BOOKS BY ALISON JAMES

*The School Friend*
*The Man She Married*
*Her Sister's Child*
*The Guilty Wife*
*The New Couple*
*The Woman in Carriage 3*
*The House Guest*
*Just the Nicest Family*

DETECTIVE RACHEL PRINCE SERIES

*1. Lola is Missing*
*2. Now She's Gone*
*3. Perfect Girls*

# THE GOOD NEIGHBOUR

## ALISON JAMES

bookouture

Published by Bookouture in 2025

An imprint of Storyfire Ltd.
Carmelite House
50 Victoria Embankment
London EC4Y 0DZ

www.bookouture.com

The authorised representative in the EEA is Hachette Ireland
8 Castlecourt Centre
Dublin 15 D15 XTP3
Ireland
(email: info@hbgi.ie)

Copyright © Alison James, 2025

Alison James has asserted her right to be identified as the author of this work.

All rights reserved. No part of this publication may be reproduced, stored in any retrieval system, or transmitted, in any form or by any means, electronic, mechanical, photocopying, recording or otherwise, without the prior written permission of the publishers.

ISBN: 978-1-80550-283-8
eBook ISBN: 978-1-80550-282-1

This book is a work of fiction. Names, characters, businesses, organizations, places and events other than those clearly in the public domain, are either the product of the author's imagination or are used fictitiously. Any resemblance to actual persons, living or dead, events or locales is entirely coincidental.

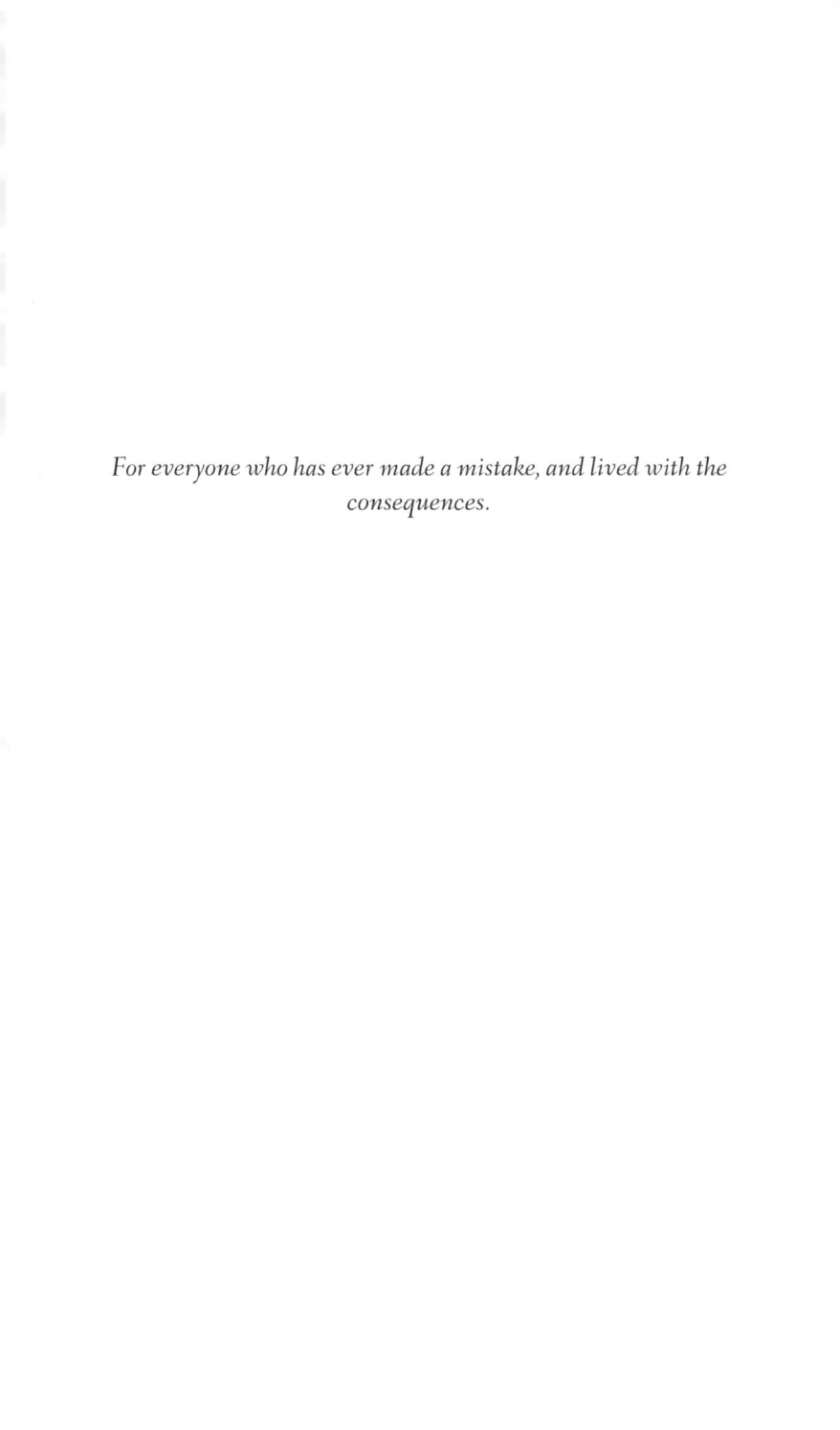

*For everyone who has ever made a mistake, and lived with the consequences.*

# PROLOGUE

The estate agent was waiting for me on the front steps of the building, clipboard in hand.

'Hi... Ms Pearson? I'm Tom. Tom Burridge. Good to meet you.'

He held out his hand to shake mine. He was a head taller than me, with well-cut golden-brown hair and dimples on either side of his mouth when he smiled. A nice face, I thought. Not Hollywood handsome, but cute. And quite young, but then most of them seemed to be young now that I had reached the age of thirty-four.

He started straight into the slick sales patter. Perhaps he needed to offload this flat to hit some sort of sales target. He needn't have tried so hard. Before I had even set foot in the communal entrance hall – which turned out to be clean and well maintained – I had already decided to buy it.

He waved his clipboard in the direction of the staircase. 'Shall we go up?'

As I looked around the flat he gave me the spiel about room sizes and natural light, and the inevitable 'opportunity to place your own stamp on it'. There was an open-plan kitchen and living space as was now the norm in flat conversions, a generous bedroom and a well-fitted shower room. Yes, the interior was a little scruffy and drab, but I wasn't worried about that. It was the block itself that was my primary concern. It felt solid and safe compared to all the other places I had viewed. The ground and first floors had one flat on either side of the central staircase, but the flat for sale was the only one on the top floor, its entrance at the end of the landing and some distance from the stairs. This made it feel separate, tucked away, which I liked. Being safe and secure was more important to me than anything else.

'This is a nice street. And a very popular location,' Tom added. 'Due to its proximity to St Anselm's Hospital.'

'Yes, I know. That's where I'm going to be working.' I was looking out of the living room window as I spoke and from there I could just about view the roofs of the hospital complex. It was a light room that included a kitchen and plenty of space for a dining table.

'So, what do you think?' he asked as he led me back down the stairs from the top floor. 'Only there's already been plenty of interest.'

'I'm going to make an offer,' I said firmly, taking in first the surprise then the pleasure that crossed his face. 'This is exactly what I've been looking for.'

'It does give you a bigger square footage than a lot of comparable flats on the market,' he agreed.

'It's not the size that interests me, it's the security. And the privacy.'

Tom nodded. 'Well yes, I know our vendor's been happy here. Nice quiet block and no issues with the neighbours.'

Ah yes, the neighbours. There was nothing about my lifestyle they could possibly object to, but what would they think if they knew the truth? Not that there would be any reason for them to guess. But there were many things about my past life that I needed to hide. A lot of decisions I regretted, some terrible mistakes made.

And one very big secret to keep.

# PART ONE

# ONE

## BRYONY

Now

Moving day was hellishly stressful. But then moving days always are, aren't they?

The first problem was with the keys. I had arranged to collect them from the agent's offices on Friday afternoon, once the purchase funds had been transferred. I was met by the handsome Tom, looking distinctly sheepish.

'Bryony, really sorry, but it looks like we've messed up.'

My heart sank.

'It says in the paperwork you're to get both sets of keys – ours and the vendor's – but at the moment I've only got one. The vendor's gone abroad and forgotten to hand theirs in. Which as you know, they're strictly speaking required to do on completion.'

'But you do have a set here?' My heart was pounding. What if I couldn't get into the property at all?

'Yes, like I said you can have our copies.' He rummaged in the filing cabinet and pulled out an envelope containing a bunch of three keys. 'That's the building front door plus your Yale and your mortice.'

'That's fine,' I said, weak with relief. 'As long as I can get access with all my stuff.'

'Apologies.' Again, the charming, dimpled smile. He really was very attractive, but probably a decade my junior. 'I hope you're very happy in your new home. And you have my absolute word of honour that I'll chase down the other set as soon as I can and drop them round to you. Promise.'

The second problem was the means of transport. I had booked a removal firm to take my stuff over to the flat on Saturday morning. Or I thought I had, but there was some mix up with the booking and the van never showed up. After a round of frantic phone calls, the original company called in a favour from one of their competitors and a van and two men eventually showed up, albeit three hours later than planned. And of course it poured with rain, nonstop. As I said, moving never goes smoothly.

Fortunately, I didn't have very much stuff, because I was renting a furnished flat before I went away. Just four suitcases of clothes and shoes, and a few boxes of books, photographs and bits of china which had been in my father and stepmother's garage for the past five years. The only piece of furniture I already owned was also there: my grandmother's old rosewood bureau.

As soon as exchange of contracts had taken place, I'd ordered a double bed and a sofa and a dining table and chairs and had them delivered to a storage unit I'd rented for the purpose. I borrowed my father's car to move my boxes from his garage to the unit in preparation for the move. In the intervening weeks I'd also bought various household essentials to add to this growing collection of worldly goods: a couple of lamps, a vacuum cleaner, a kitchen bin, a bedside cabinet, saucepans and cutlery. A coffee machine and a kettle.

The removal men were predictably grumpy about it being a top-floor flat with no lift, and started dropping heavy hints about needing cups of tea. I had the kettles and mugs unpacked at this point, but it hadn't occurred to me to provide tea bags, milk and biscuits.

'I'll just run over the road to Tesco Metro,' I told the men as they set to work assembling the bed frame. I pulled on my raincoat and grabbed my phone, purse and keys. 'Kettle will be on as soon as I'm back, I promise.'

I headed down the communal stairs to the ground floor. Like the entrance hall they were too brightly lit, giving the whole building a sterile, rather clinical feel. Some people would have found it off-putting but I didn't mind it. From the moment I first entered it, the place made me feel safe. A door opened on the first-floor landing as I passed it, and an elderly woman with a sour expression stepped out.

'Are those your removal men?' she demanded.

'Yes... hi. I'm moving in. I'm Bryony. Bryony Pearson.'

I held out my hand but it was ignored, and no name given in return. 'They keep slamming the front door. And they've tracked mud all the way up these stairs,' the woman complained.

'Yes, sorry about that, only it's so wet outside. As soon as it's dried, I'll hoover it up, don't worry.'

She made a huffing noise and retreated into her flat, but only once she'd given me a hard stare. I let the front door of the building close as quietly as I could, pulled up the hood of my raincoat and darted out into the rain. Not wanting to wait for the traffic light at the junction to change, I decided to take advantage of a gap in the traffic. I stepped out into what I perceived to be empty space, but my hood was blocking my peripheral vision. I failed to see a lorry careering towards me, and too late I heard tyres skidding over the rain-drenched tarmac, and brakes squealing.

In that split second as I turned my head to the left, I saw my life about to come to an end as three thousand kilos of metal slammed towards my defenceless body.

And then something miraculous happened.

Seemingly from nowhere an arm flung itself across my chest. It heaved me backwards, knocking me to the kerb, winded but alive. The lorry thundered past mere inches away, its horn blaring angrily.

I turned, barely able to catch my breath, and looked at my rescuer. It was a man, youngish, wearing a black trucker cap with the hood of his rain-soaked sweatshirt pulled up over it. I couldn't see much of his face in the early evening gloom, but I caught a glimpse of some neck tattoos.

'My God. Thank you!' I gasped. 'Thank you so much. You've just saved my life.'

'You should have looked, yeah?' He spoke with the local South London accent.

'I know. You're right. I was rushing. I'm in the middle of moving into one of the flats in Kenley Court.' I pointed, then reached down and felt my ankle, which throbbed from being smashed against the kerb.

'Your leg all right?'

'I'm pretty sure it's not fractured. Probably just some bruising.'

I saw him narrow his eyes slightly. 'You a doctor, innit?'

'Not exactly. But I am a radiographer, so I know a bit about fractures.' I straightened up. 'Anyway, look... I feel I should repay you somehow.'

I reached for my purse, but he put a hand on my wrist. 'I don't need your money,' he said irritably.

'Sorry, I didn't mean to offend you... I thought perhaps you might want to buy yourself a drink on me, that's all.' I was relieved that he didn't want the cash. The two twenty-pound notes I had on me were allocated to tipping the removal team. 'Thank you again though.'

He nodded, the rain streaming off the brim of his cap. He wasn't wearing waterproof clothing and his zip-up hoodie and nylon track pants were soaked through. 'Can I at least offer you a hot drink? I was just heading to Tesco to buy tea and milk.'

If I was about to make cups of tea for the two removal men, there was no reason I couldn't add one more.

'Yeah, sound.' He shrugged. 'Don't drink hot drinks though.' He pronounced it 'dough'.

'I'll get some soft drinks then.'

'Want me to come with you?'

'No, it's fine. Believe it or not, I do know how to cross the road on my own.' I smiled, to show this wasn't meant to be waspish. 'Wait here.'

I returned five minutes later armed with cans of Coke and lemonade, tea bags, instant coffee, milk, sugar and chocolate digestives. I half thought my rescuer might have disappeared, but he was waiting for me and we squelched back through the puddles side by side. To break the awkward silence, I introduced myself.

'I'm Bryony. And you are?'

'Kyle. Kyle Kirkwood. You bought the flat then?'

'Yes.'

'Nice.'

'I know. I'm very lucky,' I said, aware I sounded prim.

Once we got to the flat, the presence of the removal men seemed to inhibit Kyle, and he leaned against the kitchen counter watching them warily with a Coke can in his left hand. The little finger of that hand was adorned with an ostentatious silver signet ring featuring a spider with inset rubies for eyes. Refusing the biscuits, which the removal men were wolfing hungrily, he drained his Coke in one go, then removed his wet hoodie to reveal a spider's web neck tattoo. His hair was worn in a short bowl cut and his beard in a very sculpted Van Dyke goatee: a combination that managed to be both comical and faintly sinister. His body had the unnatural, overly inflated look of someone of slight build who has worked excessively in the gym to add bulk. His head was small, with undistinguished facial features, including eyes that were slightly too close together. And he was young, quite a bit younger than I had realised, probably only in his early twenties.

After their tea, the removal men – who had emptied their van – repositioned some of the furniture into my preferred layout, and then left with their cash tip. I thought Kyle might follow suit, but he showed no inclination to go. Instead, he walked round the flat looking at everything and pointing out things that were wrong.

'That door's sticking: needs planing down... and that shelf's not been put up right. Put anything heavy on it, that's gonna come down.'

'Are you in the building trade?'

He shrugged. 'I do bits and pieces, yeah. Odd jobs, you might say.' He gave me a sidelong smile, revealing front teeth that crossed over each other.

'I guess I'd better make a start on unpacking,' I said, reaching for a box and tearing off the parcel tape.

He took the hint. 'Sweet; I'll bounce then, yeah?'

I smiled gratefully as I went to the front door to let him out. He was wearing a lot of aftershave with an overwhelming scent that combined pine with something more like petrol, and the scent of it lingered in the flat even after he had crossed the threshold onto the communal landing.

'And really, thank you so much for earlier. If you hadn't been there...' We both let the possibility hang there. 'Like I said, I owe you.'

He was my saviour. Or so I thought.

# TWO
## BRYONY

Now

I stayed up until 1 a.m. unpacking boxes, and by the time I crawled into my newly made bed I had emptied most of them. The place still looked bare, and there was a lot I wanted to do to it. It was all going to take time, but at least I was here, and it was mine. A top-floor flat on a relatively quiet street in an outer suburb of South London. Home.

When I eventually emerged the next morning, I felt drained and hungover, even though I hadn't drunk any alcohol. I rarely drank to excess these days anyway; not like in the wild, partying days of my twenties. I plugged in my newly purchased coffee machine and while it was brewing an espresso, scrolled through my phone. A message flashed up on the screen. It was from my friend Claire.

> *How did the move go? So great that we're neighbours again!*
> *Come over for something to eat? xx*

Claire Byrne, née O'Connor, born and bred in Crystal

Palace, had lived in South London all her life, surrounded by her large Irish Catholic family who all had homes within the same grid of streets. I met her straight after university, when we shared a flat in Beckenham, and though that particular living arrangement didn't last more than a few months, I stayed in the area and went on seeing Claire socially, to the point that she became my closest friend in London. And now, after an interval of just over five years, I had moved back to our old neighbourhood. One of the things that had driven me to buy the Kenley Court flat was that I would be near to Claire and her family again.

*Just woken up*, I typed, then glanced at the time on my phone screen. It was almost midday. *Bit late for breakfast, maybe an early lunch? xx*

*Just come whenever. It's Sunday, so I guess we can call it brunch? xx*

She'd added an eye-rolling emoji, implying that at our age going out for brunch was a little beneath us. That was very Claire.


Half an hour later I was showered and dressed and making my way down the stairs. As I reached the front door, a man was coming in through it carrying a bag of groceries in each hand. I instinctively reached out and held it open for him, since he was struggling to push it while holding his shopping.

'Thanks,' he said with a slight grimace. 'Have you just moved in? Only we spotted a removal van out there yesterday afternoon.'

'*We*'. So married then, or at least cohabiting. He was tall and slim, with greying hair in a short spiky cut and the sort of horn-rimmed designer glasses you can only buy in annoyingly trendy opticians. He spoke in a mellifluous, well-rounded baritone that reminded me of the voiceovers for cruise liner and mobility aid commercials. His natural air of authority made me think he was probably a teacher, or a social worker.

'Yes, that's right. Top-floor flat. I'm Bryony.' I extended my hand, and unlike my first-floor neighbour, he shook it, having put down his shopping first.

'Welcome to Kenley Court. I'm Leo Salvesen, and I live in there.' He pointed to the door of one of the two ground-floor flats. 'Have you met any of the other neighbours?'

'The lady on the first floor, on that side.' I pointed to the flat above his own. 'I can't say she was exactly friendly.'

Leo nodded sagely. 'Ah, that'll be Lida. She can be a bit crabby, but she's decent enough when you get to know her.' He picked up his shopping. 'Better get on... we can't make a start on lunch til I've got this lot home. Nice to meet you, Bryony. Enjoy your walk: it's a lovely day.'

The door to his flat was opened by someone inside, and I caught a brief glimpse of pale skin and pale hair before it closed again. At least one of the flat's occupants had turned out to be friendly.

Autumn weather is so fickle.

The previous day had been as wet and miserable as they come, but that morning was a completely different story. There was a fresh breeze blowing leaves along the pavement, and warm, buttery sunshine came and went behind high white clouds. I decided I would walk the thirty-five minutes to Claire's house. It was fitting, I thought, as I crossed Cator Park, that she was living in Crystal Palace, a few streets from where she was born, while I had just bought a home in Beckenham where we had first flat-shared together.

The door to the neat, terraced house was opened by Ryan

Byrne, Claire's husband. That was something that had changed in recent history: Claire was now married. I had spoken to Ryan on the occasions when I had FaceTimed Claire, but this was the first time we had met in person. He was a solicitor, a square, stocky man with receding hair and warm, twinkly eyes. His manner was warm too, and I was relieved. If my best friend had married someone I didn't like... well, that would be awkward, wouldn't it? She was the nearest thing I had to a sister since my real sister had emigrated to New Zealand. The nearest thing to family really. My mother was dead and my father and I had had a rather distant relationship since he walked out of the family home when I was twelve and subsequently remarried.

'So good to meet you in the flesh,' Ryan said, releasing me from a bear hug. There was music and laughter coming from the kitchen, and he turned his head in the direction of the noise and shouted, 'Girls! Bryony's here!'

The 'girls' turned out to be Claire and Dervla, one of her sisters. I was embraced again, and a strong Bloody Mary was thrust into my hand before I could even sit down at a table covered with everything from pizzas to sausage rolls to takeout sushi.

'We thought we'd cover all bases,' Dervla said with a laugh. I'd met her many years earlier when Claire and I were both single and she was already married to an Irishman called Pauly Quinn, and the mother of young children. Children who must be teenagers now, I calculated.

'Lovely to see you again, Dervla. How's the family?' I asked.

Dervla grimaced. 'Why d'you think I'm here on my own? Desperate to get away from them all for a few hours' peace.' She helped herself to some Brie from the makeshift cheeseboard. 'But never mind me, what about yourself? It's grand you're back from Australia... is this for good now?'

I nodded.

'And how long was it you were gone in the end?'

'Five years,' Claire supplied, adding a slug of vodka to her Bloody Mary and topping it up with more tomato juice. 'Not that I'm bitter or anything,'

'Wow,' Dervla said. 'Great that you're back and all, but did you ever think about staying permanently?' She helped herself to a handful of tortilla chips. 'Your sister did, didn't she?'

'Flora's in New Zealand,' I corrected her. 'And I thought about it, yes,' I said carefully. 'But in the end, I decided I'd been there long enough. I had an employer-sponsored visa and it expired after five years. The only way I could have stayed on was to apply for permanent resident's status.'

I'd studied for a BSc in diagnostic radiography at the University of Liverpool and completed my training at Barts before making the decision to use my qualifications in Australia, where there were plenty of well-paid jobs for radiographers. I wanted to be on the east coast, and it had proved quite easy to get sponsorship from the Monash Medical Centre on the outskirts of Melbourne. An opportunity that had come along at the perfect time, and proved the perfect escape.

'Or she could have married an Australian citizen,' Claire supplied, 'Which she nearly did, didn't you, Bry?'

I thought back to Joel's proposal. We had been together for most of the five years I was in the country, and he saw marriage as the natural next step. But much as I loved him, I knew I didn't want to stay in Australia for the rest of my life, and Joel had no desire to move to the UK. It broke my heart, and was the hardest thing I'd ever done, but I turned him down and spent my last few months in Melbourne living unhappily as a single woman. I threw myself into work, doing as much overtime as I could to build up the nest egg which I eventually used as a deposit on the flat in Kenley Court.

After we'd chatted and picked at the food for an hour or so, Ryan excused himself to go to five-a-side training, and Dervla reluctantly stood up from the table. 'I'd better head home,' she said grimly. 'Better get back to the hellscape that is the Quinn family.'

'She's having problems with her eldest,' Claire explained, once the front door had closed behind Dervla. She put two cups of coffee on the table and opened a box of after-dinner mints. 'Shane.' She sighed heavily as she pushed the chocolates towards me.

'Bit of a tearaway?' I asked.

'It's worse than that. Have you heard of the Gipset gang?'

I shook my head.

'Apparently they pride themselves on being the most violent of all the South London gangs, though who that dubious accolade actually belongs to is a moot point.' She rolled her eyes as she bit into a chocolate. 'Anyway, Shane's got himself tangentially involved in their goings on. From a while back, when he was just a kid. The drug-dealing stuff more than the violence, as far as Dervla and Pauly can tell. But still; it's horrible. Scary. She's going out of her mind with worry.'

'Dear God, Claire... surely he's not old enough?' I was incredulous.

'He's seventeen, going on eighteen. And believe me, that's old enough. They recruit kids as young as twelve. Bribe them with expensive trainers, things like that, use them to do drug deliveries. Apparently, there are kids as young as eight carrying knives.'

'Jesus. Poor Dervla.'

'I know. Anyway... let's change the subject. How's your love life?'


Later that evening, I sat on my new sofa with a cup of tea while I wrote in my diary, looking round the room with a sense of satisfaction. Yes, there was a lot still to do, but with a vase full of the bright-yellow chrysanthemums Claire had given me and the lamps lit, the place was looking cosy, homely. I felt safe, just as I had hoped I would.

I'd been keeping a diary since I was about ten, and never kicked the habit. And yes, I know it's an activity that makes me sound tragically uncool, but after more than twenty years it had become an automatic task, like brushing my teeth.

*Saw Claire today, and her sister Dervla. Found out Dervla's boy Shane has been recruited by some sinister-sounding South London gang. She must be out of her mind with anxiety about it. And of course, Claire was quizzing me about whether I'm seeing anyone. Just like old times! She pointed out that there'll be hundreds of male employees at the hospital and statistically at least some of them must be dateable. Which must be true, I suppose.*

Instead of a leather-bound book I had graduated to using a journal app on my phone. The pages could be customised to look pretty, and photos and pictures inserted; something that would have delighted my ten-year-old self if the technology had existed then. Come to think of it, a passcode-protected phone would have prevented Flora from taking my old-style diary from my underwear drawer and reading it. And now there was cloud storage which meant that I could access what I had written in perpetuity, even if my devices were lost or stolen. I always made sure I backed it up for that reason.

The entry phone buzzed loudly, making me jump.

'Hello?' I asked, mildly annoyed at having my me-time interrupted.

A male voice mumbled something, distorted to a squawk by the poor quality of the handset.

'I'm sorry... who is this?'

'Kyle Kirkwood.'

It took me a few seconds to remember who that was. Then

it came to me. My rescuer from the day before. The man who had saved my life. I had to let him up; there was no other choice.

He stood at my front door, jacket zipped up and hood pulled forward so that his face was barely visible.

'Thought I'd rock up and fix your shelf.'

'My shelf?'

'The one in the kitchen that's hanging off the wall. I told you I could fix it.'

I hesitated for a few seconds, torn between gratitude and irritation. 'That's really kind of you, Kyle, but there's no need, honestly. I'll book a handyman to come round and do all the little odd jobs like that.'

'You don't need a handyman though, innit. Not when I'm here.'

I looked down and saw that he had a canvas tool bag in his hand. I wanted to tell him that I'd rather sit and do my journal writing in peace. That I was starting a new job in the morning and needed some mental space to prepare, to think about what lay ahead.

'Come in,' I said instead.

He took his jacket off, revealing arms covered with an array of tattoos: phrases, dates, symbols, skulls. I wondered what they all meant, but was not inclined to ask.

'You've got no TV,' he observed, as he wielded his drill.

'I don't think I'll bother with a TV,' I told him. 'Not yet anyway. I can stream stuff on my laptop. Or I will be able to once I've organised a broadband account.'

Kyle grunted at this, scanning the room. Was he looking for more DIY jobs, or casing the joint, I wondered?

'Hopefully this isn't going to take you long,' I said, mustering as much tact as I could. 'I don't want to take up too much of your evening.'

'No dramas,' he said, brandishing his electric drill and baring his small overlapping teeth.

'And I've got work in the morning, so...'

'You working at St Anselm's, yeah?'

I stared at him a beat. 'How did you know that?'

'You said you was a radiologist, innit. So I figured you'd be working there, seeing as it's just up the road.'

'Radiographer,' I corrected him. 'And yes, I will be working there.'

'Sweet.'

Eventually he finished reattaching the loose shelf and packed his tools away. I thanked him effusively as I showed him out, thinking as I did so that I wouldn't see him again.

But I was wrong.

# THREE

## BRYONY

Now

I woke up far too early the next morning.

After all, I didn't need time to decide what to wear: I would be in uniform at work. Nor did I have a commute to worry about, since St Anselm's was only a ten-minute walk from Kenley Court. I had worked in several different hospitals if you included my initial training, so I wasn't unduly worried at the prospect of starting at a new one. But I still had an unsettled, nervy feeling. Perhaps it was having moved house only forty-eight hours earlier, and feeling as though there were a hundred and one things that still needed doing in the flat. I showered, made coffee and distracted myself with the radio as I applied make-up, finally leaving at 8.10 a.m.

'Hello again!' said a voice as I was about to enter the revolving door at the main entrance of the hospital. I turned round to see my neighbour Leo Salvesen striding up behind me, a cycle helmet dangling from one arm. No surprise that he cycled to work. He was definitely that type.

It seemed to suddenly occur to him that I might be here for

an outpatient appointment and therefore have some serious medical issue. He hesitated. 'Are you...?'

'Starting work,' I said, with a reassuring smile. 'In the imaging department. I'm a diagnostic radiographer.'

'Aah! That's great.' He smiled back. His eyes – through the magnifying lenses of his trendy glasses – were hard to read, but there was an intensity in his expression that unnerved me. 'So we'll be colleagues as well as neighbours.'

'Are you a doctor?'

'No. One of the dreaded IT guys, I'm afraid.' He still had that intense gaze directed on my face, as though he were trying to access my innermost thoughts.

'A very important job in a hospital,' I returned. 'There's a lot of tech-related stuff that can go wrong.'

By now we had reached the bank of lifts at the rear of the main foyer. Imaging was on the second floor, I noted from the sign next to them, and IT was on the fifth. There was a coffee shop in the foyer too, already doing a brisk trade with its circular metal tables all occupied and a queue of patients and staff waiting to be served.

'I think I'll...' I pointed to the queue to indicate that I wanted to pick up coffee. The truth was I'd had plenty at home, but I didn't much fancy riding in the lift with my neighbour. It felt strange being here at my new place of work with someone who I knew and yet didn't know.

'Right, that's a good idea. And good luck on your first day.'

'Thanks. And I'll know where to come when I'm struggling to get to grips with my broadband at home.'

'Of course.' Leo nodded. 'Always happy to help if you're having any problems setting stuff up.' He got into the lift that had just arrived and gave me a little wave as the doors closed. I waited for the next lift to arrive and went up to the second floor.

I was met in the imaging reception by Angela Hyter ('Call me Ange'), the senior radiographer who would be my line manager. She was a short, plump woman with a friendly but brisk manner.

'We have a team meeting at nine every Monday, so I'll introduce you to everyone then, but first let's get you kitted out.'

I was relieved that I would be wearing pale-grey scrubs rather than the white polyester tunic and navy trousers that had been the standard radiographer's uniform when I started my training. 'We've just switched to these,' Angela told me as she rummaged in the storeroom for the correct size. 'Most of us prefer them, though we're not crazy about the colour.' She held a top up against me with an appraising look as she tried to assess which size I needed. 'I reckon you'll look bonny in it, though, with your lovely colouring.'

The next few hours were a blur of new names and faces, new systems, new equipment. There were the inevitable glitches getting logged into my email account and St Anselm's diagnostic software, and I noted in the handbook I'd been given that Leo Salvesen's details were included under the IT helpdesk information. After I'd sat in as an observer on a few patients' scan appointments, I was taken to lunch in the staff canteen by Craig and Rochelle, two of my new colleagues. Rochelle was a petite, pretty girl of mixed race and Craig a flame-haired native of Belfast.

'Who's that?' I whispered to Rochelle, as we were queuing for lasagne and chips. I pointed to a tall, absurdly handsome man who was returning his tray to one of the trolleys where used dishes were stacked. He was wearing a white coat and stethoscope over green scrubs, and with his olive skin and dark, swept-back hair, he looked exactly like the hero of a medical soap opera.

'One of the gastroenterologists, I think,' she said, swivelling her head to watch him go. 'Not sure of his name. He's hot though, isn't he?' She giggled.

'Just a bit,' I concurred.

. . .

The day passed in a blur, and although it had gone without a hitch, I was exhausted by the time I got home that evening.

After I'd showered, I examined the contents of my fridge and decided, reluctantly, that I would have to make a trip to Tesco. I wasn't particularly hungry after my stodgy canteen lunch, but I was desperate for a drink. I headed out in the dark, being mindful to cross at the pedestrian lights after my near-death experience on Saturday.

As I was coming into Kenley Court with my carrier bag containing a bottle of wine, a bag of popcorn and a bar of chocolate (the single girl's diet, I reflected gloomily), Leo Salvesen was coming out, this time with a woman. Pale, straight, mousey hair fell almost to her waist, and her face was devoid of make-up. She wore a shapeless woollen coat, baggy jeans and Birkenstock clogs.

'Hi, Bryony,' said Leo. He touched the woman's shoulder. 'This is Ingrid. Ingrid, this is Bryony, the new upstairs neighbour I was telling you about.'

Ingrid looked me up and down with ill-disguised suspicion, and the smile she gave me didn't quite make it to her eyes.

Once they'd gone into their flat, I leafed through the heap of mail on the shelf where the postman deposited it, expecting to find a sheaf of bills for myself. I noted that there were a couple of letters addressed to Ingrid Salvesen. So she and Leo were married. This was probably a good thing, I told myself, if we were to both work together and live in the same building. Simpler if he wasn't single.

Over the next few days I started to feel more confident at work, while back at Kenley Court I was getting to know a bit more about my neighbours.

The Salvesens had the flat to the left of the front door, and the one opposite them was rented by a Chinese postgraduate studying Astrophysics at University College. He would smile and nod shyly but duck his head to avoid conversation. On the first floor was the crotchety Lida who, apart from her frequent complaints, kept herself to herself, and in the other flat a fifty-something divorcée called Theresa. The latter knocked on my door one evening after I had returned home from work and presented me with a pot plant.

'Just thought I'd come and say hi.' Her voice was breathy, her manner slightly fey. She wore flowered dungarees and had a scarf wound through her greying curls. 'Has someone told you about the bin store?'

I looked back at her blankly.

'In that case, come with me,' she said firmly. 'You need to know about this stuff. People never tell you what you actually need to know when you move into a new place, I always find.'

I fetched my door keys and followed her obediently down the fire escape stairs and out of the back of the building, remembering as I did so that the estate agents still owed me a spare set. I mentally added chasing this up to my endless to-do list. Outside there was a small grassy area that didn't really qualify as a garden, more a yard. The cold evening air smelt of marijuana coming from someone's window, mingled with the aroma of frying food. Next to the fire escape door, a short flight of concrete steps led down to a basement passageway. To the right there was an opening through which I glimpsed a couple of dumpsters heaped high with refuse bags. Even in the cold night air, their smell was pungent.

Theresa caught my expression. 'Bit whiffy, isn't it? The one on the left is recycling, the other one's normal household waste. Rubbish collection is Monday mornings, and recycling Tuesday, but you can dump stuff in here any time.'

'Good to know, thanks.' I pointed to a metal door at the end of an unlit passageway. 'What's in there?'

'I think that's the bike store, but I don't cycle myself, so I'm not a hundred per cent sure.'

I tried the door, but it was locked.

'Oh no, you won't be able to get in,' Theresa told me. 'You have to apply to the freeholder for a key, apparently, so they can keep track of who has access. There's a clause in our leases saying you're not allowed to keep bikes in the hall or on the landings. Fire risk or something.'

Leo must have a key then, I thought. Presumably his bike was kept in there.

After I'd thanked Theresa and agreed to meet up with her for coffee soon, I emerged onto the top-floor landing to see a familiar hooded figure standing by my front door.

Kyle Kirkwood.

He held out a scruffy-looking plastic carrier. 'Got you this,' he said gruffly.

Inside the bag was a broadband router. It was unused, but the writing on it was indecipherable.

'You said you didn't have Wi-Fi and that.'

'That's very sweet of you,' I said helplessly. 'But there's no need, honestly. I've got a BT engineer coming on Saturday morning to install the broadband.'

I invited him in. Of course I did: this man had prevented me falling under the wheels of a lorry and I was eternally in his debt. I already knew he didn't drink tea or coffee but fortunately I had one remaining can of Coke, which he accepted.

'How's it going?' he asked me. 'You settling in and that?'

'Starting to,' I said. My arms were crossed tightly over my chest, in what I was aware was a defensive pose. 'There's still loads I want to do, of course, and it's hard to find time, having just started a new job.'

Kyle examined one of the paint colour charts I had picked up in my lunch hour one day.

'You're doing walls, innit?'

'Hoping to. As soon as I can find the time. And decide on a colour.' I pointed to a shade of greenish blue. 'I'm pretty sure I want to go with that one.'

My plan was to buy a few tester pots and daub the magnolia walls with them before settling on a final shade. In Melbourne, Joel and I had made the mistake of buying the paint first, not realising that it was important to see how a colour looked in your own home before committing.

'Yeah, sound,' Kyle said approvingly.

Another ten minutes of awkward conversation followed. We had nothing in common, nothing to talk about, and I wasn't quite sure why he was there. Wasn't it Chinese culture that believed that if you saved someone's life you were responsible for them forever? Perhaps that was what kept drawing him back: a need to check that I was still alive and had not succumbed to any further near-fatal incidents.

Eventually he scrunched up his empty Coke can, threw it in the kitchen bin and sloped off with a backward 'See you later, yeah?'

He was in my life now. And I would soon wish that he wasn't.

# FOUR

## BRYONY

Diary entries: six years earlier

*6<sup>th</sup> May*

*My twenty-eighth birthday tomorrow. It'll be the first birthday in four years when I've been single. And I expect it will feel a bit weird not waking up to flowers and balloons from Aaron. He usually brought me a glass of champagne in bed too. He's good at birthdays, Aaron. Wonder if he goes through the same routine with the new girlfriend. Jessica. God, I don't even want to think about that. But it's over, and I need to move on. Get myself out there.*

*I've thought about getting back on the dreaded apps but I can't face swiping through all the pictures of random guys holding fish they've caught. Or with Machu Picchu in the background. Why are they all obsessed with Machu Picchu FFS? Modern dating is so superficial, so disposable. Since Aaron and I broke up I've probably scored nearly fifty matches but only been on two actual dates, both of which I've written about in these pages and neither of which ever went anywhere. Chris was one, and I can't even recall the name of the other. Andy? Harry?*

*Like I said, dating is now completely broken. With that in mind, Claire's going to take me for birthday drinks tomorrow evening at some new bar she's found. Who knows what might happen. At this stage it feels like it's meeting someone socially or nothing. No more swiping.*

*7th May*

*Surprise, surprise: I did actually meet someone this evening. We went to a new dive bar in Annerley called Alibi, and there was a group of men from a tech company holding a leaving-drinks do. They were at the next table and we got talking to a few of them, then Claire made a tactful exit and left me talking to the one I'd hit it off with. He's called Robbie. Robbie Makepeace. Seems like a really nice guy. Normal, at least. And single, which is a good start. Faint Scots accent, which I find attractive. Like me, he's dated around since leaving uni but nothing's stuck. I gave him my number and he said we should meet for a drink. I'm not going to get my hopes up: let's just see what happens.*

*8th May*

*I got a text from Robbie this afternoon. Less than twenty-four hours after we met, which Claire and I both agree indicates keenness. And he signed with two kisses. Possibly too much keenness? We're going to go for a pizza on Friday night. I felt that pizza makes it seem more casual. Definitely not looking for more than casual at this stage. If we were going to a fancy restaurant I'd be ordering something new to wear online (work's manic, so no time to go shopping) and paying for next-day delivery. But pizza doesn't really justify that. So I'll probably just go with shorts and sandals. Or possibly trainers. Haven't decided yet.*

# FIVE
## BRYONY

Now

The following Monday I was in the MRI suite, treating eighty-three-year-old Ada Marsh who had been brought into Accident & Emergency with a suspected hip fracture.

After the nurses had topped up her pain relief so that she would be able to lie still, we manoeuvred her immobilisation board onto the scanner and I retreated to the other side of the viewing window and looked at the images on the computer monitor. There was no door to the control room, but while I was preparing a summary for the on-call radiologist and orthopaedic registrar, someone tapped on the dividing screen. A brisk, peremptory tap.

I looked up, annoyed, wondering who had had the gall to walk into the imaging room while the scan was in progress. And there, in front of me, was the hot doctor I had been discussing with my new colleagues.

'Hi,' he said, with a smile that revealed too-perfect teeth; almost certainly veneers. 'Sorry to disturb, but we've got a small bowel infarction. Needs imaging urgently. Can they bring the patient through now?'

He did not introduce himself, but his name badge said 'Dr Andreas Koros'.

'Yes, of course: bring them straight through. This lady will be done in a couple of minutes.'

There was a list of outpatients to be scanned that afternoon, but it was accepted practice that severely ill inpatients and urgent admissions would jump the queue, leaving the outpatients loitering in the waiting area until they were done. I knew, of course, that a bowel infarction was an acute emergency with a high mortality rate.

'You're new here, aren't you?' His eyes narrowed slightly, and he gave me a curious, appraising look.

'Yes, it's my second week. I'm Bryony. Bryony Pearson.'

A brief nod of acknowledgement. 'Good to meet you... Sorry, I'd better go and get my patient brought in.'

He turned to go, but not before making eye contact that lingered a few seconds longer than was comfortable. I felt heat rising at the back of my neck, and turned my head to look back at the grey and white images of Mrs Marsh's pelvis.

'Welcome to St Anselm's,' he added, then swept out of the room, his white coat billowing behind him.

The afternoon list ended up running late, and I was tired and drained by the time I eventually arrived home.

I flung my jacket and bag down on the hall floor (acquiring some pegs or a coat stand was on my very long to-do list) and went straight to the fridge. Pouring myself a generous glass of white wine, I decided that what I needed was a long soak. I had just turned on the bath taps when the doorbell buzzed.

It was probably a delivery, I reasoned. I had made several

online orders of things for the flat, draining my account of funds, at least until I received my first salary payment.

'Hello?' I barked into the intercom.

'It's me,' said the voice.

'Who is this?' I asked, irritated. Behind me, I could hear the water gushing into the bath and smell the lavender-scented foam. I had been about to light the Jo Malone candle that Claire had given me as a housewarming gift.

'Kyle.'

*Oh God*, I groaned inwardly. I really wasn't in the mood. But, on the other hand, I owed this man my very existence. This fact had not ceased to be true. 'Come up,' I said, trying and failing to keep the impatience out of my voice.

'I'm just about to get in the bath, actually Kyle,' I told him as soon as I opened the door. He was wearing a Stone Island camouflage puffer and a cap with 'Fendi' on the brim, which I doubted was real. He looked like a caricature of an urban gangster. Which, I was beginning to realise, was who he was

Once again he had a carrier bag with him – a larger one this time – and he reached inside and pulled out what I realised was a tin of paint.

'Got the paint, innit,' he said with a note of triumph. 'For your walls and that.'

I examined the offering. It was a dupe of the expensive brand I had intended to buy, close but not identical to the shade I wanted. Not close enough when it came down to it. From the label on the tin, I could already see that the colour was just a little too brash, a little too close to turquoise. I did not want to get into a discussion of the finer points of colour choice though.

'Thank you,' I said weakly. 'That's really kind.' I put the can down in the hallway, intending to ignore it and buy the shade I'd planned on using instead.

He pulled a roller from the bag and waved it near my face. 'Thought I could start now.'

I shook my head. 'That's so kind, Kyle—' I was starting to sound like a stuck record '—but I've just got back from a really long shift at work, and after my bath I'm planning to go straight to bed.'

He shrugged. 'All right, later then.'

'Later,' I agreed, and ushered him out of the front door before he could come up with another reason to stay.

I felt disproportionately guilty for making him leave.

You're being ridiculous, I told myself. Forget about him and move on.

After a fifteen-minute wallow in the bath, I threw on my dressing gown and went to the sitting room's bay window, which faced the street-side of the building. The pavement was in shadow, but I was sure I saw a man's figure standing against the wall that flanked the opposite pavement. His head raised briefly in my direction before he walked off, face obscured by a cap.

I shivered involuntarily, watching the street for a little longer, before eventually turning away.

# SIX

## BRYONY

Now

'To be honest, Bry, I find it all deeply weird,' Claire said a couple of evenings later when I told her about Kyle Kirkwood's visits.

We were having a drink at the Bricklayers Arms. At least, I was drinking; Claire was sticking to mineral water. She had recently confided that she and Ryan had been trying to conceive for over six months, and to increase her chances of success they had both given up alcohol. 'I mean, does he fancy you? Is that his agenda?'

I shook my head. 'I've no reason to think so.'

'So he hasn't made a pass at you? Sent you suggestive texts?' Claire bent her head and sucked her water noisily through a straw.

'He hasn't got my mobile number. But he knows my address because of what happened the night he dragged me out of the path of an oncoming truck. And he just shows up randomly. He's at least a decade younger than me anyway: can't be much older than twenty.'

Claire scoffed. 'Trust me, that's not going to stop him fancying you. If anything, the reverse. I mean, look at you.' She indicated my mini skirt and suede over-knee boots.

I took a thoughtful swig of my gin and tonic. 'Maybe he's just slowly working up to it. Trying to find the time to make his move.'

'Be honest—' Claire narrowed her eyes '—does his presence in your flat make you uncomfortable?'

I hesitated for a few seconds. 'A little, yes,' I admitted eventually.

'You should change the locks,' Claire announced. The familiar bossy tone had crept into her voice. 'You're a single woman living on your own. What he's doing is tantamount to stalking you. As I say, you should definitely think about changing the locks, just to be safe. In case he's managed to get hold of a key somehow.'

I scrunched my nose. 'That seems a little excessive.'

'Okay, well at the very least you should start discouraging him. If he buzzes your bell on the front entrance, don't let him up. Or better still, don't answer. Get a smartphone security camera installed so you can see who's there.'

'I'll look into it,' I promised her.

On my way home from the pub, I thought about my handling of Kyle's visits. Claire was right to be wary, I concluded. Any decent citizen would act to prevent someone being run over. That was a normal thing to do. But they wouldn't necessarily expect ongoing access to their home in return. I really ought to be more careful in the future. Once I was back at Kenley Court, I went to the door of the Salvesens' flat and rang the bell. Ingrid answered.

'It's late,' she said, rather unnecessarily, frowning at me. She was wearing what looked like men's flannel pyjamas, and thick socks.

'Yes, I know; I'm sorry. I wondered if I could have a quick word with Leo.'

He appeared behind Ingrid's shoulder and to my relief was not dressed for bed.

'Hi, Bryony.' He raised a hand in greeting. 'Everything all right?'

'I just wanted a quick word, if that's okay.'

'Sure, come through.' He led me into the living room, leaving Ingrid hovering in the hallway like a pale, resentful ghost. It was decorated in a pared-back Scandi chic: all natural wood, primary colours and house plants. He offered me a seat on the sofa but I assured him I wasn't going to stay long.

I told him I was thinking of installing a door camera, but wasn't sure if that was allowed.

'It's a bit tricky if it covers communal areas and potentially infringes on your neighbours' privacy,' he said. 'I think you'd need to do two things: check the legal small print, and get permission from the freeholder.'

'Thanks, that's really helpful.'

Leo narrowed his eyes slightly. 'Has there been an issue since you've moved in?'

I hesitated. 'Not exactly.'

'Only I couldn't help noticing that young lad who came into the building with you the night you moved in—'

'Kyle,' I supplied.

'You know him?'

I pulled a face. 'Sort of. It's complicated.'

'Well, I've noticed him hanging around in the street a few times. Like he was waiting for you. He's not causing you problems, is he? Only you know you can always let me know if that's the case. We should exchange phone numbers so that you can contact me if you're worried.'

I agreed that this was a good idea, and he handed me his mobile for me to enter my details.

'You don't want me to have a word with this Kyle guy?'

'No, it's fine.' I turned to go. 'Thanks, but it's really nothing I can't handle.'

On my lunch break the next day, I bought a coffee from the machine in the canteen and found a seat in the lounge area next to the dining tables. Pulling out my phone, I started to research the red tape around door cameras in blocks of flats, and composed an email to Kenley Court's managing agent, asking for an outline of their policy. If they were opposed to individual cameras, I enquired, then would they consider installing a communal entry system that included video phones.

As I was typing, a message flashed up on my screen from an unknown number.

*Hi sexy*

I recoiled slightly, frowning. This was surely a friend who had just purchased a new phone, playing a prank. My thoughts wound back to the conversation I'd had with Claire the previous evening. Was this Kyle? If so, how could he possibly have got my number? I had turned my back on him when he dropped round with the router, while I fetched him a Coke from the fridge. The only thing that made sense was that he had phoned himself with my mobile while I wasn't looking and my phone was unlocked, but it would have taken several seconds to punch in his own number in full and I didn't think my back had been turned that long. I checked my 'Recents' call log but there was nothing. Then it came back to me in a rush. I had just given my number to Leo Salvesen.

I was so stunned by the idea the message could be from Leo

that I sat staring at my phone for several minutes. From the little I knew of him this message did not seem at all like his style. And then there was the frosty Ingrid.

*Who is this?*, I typed back eventually. Yes, I knew it was best just to block and delete unwanted texts, but curiosity was overwhelming me.

A single word appeared on my screen: *Andreas*

Andreas. It took a few seconds for the penny to drop. Dr Andreas Koros. The Hot Doctor himself. I had written about him in my diary only the previous night, describing the intense eye contact he had made.

Before I had even processed that he was now reaching out to me, another text arrived.

*I like your hair like that. Looks stunning*

So he knew I was currently wearing my hair in a high ponytail. Was he looking at me right now? I glanced over at the queue for the cooked main dishes and caught a glimpse of a white coat, dark swept-back hair. My cheeks flaming, I shoved my phone back in my pocket, stood up and hurried out of the canteen.

As I walked home from work a few hours later and the initial shock had worn off, I realised I had overreacted. After all, this was just the equivalent of sliding into my direct message inbox on social media. If he'd gone to the trouble of looking me up on Instagram he could have done just that. It had happened to me a few times recently with male followers. There was no point me clutching my pearls like some Victorian spinster. On the other hand, I *was* still curious.

*How did you get my number?*, I typed as I walked.

*I've got contacts*

He added a winking emoji. When I didn't respond, he sent another, longer message.

*Seriously... I'm good friends with a girl in HR. She pulled it from your file*

*Good friends?*, I replied, and added a tongue-out emoji to show that I was matching his playful approach. *You mean she's one of your conquests?*

*That would be telling. But when I met you yesterday I was intrigued. And I could tell you were too. All in the eye contact, hey?*

This was uncanny. I had used almost identical words when I wrote about our brief encounter in my diary. I decided to up the ante.

*So why not just come up to me in the canteen and say hi?*

*The higher ups aren't keen on interdepartmental romances*

I stared at these last two words as I let myself into the front entrance of Kenley Court. Was that what this was: a romance? I felt a little frisson of excitement. But then, concerned that things were moving a little fast, I refrained from responding until I had showered and changed into sweats, and was installed on the sofa with a glass of wine.

*There must be loads of those in a hospital the size of St A*, I eventually wrote back. *If we're both single surely no one would care?*

As I typed this, it occurred to me that I had no idea if he was single or not. For Doctor Koros this was probably just a little flirtation on the side, a situationship.

*True but I'm up for a big promotion and I want management to think I have my mind on nothing but work*

I was forced to concede that this made a certain sort of sense. I took a swig of wine and was about to go and rummage through the fridge when I saw the greyed-out words under his name. *Andreas is typing...*

*Besides, it's more spicy if this is our little secret, isn't it? More fun x*

So we had moved onto using kisses now. I wasn't sure how I felt about that. I put my phone down and reflexively walked to the window to look out. I'd got into the habit of doing this, checking to make sure no one was watching me. That Kyle Kirkwood wasn't out there. There was a small movement somewhere near the main door of the building, but it turned out to be a large, scruffy-looking fox.

I went into the kitchen to prepare supper, having decided that, for now at least, I would not reply to the dashing Dr Koros. I would leave him wanting more.

# SEVEN
## BRYONY

Now

I saw Andreas in the coffee shop the next morning, as I arrived at work.

My immediate thought was relief that I'd had the foresight to make a bit of an effort. Since I'm in uniform most of the day, with my hair tied back, I usually leave the flat having done the bare minimum. But this time I had taken care choosing my outfit and spent time on my make-up, running a styling brush through my hair. Once the relief of knowing I looked put together had subsided, I fell into a panic about how to behave. Should I say something about our text exchange, or should I play along with his idea that it was some sort of secret between us?

He turned in my direction, coffee cup in hand, as I approached the bank of lifts and our eyes met. I smiled in a way that I hoped was suggestive rather than leering, and he smiled back. Neither of us spoke, and he didn't get into the lift with me, instead heading down the corridor that led towards the Accident & Emergency department.

Feeling a little deflated, I waited until I was on my break, then composed a message.

*Good to see you this morning, Dr Koros!*

I added a wink.
Ten agonising minutes later I finally got a reply.

*You too, Ms Pearson. Love those boots x*

*Aw, thanks*

I added a smiley face, and then, after a few minutes' hesitation, a kiss.

There was a full list of patients waiting for me in the MRI suite that morning, but I checked my phone at intervals and each time there was a message waiting from Andreas, which I replied to. We kept up this game of text ping-pong all day, but it was very light, flirty stuff. Banter. Neither of us gave away anything of significance. He was nowhere to be seen at lunchtime, but I passed the time by checking his Instagram. There weren't many posts on there, as you would expect with a busy, ambitious hospital doctor. There were some posts from Greece during the summer, where he seemed to be visiting family, some skiing shots, and one or two selfies with a beautiful woman who had an exotic Middle Eastern look. She wasn't tagged so I couldn't online stalk her, but the posts were from six months ago and she hadn't featured since. Certainly, there was nothing to suggest that he was married, and I was relieved about that.

I did a supermarket run on my way back from work, and as I

was unpacking the groceries, there was a knock on the front door of my flat.

My heart sank. Surely not Kyle Kirkwood again?

But standing on the front mat was Leo Salvesen, clutching a bottle of wine.

'Hi, Bryony.' He smiled hesitantly; his eyes magnified behind the designer frames. 'Sorry to disturb, but I wanted to see how you'd got on with the door camera thing?'

'Come in.' I ushered him into the kitchen area of the living room, where packets of kitchen towel, several frozen ready meals, multipack bags of snacks and six packs of soft drinks covered every surface. 'Sorry about the mess.' I continued putting my purchases away in cupboards as I spoke. 'I did hear back from the management company. I can put a personal app-based door camera on there...' I pointed back in the direction of the door he had just come through. 'But since there's already CCTV on the outside of the building, I can't do anything in the ground-floor communal area. But they did say they were going to replace the existing doorbells on the main door with a video intercom system. And when they do, obviously we'll all be able to see who's out there.' One by one, I took a dozen eggs out of their carton and placed them in a ceramic bowl. 'So mostly positive, I guess.'

'Right,' said Leo thoughtfully. 'Yes, I suppose that's pretty good news. Though when they'll get round to doing it is another matter.' He held out the bottle of wine. 'And this is just a little housewarming gift from Ingrid and myself.'

'Would you like a glass?' I opened the cupboard that held my wine glasses.

'No, thanks, I'd better get back downstairs to Ingrid.' When I looked puzzled, he pulled the sides of his mouth down in a grimace. 'She suffers from chronic fatigue syndrome.'

'Oh, I'm sorry,' I said politely, thinking this explained quite a lot.

'She has good days and bad days, but today, I'm afraid, has turned out to be one of the bad ones.'

'Poor Ingrid.'

'Yes, well... she's not with me all the time, just when she needs extra help.'

I must have looked confused, because he went on, 'Just trying to be a good big brother, you know?'

'Ah, so she's not your wife?'

Leo laughed. 'Last time I checked I didn't have one of those... Nope, Ingrid's my kid sister.' He turned to go. 'By the way, I'm assuming you haven't had any more unwanted visits. From that young guy?'

Absurdly my mind went straight to Andreas Koros before I realised that he meant Kyle. 'No, all quiet on that front.'

So Leo was single after all. I felt a little spark of interest at this news, but instantly suppressed it. A flirtation with a colleague was one thing, but with a colleague *and* a neighbour felt potentially too complicated. After he had gone, I checked my phone and found another pointlessly flirty message from Andreas. Feeling suddenly irritated, I started typing rapidly.

*Listen, this is all good fun, but I'm not really into endless texting. I don't have time and I'm sure you don't either. Happy to keep things off campus, but can't we just meet up and have a proper conversation over a drink? X*

I checked at regular intervals for the next three hours, but there was no reply.

Eventually, as I was turning out my bedside light, resolving to end this pointless liaison for good, my phone buzzed with a message.

*Sure: I'm game if you are xx*

# EIGHT
## BRYONY

Diary entries: six years earlier

$12^{th}$ May

*Currently sitting on my bed in my sports kit, trying to motivate myself to go for a run. Claire and I are going to meet up for brunch later and a post-mortem on Friday night. She's been texting me all agog to hear more and I haven't said much, putting her off by saying I'm saving it for when we meet. The truth is there isn't a lot to say. It was a pleasant evening. Oh God, that's so damning, isn't it? 'Pleasant'. That says it all. I mean, Robbie is a nice guy. He's no Chris Hemsworth, but he's not unattractive either. You probably wouldn't pick him out in a crowd. He's just a normal, average guy with nice blue eyes and a good job in tech. One who likes dogs and travel, follows football and occasionally goes to the gym at weekends. Oh, and he's signing his texts with three kisses now. Which, if I'm honest, feels a bit much.*

*Do I want to see him again? Well, I don't not want to see him, put it that way. The way I look at it, there's no need for it to be super serious, and he's fine for someone to just hang out with.*

## 19$^{th}$ May

*Work's been bloody manic this week. I've got no energy for anything other than crawling into bed at the end of the day, so when Robbie suggested doing something I almost turned him down flat, but in the end told him he could pop in here for a quick drink. Actually ended up quite enjoying it. He's good company, and he was happy just to chill here over a glass of wine. He also got my Bluetooth speaker pairing with my phone again, so we could hook up some playlists. Turns out there are some advantages to going out with someone super techy.*

*If going out is what we're doing. Not quite sure yet.*

# NINE
## BRYONY

Now

I heard no more from Andreas for a day and a half.

There was no way I was going to chase him about it, I told myself. Let him prove that he was serious. I caught a couple of glimpses of him in the hospital corridors, but he was always with other people and did not look in my direction.

Eventually a message arrived.

*Hey Ms Pearson... how about that drink? Suggest we meet at the Bunch of Grapes at the end of Churchill Road*

The pub he'd named was a short walk from the hospital grounds, and frequented regularly by its staff.

*Sure, why not*, I replied, determined to keep things light and breezy. *When?*

He suggested meeting at 6.30 the following evening. And so yes, of course, I took extra care with my appearance again, getting up early to create a bouncy blow dry using rollers, and perfecting my make-up. I left the flat in my favourite suede mini skirt and a sheer top, and at the end of my shift changed back into them from my uniform.

'You must have a hot date,' Rochelle said when she came into the locker room and found me tweaking my make-up and brushing out my hair in the mirror. She looked me up and down approvingly. 'Don't tell me it's with that gastroenterologist?'

I nodded, unable to suppress a grin.

'Wow, you're a fast worker!' She gave me a fist bump. 'Respect.'

Would she still have respected me an hour later as I was sitting alone in the Bunch of Grapes? No, probably not.

For the first thirty minutes or so, it was fine. The Grapes was a no-frills London pub with swirly carpets that smelled of cooking fat and spilled beer, but I'd just endured a long day at work, and was quite happy to sit at a corner table, nursing a gin and tonic and scrolling through news sites on my phone. I took advantage of the downtime to pay a couple of bills and have a WhatsApp catch up with my sister, Flora, who was just waking up on New Zealand's South Island.

By the time forty minutes had passed, however, I was starting to feel irritated. I tried calling Andreas's number but it went straight to voicemail. I fired off a text.

*Have I got the right day? Am at the Bunch of Grapes!*

My phone buzzed with a message alert, but it was from Claire.

*Fancy meeting for a drink? A few of us are at Alibi if you want to join xx*

It was pretty obvious by now that Andreas was not coming.

Or perhaps he still was, but I did not want to give him the impression that showing up nearly three quarters of an hour late was okay. So I messaged Claire to tell her that I was on my way and called an Uber.

As I was sitting in the back seat, my phone buzzed again. Andreas. Of course.

*So so sorry, we had a strangulated hernia come in and I had to stabilise the patient and get emergency surgery organised. Another time perhaps? Xxx*

The car was pulling up outside the dark green frontage of the bar, so instead of replying I switched off my phone and pushed it into the recesses of my bag. I found Claire alone in the room upstairs, where there was a vinyl-spinning jukebox and the walls were plastered with posters for long-forgotten bands.

'The others just left.' Claire brandished a dark 'n' stormy, her favourite cocktail. She had apparently abandoned her plan to avoid alcohol, at least for the night. 'I'm amazed this place is still open. Do you remember that night when we first came here?'

I could not possibly have forgotten it. That was the night that led to a chain of events that would change my life forever. The night Robbie and I met.

'I do indeed,' I said, glancing around. It didn't seem to have changed.

'Oh God...' Claire flapped her free hand in front of her face. 'Sorry. Should have thought. After what happened... this might not be the ideal venue.'

'It's fine.' I picked up the slightly sticky laminated cocktail menu and waved the barman over to order a Moscow mule. 'It is a bit strange to be here, but to be honest I'm just glad to be having a drink with someone who's where they said they'd be.'

Claire nodded vaguely, seeming – from my years of knowing her – a little checked out.

'Are you okay, Claire?' I scrutinised her face.

'Just got my bloody period.' She laughed bitterly at this oxymoron. 'Honestly, Bry, I just don't understand why it's not happening for us. We're doing everything right, you know? Everyone I know seems to be able to get pregnant at the drop of a hat.'

'It will happen,' I reassured her, placing my hand over hers. 'Just give it a bit more time. And try to relax. Apparently the more anxious you are, the lower your chances.'

She took a tissue from her bag and dabbed at her eyes with one hand while taking a large gulp of her dark 'n' stormy. 'Anyway, enough about me. Where've you come from?'

I told her about having just been stood up by Andreas. She waved a hand dismissively.

'Nah... fuck him.' Her words were slightly slurred. 'Life's too short to run around after fuck boys and losers.'

It was my turn to be downhearted. 'I don't know, Claire... it's just so disappointing. Someone comes along without the need for you to resort to the dreaded apps, and you assume you're on to a winner. But it's just another dead end.'

'All you can do is move on, babe. Thank you, next!'

I raised my glass in a mock toast. 'Next! Now... let's change the subject.'

So we talked about the difficulty of finding reliable painters and decorators in South London, the merits of various local hair salons and negotiating family dynamics at Christmas.

'Still a few weeks to go before you need to think about that,' I reassured her.

'But speaking of family, and because you need cheering up,' Claire draped an arm round my neck. 'Why don't you join my lot for Sunday lunch? It's Dervla's turn this week, so we'll be over at hers.'

'That sounds lovely,' I said, smiling.

'It'll be a roast, of course. It's always a roast. I know that's tricky with you being a veggie.'

'That's fine,' I assured her. 'I can still have a roast potato.'

'And there'll be Yorkshires.'

'Even better,' I said, beaming. 'I love a Yorkshire. Anyway, what else am I going to do at weekends? It's not as though my love life is going to be keeping me busy.'

'Like I say, fuck him,' Claire repeated, raising her glass tipsily and splashing a puddle of rum and ginger ale over the bar. 'And with the exception of my own husband, fuck all men!'

I sighed heavily, and raised my own glass high.


It was only when I was getting ready for bed a couple of hours later that I remembered I had switched off my phone when I was on my way to Alibi.

Turning it back on again, I half expected there to be missed calls from Andreas, or at least a further message suggesting an alternative meetup. There was nothing. At first puzzled, and then annoyed, I did something I wouldn't have considered unless I'd had a few drinks. I opened the FaceTime app on my phone and selected 'Andreas Koros' from the list of contacts.

The app's familiar chirruping ring was cut off immediately. I switched to a regular voice call, but again it was cut straight-away. He had stood me up, and yet he wasn't prepared to talk to me. That should have been all the warning I needed.

# TEN

## BRYONY

Now

Sunday dawned with a sharp frost and brilliant blue skies.

I felt cheerful as I wrapped up in an overcoat and scarf and headed out of my front door and down the stairs. As I reached the first-floor landing, Theresa's door opened and she stepped out into my path. She was wearing a baggy denim dress and bright pink Converse high-tops, and had her grey curls secured on top of her head with a complicated series of clips.

'Bryony! I'm so glad I caught you,' she declared in her breathy voice. 'Come in and have that coffee.'

I hesitated a second.

'I've got something for you.'

My hand forced, I went into her flat. Hers had a separate kitchen and living room; the latter a jumble of ethnic wall hangings, dusty spider plants, incense sticks and stacks of yellowing paperbacks.

'I'm on my way out to lunch,' I told her apologetically, perching myself on the edge of the hand-crocheted throw that covered the sofa. 'I'm afraid I really can't stay long.'

Theresa ignored this, disappearing into the kitchen and returning with a tray that had a Bialetti coffee pot and two earthenware mugs on it. I sipped on the bitter liquid, having refused milk that looked long past its sell-by date.

'And this is for you!' Theresa said triumphantly, producing a manila envelope from the pocket of her dress. I opened it. Inside was a small silver-coloured key.

'I went to the annual meeting that the freeholder and management committee hold, as the residents' representative. We're supposed to take it in turns but sadly it usually falls to me.' She gave a self-pitying eyeroll. 'Anyway, I asked about keys to the bike store, and someone from the management committee had brought along spares, so I took a couple: one for each of us.'

'Thank you,' I said, surprised. 'That's very kind of you.'

'You never know, we might decide we want to take up cycling. Stranger things have happened!' she said, and guffawed at her own wit. 'Only keep it somewhere safe, because there's a ten-pound charge for a replacement if you lose them, apparently.'

I took my key ring from my bag and brandished it, before securing the small key next to the ones for the building and my own flat.

'Who were the people who lived in my flat before?' I asked Theresa. 'Only they never returned their own set of keys, so I still don't have spares.'

'A retired couple: Don and Coral. They really only used the place as a *pied-à-terre*. Most of the time they were off on some cruise or other; always taking cruises.' Theresa gave a dramatic shudder. 'Personally, I can't think of anything worse.'

I shoved the only set I had back into my bag and stood up. 'Sorry, Theresa, but I'm really going to have to get going. But you must come up to me for coffee soon.'

. . .

After I'd left Theresa's flat, I just had time to make a detour to the local florists to buy a gift for Dervla.

Then, armed with a large bunch of hydrangeas and a bottle of red wine, I elected to walk through Cator Park and cut across to Perry Hill where Claire's sister lived with her husband, Pauly, and their three children.

I arrived to the smell of roasting meat and loud laughter from the kitchen where everyone was assembled. In addition to Claire and Ryan, the youngest O'Connell sister, Maggie, was there with her husband, toddler and newborn baby, along with their Aunt Geraldine and a tiny shrunken woman introduced as Miss Ember. Miss Ember, Claire explained, was Dervla's elderly widowed neighbour who had no family of her own and who attended all of the Quinns' gatherings.

'Dervla's roasts are the only hot meals she ever eats,' Claire whispered under her breath. 'And notice how she makes short work of the dessert, when it's served.'

Dervla's daughters were helping; twelve-year-old Aoife proudly stirring the gravy while her fourteen-year-old sister Molly set the table and went in search of spare chairs to cram in around the large, scuffed table.

'Shane is supposed to be gracing us with an appearance,' Dervla told me, handing Miss Ember a glass of sherry before yanking open the oven and giving the joint of beef a basting. She closed the oven door with her foot, reaching for a pan of potatoes and draining them.

'It'll be a miracle if he does,' Pauly Quinn said. He was a tall, rangy man with a shock of springy, dark hair. 'But you never know. Stranger things have happened. Aoife, offer Miss Ember a Twiglet with her sherry, why don't you.'

Thirty minutes later, as we were squeezing in around a table laden with plates and serving dishes, and Ryan was pouring everyone red wine, the door opened and a teenager loped in, muttering an apology under his breath. This could only be Shane Quinn. His dark hair was shaved into a fade and what was visible of his neck was covered in tattoos. He took the only empty chair next to me.

'Hi, I'm Bryony Pearson. Your Auntie Claire's friend.'

He turned to look at me, and there was no doubt that he was a good-looking young man. He had the fabled Irish eyes: dark blue with black lashes.

'Don't be forgetting your manners now, Shane,' his mother chided.

Shane extended a hand to me. There were gold chains around his wrist and a heavy gold Celtic warrior necklace on his chest. 'Nice to meet you,' he mumbled, and gave me a dazzling smile that was like the sun emerging from behind clouds, and revealed a gold tooth. 'Sure, it's good to see you too, Miss Ember,' he added to their other guest. 'Can I pass you anything? More gravy?'

I remembered what Claire had confided about Shane belonging to a gang, being involved with dealing drugs. Dervla's concerns were no doubt justified, but despite the tattoos and the bling he seemed amiable enough to me. I was a little wary of questioning him too closely, unwilling to start an awkward discussion about his lifestyle choices, but he volunteered that he wanted to train as a chef, and that his mother's cooking had inspired him.

Dervla's food was indeed delicious, and after putting away a plate heaped with roast potatoes and Yorkshires, the tiny Miss Ember managed no less than three helpings of lemon meringue pie.

'Told you,' Claire muttered as we cleared the table. 'Lord alone knows where she puts it all. Not an ounce of meat on her bones.'

Shane disappeared as abruptly as he had arrived, slamming the door behind him and heading out into the darkening afternoon. Molly and Aoife took their little cousin upstairs to watch a Disney movie while Pauly walked Miss Ember home, leaving the other adults plus Maggie's baby in the drawing room drinking coffee and eating chocolates. Eventually, I too headed home, feeling greatly cheered by this helping of family life.

As I rounded the corner and approached the front door of Kenley Court, I became aware of footsteps behind me.

Spinning round, I saw a figure step forward from the November afternoon gloom into the beam of a streetlamp. A figure wearing a shiny Moncler down coat and trucker cap. Kyle Kirkwood.

'Hello, stranger,' he said. He gave me a smile that did not reach his eyes.

'Oh... hello.' I was genuinely confused. The hours spent in an overheated house consuming rich food and plenty of wine had left me feeling thick-headed and slightly disconnected from reality. 'I wasn't... is there a problem?'

'Yes,' he said coldly. 'I'd say there was a bit of a problem. Like you having your boyfriend warn me to stay away.'

'My boyfriend?' I was even more confused. What did any of this have to do with Andreas?'

'He saw me out here and told me to stop hanging round this place, that it was upsetting you.' He gestured to the door of the building. 'So I had to remind him that if it weren't for me, you wouldn't even be in a position to be upset because you'd be dead.'

He spat this last word, and I felt drops of saliva on my cheek. Then I realised that he must be referring to Leo Salvesen. It was funny, I thought incongruously, but despite discovering Ingrid was not his wife, I still didn't think of Leo in that light. As someone who might be interested in me. I liked him, yes, but the presence of his sister in his flat was a stumbling block to developing further intimacy.

'I'm sorry about that,' I mumbled. 'But for starters Leo isn't my boyfriend; he lives in one of the other flats; that's all. And I didn't ask him to speak to you. He got that idea into his own head.'

'Yeah? And why did he do that?' Kyle pulled out a disposable vape and started puffing on it aggressively.

'I don't know... just being a protective neighbour, I suppose.' I badly wanted to go inside, but Kyle had placed himself between me and the front door. 'I'm sorry, Kyle,' I repeated. 'And of course I'm still incredibly grateful for what you did the other day. I'll always be in your debt. But you really don't need to keep checking up on me. It's not like we're friends or anything.'

'No,' he agreed, with a strange little smile. 'We ain't friends.'

And with that he turned abruptly and strolled off, still puffing on his vape.

Once inside my flat, I felt drained and out of sorts. I couldn't face eating anything and I certainly didn't want any more wine. I made myself some herbal tea and threw myself down on the sofa, surfing through channels on my newly acquired TV to find something undemanding to watch. My phone buzzed with a text.

> *Hi Bryony, can we give meeting a second try? Maybe dinner this time. Somewhere special, to make up for last time? A xxx*

I wanted to tell him to go to hell, of course I did. But my natural instinct to right a wrong kicked in. Yes, I told myself, I did deserve a fancy dinner at the very least. Something that would compensate for waiting nearly an hour in a pub. Call me a fool, but I texted him back, telling him to let me know when he had made the reservation.

I deliberately kept the tone light, but when I typed '*Last chance!*', I was deadly serious.

# ELEVEN
## BRYONY

Diary entries: six years earlier

*28<sup>th</sup> May*

*Robbie and I went out yesterday. It was quite a fun night. We met up with a mate of his called Dev and his girlfriend (I've already forgotten her name: my bad). The four of us had drinks at a bar I haven't been to before, then went bowling. Afterwards Robbie and I went to the Bricklayers Arms on our own. We talked about all sorts of stuff. He's pretty easy to get along with. He asked if he could come back to mine, and I can't say I wasn't tempted. A girl has needs and all that. But in the end, I used having an early shift at work to duck out of it. Let's face it, though; sleeping together is going to have to happen at some point. We can't put it off forever if this thing is going to progress. But he also told me during our rambling conversation that he's only ever had one girlfriend, and that was when he was at school. I know he's still in his twenties, but even so. Red flag? Claire says he gives her incel vibes. A bit harsh, but he's maybe a bit too intense for me.*

*It might be better to stop things before they go further.*

## TWELVE
### BRYONY

Now

On Monday morning I went on a foray to the third floor in search of fresh supplies for the cannula trolley.

As I came out of the lift, I caught sight of Andreas striding past with a gaggle of medical students in tow. His eyes swept over me and as they made contact with mine, he gave me a knowing smirk. I thought about winking, but decided that would be way too cheesy and gave a faint lift of my eyebrows instead.

An hour or so later I received a text.

*Morning, gorgeous! La Colombe Blanche on the high street, Wednesday at 7.45. How does that sound? Xxx*

I stared at this for a few seconds, unsure how it did sound. My first reaction was that it felt too good to be true. My second was gratitude that I'd been given two days' notice. When I had a brief break between patients, I used the time to find the website of a local blow-dry bar and book a wash and style for my lunch hour on Wednesday. I also booked a manicure for that evening at a nail salon I walked past on my way home from work. Only then did I reply to Andreas.

*Sounds perfect... don't you dare be late this time! X*

As I patiently felt for a patient's vein to cannulate for a contrast CT scan, I brooded on whether I should tell Claire my news. But I knew only too well what she would say. That I was an idiot, and that Dr Koros didn't deserve any more of my time. That he probably wouldn't even show up. And so I didn't share this latest development with her, or with any of my colleagues in the radiography department. Instead, at the end of my shift and after my visit to the nail bar, I took myself and my newly manicured scarlet talons home for an early night.

When Wednesday rolled round I still hadn't decided what to wear, so I had no choice but to head to work without an outfit picked out.

My plan was to return home at the end of my shift (with freshly styled hair), then change and get a cab straight from home to the restaurant. Not only did that give me all day to mentally run through my wardrobe choices, but it also meant none of my colleagues would see me teetering out of St Anselm's in high heels and a sexy dress. Nothing would scream going on a date as loudly as that. Even so, Marat, one of the male technicians on the unit, did a double take when I returned from my lunch hour. I always wore my hair tied back at work, but I was worried about spoiling the lovely bouncy waves, so had left it loose.

'Wow, girl, nice blow out!' He reached out and touched a curl. 'Going somewhere special?'

'Not particularly,' I lied, feeling colour wash over my

cheeks. 'Just fancied treating myself.' I curled my fingers inwards to hide my red fingernails. The rules stated that we were to have unpainted nails at work, but I had worked around this by wearing disposable gloves when I was with the patients.

'Uh huh.' The look on his face told me I wasn't convincing anyone.

Still, I quite enjoyed the thrill of subterfuge as I said good night to my colleagues and hurried home to change. Andreas was right: conducting a liaison in secret was more fun than going public. I took thirty minutes over my make-up, put on a plunging black dress and heels and, grabbing my trusty faux fur coat, set off in an Uber to La Colombe Blanche.

The interior was subtly lit with a combination of hanging globe lights and tiny shaded lamps on the tables. There were green and white tiles on the floor, and the banquette seating was upholstered in dark green velvet. It was simple, yet sexy. The maitre d' assured me that yes, he did have a reservation for two in the name of Koros, and led me to a table. The other party had not yet arrived, he said smoothly, handing me a wine list and a menu. So far, so good.

After I had ordered a bottle of water and a glass of champagne to steady my nerves, my phone buzzed with a text.

*Still at work and running a tiny bit late – be with you in 10 xxx*

My heart sank. Because it wouldn't be ten minutes, would it? When people said they were running ten minutes late, what they really meant was twenty. Still, at least he was coming. He hadn't forgotten. I slowed down my champagne consumption, determined not to have finished the glass before Andreas arrived.

Twenty minutes went by and sure enough, no Andreas.

The waiter hovered, and as much to get him to leave me alone as anything else, I ordered a second glass.

As it was about to arrive, I received a text.

*So sorry, lovely, but we've had an acute peritonitis come in, and the on-call gastro registrar is tied up in A&E. I'm going to have to deal with this one xxx*

I tossed down the menu and pushed my chair back, straight into the path of the waiter bringing my glass of champagne. It slopped over my skirt and the toes of his shoes, making me look gauche and foolish. A tidal wave of fury started to rise up inside me.

'Can you get the bill,' I snapped, then modulated my tone. 'And my coat, please.' After all, it wasn't the staff's fault that I had been stood up. Again.

They took pity on me and only charged me for the first glass. Seconds later I was outside on the street in an icy drizzle that settled in my lustrous waves of hair, making it frizz. Pulling up my coat collar I started off towards Kenley Court, then abruptly changed my mind and instead walked to St Anselm's. I wasn't going to let this go. I was going to have it out with Dr Koros.

The gastroenterology ward was quiet. The patients' evening meals had long since been served and final drugs rounds were being carried out.

I stomped up to the nursing station, aware I must look strange and incongruous in my fake fur coat and Louboutins. I tried to remember if my staff ID was in my bag or not.

'Sorry, visiting hours ended half an hour ago,' the nurse at the desk told me.

'I'm staff.' I rummaged in my bag and found the card that

bore my photo along with '*Bryony A. Pearson, Senior Radiographer*'. 'Is Dr Koros here?'

She examined my card, frowning slightly. 'No, Andreas isn't on duty, sorry.'

'I know his shift has finished, but he's here dealing with the emergency admission. The peritonitis.'

'We haven't had any emergency admissions.'

'Are you sure?'

'Yes, I'm sure.' She gave me a wintry smile. 'And if we did, Dr Koros wouldn't be dealing with them. He's on annual leave. Has been since yesterday.'

I felt a strange, cold unravelling sensation in my gut. 'He's off work? But he is around?'

She shook her head. 'He's gone to his brother's stag do in Slovenia. I think he said he was flying back to London on Sunday, so I expect he'll be back on the ward on Monday. Or you could always phone him, if you've got his number.'

'Oh yes,' I said bitterly, 'I've got his number.'

She was staring at me with a mixture of curiosity and pity. Forcing a smile, I said, 'It's fine, it wasn't important. Sorry to have bothered you.'

I was struggling to make sense of what had happened. Had Andreas booked the table before leaving the country, perhaps forgetting he was going to a stag do, or being persuaded at the very last minute to attend? But that still didn't explain the texts saying he was at work. Was he too embarrassed to admit to being double-booked and hoping I would just give up on him and go home?

*You're in Slovenia?*, I typed furiously as I took the lift back to the ground floor. *WTF?*

Head down, I hurried out of the hospital building before I was spotted by anyone I knew. I was close to giving way to self-pitying tears. Only the surge of fury prevented me from doing so. That and a sense of utter bewilderment. Was I the victim of some sort of malicious prank?

Once I was home and had kicked off my heels and removed my black dress in favour of my dressing gown, I went onto Instagram and sure enough, the day before Andreas had posted a photo of himself and a handful of male friends on the banks of a river, tagging the location as Ljubljana. I felt as though I had entered a looking glass world. What the hell was going on? I wondered, dragging my hand through my dishevelled hair.

One thing was certain; I wasn't going to rest until I found out.

# THIRTEEN
## BRYONY

Now

By the time I arrived at work the next morning, I had calmed down a little.

If not exactly seeing the funny side, I was at least more ready to chalk up the previous evening's fiasco and move on. Claire had been right: Dr Koros was a loser and best avoided. Lesson learned. At least I wouldn't have to bump into him for a few days, I thought, as I queued at the ground-floor coffee shop. That was a small mercy to be grateful for.

I was working in the MRI suite that morning. I took my takeout coffee cup with me into the control room and sat down at the terminal to log in. A pop-up appeared on the screen, with a large red danger symbol and the words 'Your password has not been accepted'.

I stared at it. I was quite sure I had entered my password correctly, but even if I hadn't, then the message would just say it was incorrect. What did 'not accepted' imply?

Craig was looking over my shoulder. 'That doesn't look right!'

I moved to try and re-enter my password but he grabbed my wrist. 'No, don't touch it, Bryony; looks like you've been hacked!'

I swivelled round in my chair to face him. 'Have you managed to log in okay this morning?'

'I'm logged in at the reception desk.' He pointed. 'Looks like it's just your login, which is weird. Call the IT guys.'

Fifteen minutes later, Leo Salvesen appeared in the doorway of the control room. He was wearing dark jeans and a navy sweatshirt and different, less flamboyant glasses in which – to my mind at least – he looked more attractive. I let him look at the screen, which was exactly as I had left it.

'Yup, looks like you've been hacked.' He sucked his teeth. 'Haven't heard of it happening to anyone else. Strange. Things like this are usually system wide.'

He pressed a few keys, then shook his head. 'I'll have to go and override your account on the mainframe and set it up again.'

'Will you need my old password?'

'It's okay.' He smiled, and I noticed for the first time that he had good teeth. He was quite handsome, really, in a silver fox kind of way. 'We have a record of all of those.'

Glancing over his shoulder to make sure we weren't being overheard, he lowered his voice. 'By the way, Bryony, I saw that Kirkwood guy skulking around outside and politely suggested he should leave you alone.'

'Yes, I know. He told me.'

Leo groaned. 'Oh God, sorry! I hope I haven't made things awkward for you.'

'No, it's okay. I think.'

'Only I discovered a very good reason to give him a wide berth.' He glanced behind him again. 'Did you notice the tattoo on his left hand, between his thumb and forefinger?'

I shook my head.

'The ace of spades symbol. Associated with the three-one-two. One of the South East London gangs.'

My eyes widened slightly.

'Trust me; if he is a member, you want to stay well away.'


It would be a good idea to get out of London for the weekend, I decided, even though the walls in my flat were still unpainted.

I phoned my father and stepmother and invited myself to their house in Sussex. My mother had died of breast cancer when I was fifteen, and around the same time my father – who had left several years earlier – married Gayle, a thirty-something buyer for a large department store. I liked her well enough, but left for college soon after she became a fixture in my father's life. We had never had the chance to become close.

Still, she always made an effort with me on the rare occasions I visited, and I enjoyed an undemanding two days of home-cooked meals and long walks on the South Downs. I even fitted in a trip to Lewes to do some early Christmas shopping. The previous week's dramas at St Anselm's seemed far away and rather petty, and by the time I returned on Sunday evening I was feeling the benefits of the break. I had already blocked Andreas Koros's number during my train journey on Friday evening, and resolved to waste no more time on him.

And then on Monday I saw him in the staff canteen during my lunch break. He was sitting at a table with a couple of his colleagues, and all of them were laughing raucously. It wasn't the laughter that tipped me over the edge – galling as it was – but the fact that he looked up, caught my eye and smiled seductively in my direction.

I waited until his two friends had left, then abandoned my sandwich and stormed straight over to him.

'You've got a fucking nerve!' I hissed.

He cringed away from me like a dog that had just been kicked. 'Woah! What am I supposed to have done?'

'Oh, you know exactly what you've done,' I spat.

'I can assure you I don't...' He leaned forward to read my name badge. 'Bryony, you and I have only spoken once, that I recall. About that infarction. You are in radiology, yes?'

'What about our drink at the Bunch of Grapes? When you kept me waiting for nearly an hour before flaking? Or our dinner last Wednesday?'

His face registered genuine confusion. 'I'm sorry but I think you've got me mixed up with somebody else. To my knowledge I've never arranged to go anywhere with you.'

He wasn't faking ignorance, I could tell. The freaked-out look in his eyes was no act. Now it was my turn to be confused. I pulled up the text thread on my phone and showed it to him. He read it, screwing up his forehead. 'I never wrote any of this, I swear. Show me where you've saved the number.'

I opened my contacts and showed him. 'Look – Andreas Koros. You're not about to tell me you've got an identical twin?'

He shook his head. 'No. But that's not my number.'

I continued to look sceptical. 'Here...' He took my mobile from me and punched in a different number, then took his own mobile from the pocket of his white coat. It was ringing, the screen flashing with my number registering as 'Unknown'.

'How did you get that number anyway... the one you've saved on your phone as me?'

'It was a couple of days after you came to the CT suite that time. Someone messaged me saying they were you, claiming they'd got my number from a contact in HR. We started talking, and whoever it was asked me out for a drink and then dinner.'

'But no one showed?'

I shook my head slowly.

'Well, of course they didn't because whoever was texting you wasn't me. Sorry, but it looks like you've been the victim of a rather unkind joke. I think they call it being catfished. My guess would be that it's someone who works here.'

'How on earth did they get my number?'

Andreas stood up to go, clearly losing interest in my dilemma. 'Someone who can access staff records? Someone in IT maybe?' He picked up his tray. 'Anyway, I'm really sorry that happened, Bethany—'

'Bryony.'

'Sorry – Bryony. But at least now you know why you were stood up, right?'

*And why whoever it was never wanted to voice call or FaceTime.*

I watched Andreas dump his tray on the trolley, turning over his shoulder to give me a rueful little wave. He was right, I thought, as I returned to the remains of my sandwich: at least I now knew that the real Andreas had not been messing me around. But who on earth would pose as him and start a relationship with me, albeit a fake one? Surely it had to be someone who knew that I'd been interested in him when I arrived at the hospital. Apart from Claire, I had only ever mentioned him to a couple of my colleagues. Could one of them really have done something so manipulative, so malicious? And why would they?

When I left the canteen, instead of making my way back to the PET scanner where I was working that afternoon, I headed up to the IT department on the fifth floor. Leo was at his desk, and broke into a smile when he saw me.

'Bryony! What brings you to the nerds' lair? Don't tell me your login has been hacked again?'

I shook my head. Then I hesitated. I didn't really want to recount the whole humiliating Andreas saga. If he'd just been a work colleague it might not have mattered, but the fact was we lived in the same building, and therefore our relationship spilled over from the professional and into the personal.

'If I gave you a mobile number, do you think you could use your cyber skills to trace who it belongs to?'

He leaned back in his chair and gave me a long appraising look.

'I take it this is an unofficial enquiry?'

'It is, yes. Well, kind of; someone's been using it to send me nuisance texts while I'm at work, so...'

'And you haven't reported it to HR?'

I shook my head. As a new employee, I didn't particularly want to draw attention to the fact I was texting people during my working hours.

He sat up again. 'Sure, I'll give it a try, on the understanding that my involvement is strictly off the record. And I can't promise anything.'

'Will you at least be able to tell me if it belongs to someone employed here?'

Our eyes met. 'Probably,' he said.

I picked up a biro from his desk and transcribed the fake 'Andreas' contact number from my phone onto a Post-it note, handing it to him.

Another member of the IT team appeared in the doorway, and Leo touched a finger to his lips. 'I'll get back to you,' he mouthed.

I touched my own finger to my lips, sealing our pact of silence, then turned and left.

As I was leaving for home a few hours later, I spotted someone who looked familiar on the front steps of the hospital.

His hair was covered by a black woollen beanie and a jacket with a fur-lined hood, but despite the evening gloom, as I approached I realised I had identified him correctly. Dervla Quinn's son, Shane.

He smiled broadly when he saw me, though I sensed he couldn't quite place me.

'Shane... it's Bryony. Bryony Pearson. Your Aunt Claire's best mate.'

'Oh yeah,' he said. 'Right, sure. Good to see you. How are you?'

Those Irish eyes really were stunning, I thought. Destined to break some hearts, no doubt.

'What are you doing here... you're not ill, I hope?'

He shifted from foot to foot in the cold, thrusting his hands in his pockets. 'Nah, nah I'm fine. I'm here with my nan. Dad's mum: Nanny Quinn. She's here to see the... the what d'you call it, for her feet?'

'The podiatrist?'

'Yeah, that's the one.' He grinned, and the gold tooth caught the light from the entrance porch. 'She doesn't drive you see, Nan, and I've got my licence now. So I've borrowed Mum's car and I'm going to drive her home after she's finished. I just came out here for a bit of... you know, fresh air.'

We both looked down at the cigarette butt at his feet.

'She's a lucky woman to have such a devoted grandson.' I smiled at him and touched his sleeve briefly. 'Well, I'd better get off home.'

'Yeah, I'd better go and check if Nan's ready to leave. Nice to see you again.'

Hands still in pockets, he shrugged his shoulders and ambled back into the building. Whatever trouble he was giving his parents, it surely couldn't be that serious, I reflected as I trudged back to the main road. Surely nothing dangerous. From what I had seen, he was a perfectly decent young man.

But yet again, the events that followed would prove me wrong.

# FOURTEEN
## BRYONY

Diary entries: six years earlier

*1st June*

*Oh God – last night was a disaster! Okay, scratch that. Maybe disaster is too strong a word. But it wasn't great. I slept with Robbie, and... well let's just say the earth didn't exactly move. We went out to dinner and probably because we both subconsciously knew this was on the cards, had quite a bit to drink. Over dinner he told me he's got a friend's wedding coming up in a couple of weeks, and I agreed to go with him as his plus one. It seemed like a positive step.*

*And of course, after a couple of Pornstar Martinis and half a bottle of wine, sex seemed like a brilliant idea. Or an inevitability, at least. We went back to his place because I have a flatmate and he doesn't. I'm not saying the sex was terrible. He didn't suffer from erectile dysfunction and he wasn't into anything weird. Nothing like that. But he was all sweaty and intense, staring at me the whole time during the deed, and when it was over he used the 'L' word. We've only known each other a couple of weeks – if that – and he's telling me he loves me? To use Claire's words, that's a whole bunting of red flags.*

*It's not that I don't like him. I do. He's a nice guy. But love? WTF. That's way too much for me at this stage. I'm worried Claire is right.*

*11th June*

*Claire came round to the flat for a quick cup of tea on her way back from work, and she talked me out of ending things with Robbie before the wedding. As I've already written here, he's fine as someone to just hang out with, and C quite rightly pointed out that since this wedding is going to be quite a big do it will be what she called 'a target-rich environment'. By which she means there will be plenty of other men there. More promising men. Also, I know it means a lot to Robbie to be attending with a plus one, so it would be a bit cruel to cancel now. I'm not that much of a cow. I've been to a couple of weddings solo since I broke up with Aaron and it's no fun being stuck on the sad singles table at the reception.*

*For that reason, I'll wait until after the wedding to finish it. The Park Hill hospital imaging unit is merging with ours and we're going to be crazy busy, and I can just blame it on the pressure of work.*

*The wedding's at some swanky venue in the Kent countryside. It's less than an hour away, and I'm keen not to give Robbie the wrong idea by arranging to spend the night. Instead, he's going to hire a car and drive us both there and back. And then hopefully we can part amicably. Draw a line under it.*

# FIFTEEN
## BRYONY

Now

A couple of days later I was trudging up the sloping approach to the hospital when I heard someone calling my name.

It had rained heavily overnight, and a layer of sodden leaves was making the pavement slippery. It was one of those overcast November days with an oyster-grey sky that never gets properly light. My mood matched the weather: I felt flat and heavy. I'd been enjoying my new job but that morning I just wanted a break from it. I was wishing I could have stayed at home and made a start on the decorating.

'Bryony!'

I turned round and saw Leo Salvesen wheeling his bike. He was wearing a black Lycra cycling top with silver reflective stripes. 'Didn't you hear me?'

'Sorry, I was miles away.' I forced a smile that probably looked more like a grimace.

'I was going to call round to your flat later actually, but now is as good a time as any, if you've got a minute?'

'Sure.' I fell into step beside him as he pushed the bike up the slope.

'That mobile number you asked me to look into: it's a burner phone. One that was purchased in a supermarket or a convenience store with prepaid minutes and data. So while it could in theory belong to someone who works here, I've no way of confirming that. Sorry.'

'You're saying it can't be traced?'

'It's possible to retrieve information about the phone's usage and location, but only law enforcement can access that, and they'd have to have a good reason to do so.'

'Oh well.' I shrugged my shoulders. 'When all's said and done, I was stood up on a date. It's hardly Single White Female.'

Leo glanced up at me as he was bending to chain his bike. 'Why, do you think it could be a woman sending those texts?'

'It did occur to me, yes.' We walked into the reception area together. 'Anyway, thanks for trying, I appreciate it.'

'Any more unwanted messages; just block the number straightaway, okay?'


I remembered this advice a couple of hours later when I was sitting in the control room of the MRI suite, looking at some images of a particularly nasty herniated spinal disc, and my phone buzzed with a text. From an unsaved number.

*Hi, it's Andreas Koros. The real one! Wondered if you fancied going for a drink sometime... a real one, of course! X*

I slipped my phone back into the pocket of my scrubs, unsure what to think. Once I was on my break, I opened it and read it again. It seemed unlikely there were two Andreas impersonators out there, harassing me. And then it occurred to me that I could check. He'd used my handset to call his own phone and make it ring, so that I could see he had a different number. Which was now stored in the call log of my phone. I pulled up the log, and sure enough, it was the same number used to send the text I'd just received. I saved it in my contacts as 'Real Andreas'.

And yet I was still wary for some reason; paranoid even. I realised that if someone was prepared to hack my work email, they could also have hacked Andreas's phone, or cloned his SIM card, though why anyone would go to such lengths remained a mystery.

*If we do*, I typed, *any arrangements will have to be made face to face. Just to be on the safe side after what happened. Sure you understand.*

I thought this might put him off, but just as I was logging out of my computer terminal and pulling off my staff lanyard in preparation for changing out of my scrubs, there was a flash of a white coat outside the control room and Andreas appeared.

'Hi,' I said, grinning. 'It worked.'

'Okay then, let's do it face to face,' he said. Rather than being amused by my demand, he seemed faintly annoyed. 'Where would you like to go?'

'Um, you choose,' I said weakly.

'How about La Molina?' He named a tapas bar about half a mile from the hospital.

'Perfect. When?'

He whipped out his phone and looked on the calendar app. 'I've got nothing before next week... how about next Wednesday. Seven o'clock?'

'It's a date,' I said. 'Let's hope it's a real one.'

He gave me the sort of smile I was sure he used on his patients and swept out of the room.

. . .

'I still reckon he's a waste of space,' Claire said, when she dropped round to my flat for a glass of wine that evening.

'How can you say that?' I protested. 'Someone was pretending to be him before, remember. This is the real person. The real hot person. And for all we know, he's going to show up.'

Claire curled her lip. 'Well now, will he though?' she said in her thickest Irish accent, which she trotted out for comic effect from time to time.

'He will,' I said firmly. 'Because he knows that if he doesn't, I'm going to harangue him in public again.'

'So who do you think did send those messages? You any the wiser?'

I shook my head, sloshing Pinot Noir into my glass.

'What about your man downstairs? What's his name... the one who works at the hospital with you?'

'Leo?' I shook my head firmly. 'No way. He wouldn't do something like that. At least, I'm pretty sure he wouldn't.'

'Bry, you don't know that,' Claire scoffed. 'I bet he fancies you. And didn't you say he works in the IT department?'

'He does.'

'Well, think about it... he knows how to hack into stuff. And he's got access to your personnel file, so presumably he could have got hold of your mobile number.'

'He's already got my number. But no,' I insisted. 'It wouldn't be him.'

But as I watched Claire walking down the steps of the building when she left an hour later, I thought I caught sight of a tall figure looking up at my window, and a flash of something silver. Silver stripes, on a black jacket.

I spent the next few days nesting.

I decided the blue-green colour I had selected was too cold for the light in the living room. Perhaps Kyle Kirkwood presenting me with a similar shade of paint had also put me off it. Instead, I painted the walls a warm ochre colour and bought a shaggy cream rug and cushions in shades of olive green and russet, and a large gilded mirror in the shape of a sunburst. I poked about in local second-hand shops for books and pieces of kitsch ceramic, sourced a hatstand for the hall and brought home several large pot plants from the garden centre. The bedroom was next on the list for an upgrade, and I ordered test pots in shades of plaster and shell pink, daubing them on the walls and starting the search for the perfect blind. During the process of installing my purchases, I left some of the packaging in the communal stairwell and earned myself a telling off from Lida, even though it was nowhere near her own flat.

'Recycling is collected tomorrow,' she told me crossly, in her *mittel* European accent. 'Unless you're taking it straight to the bin store it should remain in your own apartment.'

I was so absorbed in my domestic bubble that suddenly Wednesday had rolled around without me spending much time thinking about my date with Andreas. I realised I had been half expecting him to message me in the interim, build up a little anticipatory tension, but there was nothing. As a result, I set off to La Molina fully prepared to be stood up again. Instead of the sexy black dress and spiky heels I had played it safe this time, wearing a dark grey blazer with jeans and ballet pumps. As I approached the entrance to the tapas bar, I did a double take. No, it couldn't be... was it?

Leo Salvesen was standing outside the Hopsquad taproom a couple of doors down, with his arm wound around the neck of a woman. A petite, dark woman. Just a friend, I thought; then as though he'd read my mind, he bent his head and kissed her full on the lips. A lingering kiss, and definitely not the kind that you gave to a friend. I felt oddly flustered, but I couldn't have said why. Whatever the reason, I really didn't want him to see me. Ducking my head, I darted into La Molina. I was anticipating being led to an empty table to begin an enervating wait, but straight away I saw Andreas, his hand raised in greeting.

This time, it was real. This time he was waiting for me.

# SIXTEEN
## BRYONY

Now

He'd already ordered cava for both of us.

'Forget the cheap cava you get in the supermarket, the stuff they serve here's the real deal,' he said smugly. Did he bring all his first dates here? I wondered.

I sipped the cold liquid, and smiled, although I found it bland and faintly soapy. When the waiter finally arrived, pad in hand, Andreas ordered for us without consulting me about what I liked, or even what my dietary preferences were.

'You've got to try these,' he said, pushing *gambas al ajillo* and Iberico pork in my direction. 'I've had them here before; they're really, really good.'

'I don't eat meat,' I said pointedly.

'The prawns though: you can have those.'

'I don't eat seafood either. I'm a vegetarian.'

'Right.' He seemed personally affronted. 'Right, right, okay. You should have told me.'

*Like you gave me the chance.*

Once the waiter had been called back, I ordered some patatas bravas and cheese croquetas. Andreas was shovelling slices of pork into his mouth.

'This won't help with my cutting,' he said with a rueful grin.

'Your cutting?' I asked, confused. I was pretty sure he was a physician, not a surgeon.

'Cutting, you know...' He frowned. 'So you're not into the gym then?'

I shook my head.

'Cutting involves reducing your percentage body fat by reducing calorie load. The opposite of bulking.'

'Ah, I see,' I said. I wasn't interested but now felt obliged to ask, 'So do you spend much time in the gym then?'

And that was it. The floodgates had opened. Over the next forty minutes I was treated to a detailed breakdown of Andreas's gym habit: the hours, the reps, the sets, the gains. I was completely bored; my face aching with the effort of trying to look interested. Eventually I managed to switch the subject to his Greek Cypriot family, and his medical career. I learned that his father and grandfather were both doctors, that he had attended Athens Medical School before successfully applying to do his final three years of training in London. That he had a specialist interest in hepatology, and had published several research papers on the subject. By the time we got to coffee I had a detailed breakdown of the subject matter of that research, and his future career plans. I even learned the name of his sister (Chara) and his childhood pet dog (Bojo).

He, on the other hand, learned absolutely nothing about me. Not one thing. Because apart from demanding to know whether I attended a gym, he didn't ask me a single question about myself.

'Let's go on for a drink somewhere else,' he said once the bill had arrived and I had insisted on paying half. 'There's a couple of bars in this street.'

My mind went back to Leo, possibly in one of them with his new love interest.

'No, it's fine,' I said. 'I've had enough to drink.'

This apparently was all the encouragement he needed. He wound an arm round my waist. 'In that case let's go straight back to my place.'

I removed his arm, giving him my sweetest smile as I shook my head. 'It's a no thank you from me.'

As I was walking back to Kenley Court, grateful that I hadn't bothered with high heels, it occurred to me that when it came to communication style I had preferred the first, catfish version of Andreas Koros. Unlike the real thing, they – whoever they were – had seemed a little more fun.

The truth of this was disturbing. 'There's a lesson in there somewhere,' I told Claire when we met for a debrief over coffee on Saturday morning. 'I'm just not sure what it is.'

'That if someone behaves like an arsehole then they probably are?' she suggested. I noticed she had ordered a decaf.

'Yes, but the real Dr Koros wasn't the one who stood me up twice,' I reminded her. 'He showed up exactly when he was supposed to, just turned out to be a self-obsessed bore. That's part of what makes this whole episode so...' I reached for the right word. '... unsettling.'

'Maybe the lesson is that you should not get involved with anyone you work with,' Claire said, dragging her spoon round and round her cup. 'Stay the hell away when it comes to dating.'

I sighed. 'You're probably right. And it's been nice just concentrating on getting the flat how I want it. I quite enjoy doing the homemaking bit.'

'So you're glad you bought it?'

'Very, especially now it's starting to come together. It's my sanctuary. I feel safe there.'

Claire was nodding, but she had a faraway look on her face.

'How about you?' I probed. 'What's the latest?'

'Don't tell anyone, but I think I might be pregnant.' The words came out in a rush and she hunched forward, her hands clamped tightly between her thighs.

'Oh, sweetie, that's so exciting!' I went to hug her but she extricated her hands and pushed me away. 'Don't, Bry, no celebrations yet, okay? It's very early and things could still go wrong.'

'Of course,' I said, adopting a more sober expression. 'I'll be keeping everything crossed for you though.'

It was exciting, I thought, as I headed back to the flat after doing some shopping: new life starting. And despite the Andreas fiasco, I felt I was on the way to creating a new life for myself too. The decision to return to the UK from Australia had not been an easy one, but things were starting to fall into place. I had friends nearby; the job was going well and I loved my cosy little flat. After what had happened to me, I was lucky to be in this position.

I let myself into the building and climbed up the stairs to the top floor. As I rounded the corner into the stretch of corridor that led to my own door, I could tell from a subtle shift in the way that the light fell across the carpet that someone was standing in front of it.

Kyle Kirkwood.

'How did you get in?' I demanded ungraciously, then tried to force a smile.

*You still owe this man your life, remember?*

'Didn't mean to scare you...' He gave a slow grin, revealing his crooked teeth. 'One of your neighbours buzzed me in.'

'Was there something you needed?' I reached in my bag for

my key and inserted it in the lock. 'Only I've got a ton of stuff to do.'

'Yeah, there was, as it goes.' He reached over me to push the door open, and was inside the flat before I could do anything about it. 'It's high time you and me had a bit of a chat.'

# SEVENTEEN
## BRYONY

Diary entries: six years earlier

*17th June*

*Saturday night was the worst night of my life. Just a catastrophe. There's no way I can even put down my thoughts about it properly yet. Why did Robbie agree to drive back afterwards if he intended on drinking? Why didn't I raise that with him beforehand? Why didn't I just book somewhere to stay overnight anyway, regardless of the message it would send?*

*All I know is that what happened can never be undone.*
*Too late now. Far, far too late.*

# EIGHTEEN
## BRYONY

Now

I reached for the kettle and set it to boil.

It was too early in the day for an alcoholic drink, even though I found myself wanting one.

'Tea or coffee?' I asked Kyle, managing to keep my tone just on the friendly side of brisk.

He shook his head. 'Nah, you know I don't mess with that shit.'

There were some soft drink cans in the fridge but I wasn't going to offer him one. I suddenly felt impatient and irritated, unwilling to engage with whatever game he was playing.

'So you said you had something you wanted to talk about?' I asked, tossing a teabag into a mug and pouring boiling water onto it. 'Something I can help you with?'

Kyle pulled out his vape and took a puff. 'I suppose you could put it like that, yeah.'

He had wandered into the living room and was taking in the new décor. I followed him with my mug of tea. 'Like what you've done with the place by the way. Got a telly now, innit.'

He picked up a tangerine velvet cushion and fingered it. 'Looking good.'

He now peered out of the window onto the street below. 'It's nice round here, isn't it? Mind you, finding a parking space must be an absolute fucker. Do you drive Bry-oh-ny?'

He placed heavy emphasis on my name, sounding each syllable separately.

I shook my head, wondering where this was leading. 'I mean, I do have a driving licence,' I clarified. 'But I don't currently own a car.'

'Probably wise, given there's no parking, and the speed bumps down these roads are a real pain.'

He continued to stare outside; his eyes narrowed as though he was focussing hard on something. When he eventually turned back from the window his face was partly obscured by a fog of vapour, but there was a new expression on it that I'd never seen before. A look of disdain, disgust almost. 'What was it they said on that old road safety advert? Oh yeah, "Kill your speed. Not a pedestrian."'

'What?' My heart had started hammering in my chest.

'That's what they said, wasn't it?'

The vapour had cleared and I could see his face clearly now. That look of disgust, curdling into hatred. My blood turned to ice at the words he spoke next.

'... but you'd know all about that, wouldn't you, Bryony Pearson?'

There was a hard, dry lump in my throat, but I somehow managed to remain outwardly calm.

'I have no idea what you're talking about.'

'Oh, I think you do.' He grinned, but his expression remained grim. Menthol-scented clouds escaped from the corners of his mouth. 'Reece Parker. Name not mean anything to you? Fifteenth of June, six years ago. You were driving the car that killed him. Thing is, that guy was my cousin.'

I set down my mug of tea on the table, because my hand was shaking so violently that the liquid was slopping onto the carpet. My first impulse was to deny that I knew what he was talking about. But clearly that wasn't going to work, and what I wanted more than anything was for him to leave my flat, to leave me alone. So I settled on repeating the accepted legal version of events, hoping that it would satisfy him.

'I remember that night, of course I do,' I said quietly. 'But I wasn't the driver of the car.'

'Oh yeah, yeah... I know that was the official story.' Kyle thrust his vape back in his pocket and walked over to my fridge, yanking the door open and helping himself to a can of Coke. 'But we both know that's not what really happened.'

My legs were shaking so violently now that I had to grip the edge of the table. How can he possibly know this?

He pulled the ring pull off the can with a loud snap and lifted it to his lips, his eyes still on me, waiting for me to speak. I said nothing.

'The guy who took the rap for you was sent down for it, wasn't he? Robert Makepeace...' He rolled the name around his mouth as though he was trying it out. 'Eight years, he got, didn't he? Pretty steep for a first offence, but I guess the judge wanted to make an example of him, because he'd been drinking and judges ain't too keen on drinking and driving, are they? Specially not when there's a dead body involved.'

He took a loud slurp of the soda, smacked his lips. 'Anyway, what happened next was quite interesting, as it goes. When he was banged up in HMP Rochester, he shared a cell with a geezer called Cliff. And your mate Robert got quite pally with Cliff and told him that he hadn't really been behind the wheel, but that his girlfriend had. A bird called Bryony Pearson. And when Cliff got out of the can, he told his family all about it, including his nephew, Lee Sweeney. And then Lee comes straight to me and tells me—'

Kyle jabbed a finger at his own chest. 'Because Lee happens to be a mate of mine, and he knew my connection to Reece. My blood connection.'

Once more he waited for me to speak, and once more I said nothing.

'So I think to myself, this is some useful information, innit. Could be very useful indeed, if I can find the whereabouts of this Bryony.' Giving me a sly grin, he tossed the can in the direction of the kitchen bin, and missed.

My voice came out in an odd croak. 'Are you saying that when you pulled me out of the road that time...?'

'Yeah, I'd been following you. Still saved your life though, as it goes,' he added a little defensively. 'Still lucky for you I was there, right?'

I ignored this, unwilling to think about the alternative scenario; the lorry colliding with the side of my body, smashing through skin and bone. 'But how did you know where I lived? I'd only just bought this place.'

'Come on now, smart bird like you.' He scoffed. 'Don't you know any information you want is available now, at a price. Ways and means, innit.'

I hesitated a beat, weighing up my predicament. 'I'd like you to please go, Kyle,' I said firmly. 'Whatever you did when I was crossing that road, this amounts to harassment.'

'Suit yourself.' He shrugged and set off towards the front door, shoving his vape in his pocket. 'Only the thing is, you lied to the feds about what happened to Reece, yeah? You let someone else take the blame. Perverting the course of justice, innit.' He had one hand on the front door catch, swinging round towards me as he pulled it open. 'And the thing with that is, it carries a sentence of up to life? Did you know that?'

I followed him to the front door. 'What do you want, Kyle?' My voice was barely above a whisper.

He had his back to me, but turned and glanced over his shoulder. 'Justice.'

'And what does that mean?' I demanded, following him out onto the staircase.

'It means that now it's time for you to pay. To pay for Reece's life.'

# NINETEEN
## BRYONY

Diary entries: six years earlier

*5th August*

*It's been six weeks, and I'm only just now able to write about what happened on 15th June.*

*I've started seeing a therapist, and that's helped me get my head straight, because until that point I hadn't even been able to talk to Claire about what I was going through. Well, she knows the official version, but not what really happened. Dr Drummond (I've been assuming she's a doctor – maybe not?) has been very helpful in allowing me to process my emotions, but I daren't tell even her the entire truth, because I'm not convinced a fatality falls within the bounds of patient confidentiality. She asked me if I felt I was somehow to blame for what happened to the accident victim. I re-ran what happened in the car that night like rewinding video tape. No, I was able to tell her with complete honesty, it wasn't my fault. But still I felt horrible*

*The wedding was lovely. Lovely bride (Ruby) and groom (Brett), gorgeous venue just outside Sevenoaks. Booze flowing. I didn't really drink all that much because too much champagne makes me feel sick, so when Robbie said he wanted to leave I'd been dancing for a couple of hours and had pretty much sobered up. But when we got to the car it was clear that Robbie had drunk far too much to be driving. I was pretty annoyed with him. He said he 'didn't really notice' how much he'd had. Yes, the wedding reception had been fun, but I didn't know anyone apart from Robbie. I was over the whole thing at this point, just wanted to get home. So I said I'd drive. I wasn't on the insurance for the car, but we agreed that a short journey on quiet roads would be fine.*

*But the roads were dark and twisty, and it started to rain. Visibility wasn't great, Robbie was all over the place, distracting me, and then suddenly out of nowhere the front of the car hit something. Robbie said it must have been a deer so I just kept driving. But after a couple of minutes there were police lights and sirens in the distance behind us. Robbie barked at me to pull over, and before I could even think, he'd jumped out and run round to the driver's side of the car, opened the door and shoved me across to the passenger side. He told me that if the cops stopped, I was to say it was him who was driving. I wasn't insured for the vehicle and he didn't want grief from the car hire people. I told him that he must surely be over the limit but he insisted he'd sobered up and would be fine.*

*So that was exactly what we told the police when the patrol car pulled into the layby behind us. They asked Robbie if he was aware he had hit something. He said yes, and that was when they told us it wasn't a deer. It was one of the other wedding guests; a man who lived locally and had decided to make his way home on foot. We were both too stunned to say anything, so of course they carried on in the assumption that Robbie was driving. They breathalysed both of us. I was just inside the legal limit and Robbie was well over. We were taken to Biggin Hill Police Station and separated. I gave a statement and eventually at about 2 a.m., an officer drove me home. I don't know what happened to the hire car, but I'm guessing it was impounded. Robbie was kept in a cell overnight. In the morning when he'd sobered up, he was told the man he'd hit had died in hospital, and he was going to be charged with causing death by dangerous driving.*

*I only found this out a couple of days later when he called me from a new phone. He said it was safer not to use his regular phone, that we could speak without being monitored. It seemed a little paranoid, but he was probably right. He told me he was okay, and that we needed to stick to the story that he was driving. That this was all his fault for getting drunk. That if he hadn't been none of what did happen would ever have happened. He was completely insistent that we couldn't go back on it now and risk adding perverting the course of justice to the charge he was already facing. On the one hand I feel terrible about what he's going through, but on the other hand yes, he's right: it was all his fault. So I did the only thing I could do in the circumstances, and assured him he had my full support: whatever he needed.*

*As for the man who died: I can hardly bear to think about him. His name is Reece Parker; it's in the local news. The remorse I feel is relentless and overwhelming. I hear the sound of the car impacting flesh and bone over and over again in my head. If only I had seen him. If only. If only.*

*Dr Drummond stressed that I need to remember this was an accident. That road traffic accidents happen all the time and no one had any intention of causing harm. That the post-mortem showed the victim had been drinking heavily at the wedding and was probably not paying attention and straying into the path of the vehicle. When you put all the facts together like that, I know rationally that his death is far from entirely my fault.*

*But that doesn't stop me feeling wretched with guilt.*

# TWENTY
## BRYONY

Now

'What do you want, Kyle?'

'Justice.'

'And what does that mean?

'It means that now it's time for you to pay. To pay for Reece's life. He was only a couple of years older than me. He should have had years.'

'But what do you want from me?' I repeated. I had followed Kyle out onto the landing, shouting after him as he headed down the stairs. 'You can't just leave things like that!'

He held up a hand, as casually as though we were discussing ordering a pizza and shouted back: 'I'll let you know, yeah.'

On the landing below, I heard the scrape of a door chain. That would be Lida, about to stick her head out and see what the commotion was about. I hastily retreated into my flat and shut the door. I leaned on the kitchen counter for a few minutes, trembling, before rummaging in one of the cupboards and finding the bottle of Scotch I kept for emergencies. With shaking hands, I poured some into my empty teacup. Kyle was calling my bluff, I told myself. His life was lived on the fringes of criminality. In fact, hadn't Leo Salvesen said he probably had gangland connections? He surely wouldn't go to the authorities?

And yet, I couldn't rule it out.

Desperate to distract myself, I put on a wash cycle and cleaned the flat from top to bottom, scrubbing the bathroom floor over and over with frantic movements as though trying to exhaust myself. When my physical energy started to flag, and it was growing dark, I slumped on the sofa and found a fifteen-year-old period drama on my streaming service that I'd never got round to watching. And I continued to work my way through the Scotch, until eventually I fell asleep on the sofa.

When I woke up, it was to the sound of sirens.

The blinds were still open, and the red and blue of a police car's lights strobed lazily across the living wall. My body seized as though in some form of arrest, and my lungs burned with sudden panic. The police had come for me. Kyle had already been to speak to them.

I somehow willed my legs to work and staggered over to the window. In the intermittent beam from the flashing light, I could see two officers climbing out of the vehicle and hear the crackle of a police radio. They walked over to the house opposite Kenley Court, a rundown building converted into bedsits, and rang one of the doorbells. They weren't here for me. Of course they weren't.

I undressed and climbed into bed, but it was the early hours of Sunday before I fell asleep again. I needed to tell someone about what had happened with Kyle. That evening's overwhelming physical panic was enough to convince me that I couldn't carry the burden alone. But who could I share it with, given that no one in my life other than Robbie Makepeace and his former cellmate knew that I had been driving the car that had killed Reece Parker? And Kyle Kirkwood, of course. Not even Claire knew. She was the obvious person to confide in, but also newly pregnant after trying to conceive for a long time. I didn't want to subject her to any additional stress. No, even telling my best friend was too risky.

My mind turned to Leo Salvesen. He was the one who had tried to warn off Kyle, after all. And although I'd ruled out a romance with him, I liked him and wanted to consider him a friend. I pondered this for the rest of Sunday, but remained unsure. The fact was, speaking to anybody about what had happened in the car with Robbie was a risk. As I tramped disconsolately to the supermarket, I remembered something my mother used to say to me as a child.

*'If you have nothing nice to say, say nothing.'*

For now, I would keep my own counsel.

'Are you on your way to the meeting?'

'Sorry?'

I turned to find my line manager, Ange Hyter, standing at my elbow. It was Monday morning and I was in the hospital's ground-floor concourse, still feeling dazed. Behind me the bank of lifts pinged constantly as patients and workers started arriving. A gaggle of medical students formed a disorderly queue at the coffee shop, chattering and laughing.

'The nine a.m. team meeting... Are you all right, Bryony? You look miles away.'

'I was just looking at this.'

I pointed at the staff noticeboard where there was a poster for the hospital Christmas party, due to take place on Friday evening.

'Are you going to go to that? It usually gets pretty wild.' Ange raised her eyebrows in an 'if you know, you know' gesture.

I pulled a face. 'Not sure. For starters, I hadn't realised there was a theme. I don't know where I'd even start with "Steampunk Gothic".'

'Think corsets and top hats,' Ange suggested as we walked together to the lifts. 'You're tall: you'd look great as a Victorian goth.'

'What was it last year?'

'*Game of Thrones*. Lot of men with swords and sheepskin rugs draped round their shoulders. And the year before was Harry Potter.'

'School uniforms and witches' hats,' I supplied as we got into the lift and headed to the second floor. 'To be honest, that would be a lot easier.'

I did my best to focus on the department's weekly meeting and then on my patients, but I was jumpy and inattentive: my mind spinning. In the cold light of day, it was hard to give credence to the idea that Kyle would choose to go to the police about me. If he did so then he would have played his trump card, when what he really wanted was to wield power over me. He needed something from me, but for the life of me I couldn't work out what that could be. Was this straightforward blackmail? In other words, did he want money? If that was the case, surely he would have just come straight out and asked for it? And what money could I give him anyway? I was cleaned out by the flat purchase. As a desperate measure I could ask my father, but that would mean telling him that I was being blackmailed for a hit and run that nobody knew about. I hadn't told him and my stepmother what really happened that night, just as I hadn't told my sister, or Claire.

By the end of the day, I was exhausted and strung out, and far from in the mood to engage with Andrea Koros. And yet there he was as I walked through reception on my way home, his sweep of dark hair gelled back, his white coat unnaturally clean. He stepped into my path so I was forced to stop.

'Hey you!'

I decided this greeting meant he had already forgotten my name.

'How are you, gorgeous?'

'Fine,' I lied.

'We should really go for that drink.'

'"That" drink? What drink? I looked up at his face, all square jaw and chiselled cheekbones. I took in what I was now sure were veneers, badly done ones that were a little too large for his mouth and wondered what I had seen in him. I shook my head.

'I really don't think that's a good idea.'

'Why, have you met someone else?'

'Something like that.' He was still blocking my path but I sidestepped him deftly and headed for the revolving door, pulling my coat on as I went.

As I approached Kenley Court a few minutes later, I half expected to see Kyle Kirkwood loitering in the shadows. But there was no sign. I heated up a ready meal in the microwave and drank more Sauvignon Blanc than was wise before collapsing into bed. Despite the three quarters of a bottle, sleep eluded me. I was alert to every tiny sound, from the rattle of the window frame to the distant clunk of the street door closing two storeys below. I found myself wishing I had an address or phone number for Kyle, so that I could contact him and demand to know what his intentions were. As things stood, I had no means of doing so. Just before I eventually drifted to sleep, it occurred to me that if Kyle could find out all about me, then there was no reason I couldn't do the same. I switched on my bedside light and tried googling 'Kyle Kirkwood'.

The results revealed a Snapchat account with an avatar of a sinister-looking hooded figure. There were also a few Facebook accounts in that name, but after ruling most of them out, the only possibility had impenetrable privacy settings. And there was an online news item from a few years earlier mentioning an appearance in Bromley Magistrates' Court by a Kyle Kirkwood, 19, from Eltham, charged with affray.

I put my phone down and switched off my light. None of this was going to help me locate Kyle. I had no idea how to go about finding more up-to-date information, but I knew someone who would. Someone who could help me.

# TWENTY-ONE
## BRYONY

Now

The following morning, I stopped on the ground floor on my way to work and rang the Salvesens' doorbell.

The door was opened a crack by a whey-faced Ingrid. She was wearing a grey fleece dressing gown and her hair was in need of a wash.

'Sorry to disturb you,' I said, smiling in the face of her hostile glare, 'but could I have a quick word with Leo?'

'He's not here.' Ingrid made to shut the door again.

'Has he left for work already?' I said quickly, moving in closer but stopping short of inserting my foot in the doorframe. 'Never mind, I can try and catch him there.'

'He's away this week,' Ingrid said bleakly. 'On a course.' And then she really did close the door in my face.

Pushing thoughts of Kyle Kirkwood's threat from my mind, I trudged to work through swirling sleet. I was in need of a distraction, so when Rochelle asked me to go to the Christmas party with her, I agreed. We spent our lunchbreak in the canteen, hunched over her phone while we tried to source items which would fit the steampunk theme. Halloween costume suppliers were a rich hunting ground, and before long we'd each made an order and paid for next-day delivery.

'We're going to look iconic!' Rochelle said, rubbing her hands with glee. 'It should be a really good night.'

'As long as everyone else sticks to the theme too,' I pointed out. 'Otherwise, we're going to look more idiotic than iconic.'

'Are you going to bring someone?' Rochelle asked, as we headed back to the imaging department. 'Only a lot of people bring a plus one.'

I shook my head.

'Not even hot Doctor Koros?' Rochelle said with a giggle.

'Especially not him. Although...' I conceded, as I read through that afternoon's list of patients, 'he would look quite good in a Victorian frock coat.'

Rochelle and I needn't have feared looking foolish.

The party was held in the staff canteen, which had been cleared for the purpose. There was laser lighting, metallic streamers and banks of black and gold balloons, while a sound system played early-2000s pop. By the time we arrived, two or three hundred of St Anselm's staff were crushed into the room, which felt hot and airless. Hospital porters were dancing with doctors, receptionists with lab technicians. The steampunk theme had been enthusiastically embraced, and the results were nothing short of spectacular. The men were wearing breeches and military-style coats, top hats adorned with feathers and flying goggles. The women had invested in a glorious mish mash of corsets, riding hats, petticoats and pantaloons. My own red velvet corset was uncomfortably tight and the calf-length lace-up boots pinched my feet, but after a couple of glasses of rum punch I managed to forget the pain and lose myself in the party spirit.

I'd twisted my hair into an extravagant arrangement of curls, which started to look bedraggled after I'd been dancing wildly for an hour. The red-black lipstick I'd used was rubbing off, so I found my bag and pulled out a compact in order to reapply it. As I looked at my mouth in the mirror, I caught sight of a familiar figure among the blur of dark coats and gold braid. He was dressed in striped breeches, a highwayman's shirt and waistcoat, and without his glasses and with black kohl outlining his eyes, I almost didn't recognise him. Leo Salvesen.

I put away the compact and turned to push through the crowd in his direction. Now that he was back from his course, I decided I might as well take the opportunity to speak to him. Then I saw that he was not alone. He had his arm draped round the shoulders of a woman. The same petite, dark-haired woman I had seen him with on the night of my date with Andreas Koros. I realised with a flash of irritation that I felt slightly jealous.

Rochelle appeared at my elbow bearing two plastic cups of punch. She looked spectacular in tartan bustier and matching flounced skirt, a black silk patch over one eye.

I pointed to Leo's companion. 'Do you know who that is?'

Rochelle removed her patch and narrowed her eyes. 'I know her by sight, yeah.'

'Does she work here?'

'I think she's one of the dieticians, but I couldn't swear to it. Monique? Monica? Michelle? Something like that.'

I swigged the sticky, lukewarm liquid and felt suddenly nauseous. I was sweating under my corset and my limp curls were sticking to the back of my neck.

'D'you know what, Roche? I think I'm going to go home.'

But she was already deep in conversation with one of the male nurses from the neurology unit. I found my bag and coat, and pushed my way through the double doors into the cool of the corridor, grateful to escape the noise and the crush.

'Bryony! Hang on a minute.'

I turned to see Leo behind me. With his eyeliner and gelled hair sticking up in spikes he looked like the lead singer from an early-80s new romantic band. I reluctantly conceded that it quite suited him.

'Hold on, are you leaving?'

I nodded. 'It was fun for a bit, but I'm feeling a bit overheated. And a bit drunk, if I'm honest. That punch is lethal.'

'Ingrid said you came by wanting to speak to me.'

'It's fine.' I forced a smile. With my smudged lipstick it probably looked more of a leer. 'Really, it's fine. It can wait.'

'If you're sure?'

'I am. Get back to the party.'

*Get back to your girlfriend.*

'Okay...' He turned to go. 'You've got my number if you need anything.'

I gave him a tipsy salute and headed out into the night, humming the words to 'Stand and Deliver' under my breath.


I was still singing when I approached Kenley Court, so wrapped in the post-party glow that I almost didn't notice him leaning against the side of the building.

Kyle.

Of course he was there, just as I had successfully put thoughts of the crash and Reece Parker's death from my head. By managing to forget about him for the night I'd succeeded in summoning him, like a gangster Rumpelstiltskin. I wasn't afraid. Not then, at least, but because I'd been drinking, any chance of being conciliatory or cooperative had evaporated.

'What are you doing here?' I slurred angrily. 'Fuck off, Kyle. Just fuck off.'

'That ain't very nice.' He looked me up and down. 'Nice 'fit.

Very sexy.' He dragged the word out in a way that made me feel uncomfortable.

I was fumbling with my keys. 'Can't this wait until tomorrow?'

'No can do, I'm afraid, Bryony.' He was already reaching over my head to push the front door open, forcing his way into the building ahead of me. He was dressed all in black: black down jacket, black sweatpants, black baseball cap. 'No need to panic, it won't take long.'

I trudged up the stairs after him and let us both into the flat. I did not offer him anything to drink but leaned on the counter, my coat pulled closed over the lowcut corset.

'So...' I looked him in the face with what I hoped was a business-like air, when in reality the rum punch was still making it hard to focus. 'Let's get this over with. What do you want, Kyle? Because you still haven't told me.'

'Ah, that's the thing, innit.' He tapped the side of his nose. 'It's not *what* I want. It's who.'

## TWENTY-TWO
### BRYONY

Now

I frowned at Kyle. 'What are you talking about?'

'You know a geezer called Shane Quinn, don't you?'

I sobered up immediately. I hadn't been afraid; now I was. My mouth felt like sandpaper and I could hear a ringing in my ears. I reached a glass down from one of the cupboards and filled it from the cold tap. Anything to avoid answering him.

'You're not denying it. Because we both know you know him. Don't you, Bryony?'

I gripped the glass so hard my fingers turned white. 'Where are you getting your information from?'

'He's your best mate's nephew, innit? Come on, I managed to find where you live, how hard could it be to find out who you hang out with?' He'd pulled his vape pen from his pocket and was filling the flat with a sickly watermelon scent.

I was casting my mind back, frantically trying to recall if I'd posted pictures of Claire and myself on social media. Possibly I had some years ago, before Australia, but not recently.

'That geezer in the nick; the one who took the rap for

you... he talked to my mate's Uncle Cliff about you having a girlfriend you were with when he met you. Like I said, not hard to work this shit out... so you know him, yeah? Shane Quinn.'

I took a gulp of water, but said nothing.

He cocked his head on one side. 'I said: you know him?' There was more aggression in his tone now.

Reluctantly I nodded my head. 'But barely at all. I've met him a couple of times briefly, yes.'

'Thing is, Shane's been causing grief for... friends of mine. Getting in their business. Keeping company that he shouldn't be keeping, if you know what I mean.'

'No. I don't.'

Kyle smirked. 'So far he's done well at keeping himself out of trouble, your Shaney boy. What is it they talk about... the luck of the Irish. But I need you to help me mark his card.'

A finger of ice ran down my spine. 'What do you mean?'

'Let's just say he needs to be told to keep this shut, yeah.' He drew his hand across his mouth before zipping up his jacket and thrusting his vape back in his pocket. 'Not be spilling any secrets.'

'What have I got to do with any of that?'

'Still need to work out the logistics.' He lingered on the word, savouring it. 'But I'll be back, yeah, with your instructions.'

'Can't you at least give me a number I can contact you on?' I pleaded desperately. I had wanted to know what Kyle was after, and now I desperately wished I did not know.

He tapped the side of his nose. 'Need-to-know basis, innit. And in the meantime, don't go getting any smart ideas,' he added as he reached the front door. 'You don't want me going to the pigs, do you?'

. . .

I sat on the sofa once he was gone, waiting for my shaking to stop.

The alcohol I had drunk was wearing off, leaving me jittery and tense. How had I ended up in this hideous position? If I spoke up, the truth would come out. The truth that I had killed Reece Parker. If I said nothing, something terrible was going to happen to my friend's nephew. Because it was clear that Kyle Kirkwood meant to harm Shane in some way.

I would speak to Claire, I decided, as I lay on my back staring at the bedroom ceiling. We'd known each other years; we trusted each other completely. I wasn't sure yet exactly what I would say to her, but she was my link with Shane Quinn, so that was where I would have to start.

As soon as I was awake on Saturday morning and had washed down two paracetamol tablets with a pint of water, I texted her.

*Fancy getting together for a coffee? xx*

She replied as I was drying off after my shower.

*Don't feel like going out, but come over to ours xx*

I looked out of the window to check the weather. The sky was pale blue; the sun glancing off a sparkling dusting of frost on the roofs and pavement. I pulled a ski jacket over my hoodie and added a bobble hat before walking to Crystal Palace, stopping at my favourite bakery to pick up a bag of croissants and Danish pastries.

Ryan took them from me after opening the door. 'I'll put the coffee on. She's through there.' He indicated the sitting room door.

Claire was lying on the couch, a blanket spread over her legs. She looked pale and drawn.

'Sorry, I didn't feel up to coming out.' She didn't stand up.

'You poor thing.' I perched on the sofa next to her and gave her a hug. 'Have you got this horrible flu bug that's doing the rounds?'

She shook her head. 'I've had some bleeding. And a bit of cramping. They call it a threatened miscarriage.'

My hand flew to my mouth. 'Oh my God, Claire! But you haven't actually...'

She shook her head. 'I haven't lost the baby, not yet anyway. They said over the phone to rest and do as little as possible, and it might all calm down.' Her lip trembled. 'But I'm scared, Bry.'

I hugged her, employing as much gentleness as I could. 'Of course you are, you poor girl. Let's pray it turns out to be a false alarm. Are you going to go to hospital to get checked?'

Claire nodded. 'I'm going for a scan tomorrow. Anyway, let's talk about something else. Dwelling on it isn't going to fix anything.'

Ryan came into the room carrying a tray with a coffee pot and the pastries on a plate. There were two mugs, one of which had a peppermint tea bag floating in it.

'I'm still not allowed coffee,' Claire sighed. 'And I specially daren't have it now.' She struggled up to a seated position and helped herself to a pain au chocolat. 'So, what's new with you?'

*I can't tell her about the Kyle threat*, I thought desperately. *Not now*.

'It was the hospital Christmas party last night,' I said, pouring coffee into the second mug. 'A Gothic steampunk disco. Which was about as crazy as it sounds.'

'Was it fun though? Claire asked through a mouthful of pastry, wiping flakes from her chin. 'Seeing as I've got to live vicariously through you now.'

'Yes, it was quite a good laugh,' I replied carefully. Well, it had been: to start with at least. I was about to launch into the horrors of my hangover but decided that would be tactless. 'How's the rest of the family?' I asked instead. 'All okay?'

'Grand as far as I know.'

I decided to subtly steer the conversation towards Shane. 'Have you seen Dervla and the kids lately?'

'Ryan and I saw all of them when we were round there last weekend. I say all of them: the girls were there but Shane was out with his girlfriend.'

She had my full attention now. 'He has a girlfriend?'

'It's a relatively new thing, I think. But you know what, according to Dervla he's doing ever so much better lately. He's got some part-time work; delivering pizzas for that new place, Stonebaked, on Gypsy Hill. Whether it's that or being loved up, he seems to have settled down a bit. Who knows; maybe this girl is a good influence.'

'Stranger things have happened.' I sipped my coffee. 'What's she called?'

'Dervla didn't say.' Claire started on a cinnamon roll. 'Talk about comfort eating...' She gave a rueful grimace. 'Anyway, you must come over for another Sunday roast sometime soon, then you can grill Shane about it yourself.'

'I'd love to,' I said, wondering if I had the luxury of time for this to happen before Kyle acted. Probably not.

'Let's make it soon. How about weekend after next? At Dervla's.'

Talking to Claire about my problem was now completely out of the question.

I trusted her, of course, but there was no way I was prepared to burden her with the stress of keeping secrets from members of her family. Nor could I wait until her pregnancy was out of danger in a few weeks' time. I didn't know how long I had before Kyle would surface again, but I was pretty sure it would not be that long.

I thought about confiding in my sister, Flora. We had been close growing up and – like Claire – I knew I could trust her completely. But she was twelve thousand miles away in New Zealand's Southlands, living on an isolated farm with three thousand sheep and three children under the age of ten. With the best will in the world, there was nothing practical she could do to help me. The time difference alone made support from her end nigh on impossible.

I thought all this through as I sat on the 227 bus back to Beckenham, and by the time I disembarked at my stop, I had made up my mind what I was going to do. After all, he at least had met Kyle Kirkwood and knew a little about him. I was going to enlist the help of Leo Salvesen.

## TWENTY-THREE
### BRYONY

Now

What I could not do was talk to Leo within earshot of Ingrid.

For that reason, I avoided calling at his flat. In fact, I avoided him all weekend, making sure to stay inside my own flat unless I was certain that there was no one in the building's communal areas. I decided I would have to approach him at work, with a view to having a conversation somewhere outside of both the hospital and Kenley Court. On neutral territory.

On Monday morning I waited until I was on a break between scan lists and took the emergency exit stairs to the fifth floor. I found Leo at his desk, looking reassuringly himself. Glasses and a dark grey sweater instead of eye make-up and swashbuckling costume.

'Hey, stranger,' he said cheerfully. 'What can I do for you? Or are you going to run off again without explaining it to me?'

'I'm sorry,' I said, smiling ruefully. 'Ingrid was right: I did want to speak to you, but the party wasn't the right time and place.'

He leaned back in his chair. 'I'm all ears.'

'The thing is...' I glanced round at his colleagues, at least two of whom were casting curious glances in our direction '... I can't really talk to you here either. Can you take a lunch hour and meet me at the Bunch of Grapes.'

Leo rubbed his hand over the back of his head. 'I could, but there'll be loads of people from the hospital in there, and you know how our colleagues love to gossip.'

I rolled my eyes to show that I was all too aware.

'I'll tell you what, why don't you meet me in the Salter wing?' He named the purpose-built annexe used for academic meetings and conferences by the doctors and medical students. 'I'm setting up the IT for a research symposium, so I've got the keys, and no one will question me being in there. Come to the small meeting room on the top floor: it's called the Cadogan Room.' He glanced at his watch. 'One fifteen okay?'

I had a PET scan list that started at two, so time would be tight, but I nodded. 'See you there.'

'Can't wait,' Leo said with a faint smile. 'I love a mystery.'


'You must think I'm very strange,' I told him two hours later, as I sneaked into the Cadogan Room and closed the door behind me.

It had plush almond green carpet and soft furnishings, a large pale wood conference table and floor-to-ceiling windows on one side with a view across the park. Leo took a seat at one end of the table and indicated that I should do the same. 'Not exactly,' he told me, 'but I am intrigued.'

'First I have a gangster calling on me at the flat, then my email is hacked and someone starts using a burner phone to stalk me... it all makes me look like a total nutjob.'

'I admit I'm starting to think you lead a rather... colourful... life. Compared to most of us.'

I sighed heavily and buried my face in my hands. 'You don't know the half of it,' I said, my voice muffled by my fingers. I lifted my head and looked straight at him, aware there were tears forming in my eyes.

'Bryony...' Leo reached out and touched my right forearm. 'Are you okay?'

'It's a thousand times worse than anything you'll have imagined.'

My voice barely above a whisper, I told him then. I told him about going to Ruby and Brett's wedding. Driving the hire car home because my date was drunk, and hitting and killing a young man. Robbie telling the police he was to blame and going to prison for it. Fleeing to Australia and returning to London five years later to be rescued from potential lethal injury by Kyle Kirkwood. Only to discover that he was related to the boy I'd killed.

'And so... he's blackmailing you?' Leo asked, after a long silence.

I shook my head. 'It's worse than that. Although I suppose you could call it a form of blackmail. He's using me to get to my friend's nephew, Shane.'

'Why him?'

I looked up at the ceiling, looked down again. 'You know you said you thought Kyle had a gang tattoo? Well, Shane has links to a South London gang himself. A different gang though. So I think it's something related to that.'

'What's his surname? Only I think we need a clearer picture of Kirkwood's motives if we're going to figure out a way to stop him.'

'Quinn.'

I was reassured by the way Leo said 'we'. It made me feel less alone in this terrible mess I had landed in. He had taken out his phone and was searching through images on his browser. 'This him?' He held up the screen. It showed a brooding selfie of Shane, his blue eyes almost closed, the tip of his gold tooth just visible.

'Yes.' I nodded.

'Right; okay...' Leo resumed his scrolling. 'Useful the way everyone under the age of twenty-five puts their entire life online...' He then showed me a picture of Shane with his arm wrapped around a pretty, very young-looking girl. She had glossy black hair, olive skin, and eyeliner flicked into dramatic cat eyes.

'Looks like he's dating this girl who is tagged as...' Leo tapped the screen '... Kayla Jevons. Know anything about her?'

I shook my head.

'Well, that's something we need to look into.'

'Should I warn Shane?'

'Not yet. I wouldn't say anything to him until you have more of an idea of what Kirkwood has planned. Did he say when he'd let you know?'

'No,' I said despairingly, pressing my hands between my thighs. 'He never tells me when he's coming round. He just shows up like the bad fairy at the christening.'

'If this was a TV drama, you'd be trying to find a way to silence him.' Leo tapped his phone on the edge of the table, thinking. 'But sadly it's not. I know it's hard, but I think you're going to have to sit tight until you know more. That's all I can suggest. And keep me in the loop, obviously, if it helps.'

I gave him a grateful smile, and he stood up, pocketing his phone. 'We should get going. Someone's booked this room at two.'

'Can you at least use your IT skills to help me find out more? About Kyle, I mean. I know nothing about him: where he lives, what he does.'

'I'll give it a go, I promise.'

'Thanks.' I got to my feet. 'And it goes without saying that you mustn't tell anyone. About my past, I mean. Well, any of it.'

'Don't worry about that.' He touched my arm briefly as we headed through the conference room door. 'I can keep a secret. That's what friends do.'

'So we're friends?' I asked. It was true that we had not spent much time together, but I instinctively trusted him. Even so, I felt guilty that so far our friendship had been a one-way street: me asking Leo for help with my own problems. I resolved to do better. As soon as I got the chance I would ask him over for supper. Him and Ingrid.

'I think so,' he said equably. 'I'd like us to be.'

I smiled. 'So would I.'


It was dark when I left work that evening, the days growing shorter now that we were well into December.

As I walked home, I had a vague sense that someone was following me. There was no evidence for it, just a feeling. I slowed down. Footsteps a few yards behind me also slowed. Not daring to turn and look back, I picked up my pace. The footsteps quickened too.

Once I had turned into my street, and with only a few metres left to go, I plucked up the courage to look over my right shoulder. Sure enough, a tall figure was rounding the corner, his face obscured by a black cap. I reached into my bag for my keys, so that they were already in my hand as I ran up the steps to Kenley Court. My fingers were trembling so much that they slowed me down as I tried to insert the keys in the lock. As I finally turned it and pushed the front door open, an arm reached over my head to grip the doorframe. I was elbowed aside, as the black-clad figure pushed past me into the building.

'Room for a little one?' Kyle asked, turning to face me with a leer.

I closed my eyes briefly. I still needed to know what it was he wanted from me, but it had been a long day and I was in no mood for games.

'What do you want, Kyle?'

'You know what I want,' he said, no longer smiling. 'It's time you and I had a little chat.'

## TWENTY-FOUR
### BRYONY

Now

Kyle usually stood at the centre of the kitchen when he visited, but today he pushed back his cap and took up a seat on my sofa. He sprawled across it with one arm extended along its back and his chunky black trainers in the middle of my immaculate cream rug. They looked sinister, like two huge insects.

I busied myself with filling the kettle and setting it to boil, saying nothing.

'Your mate's nephew, Shane... you know where he lives, yeah?'

My mouth was too dry to speak, but I nodded.

'The thing is, I need to have a little word with him, in private like. If it's me that asks him, he's not going to come, is he? But if you do, well, he trusts you, doesn't he?'

'I suppose so,' I croaked. 'I mean, he barely knows me.'

'But he's close to his family,' Kyle persisted.

'I suppose so. I know he drives his grandmother to her hospital appointments.'

'Sweet. In fact, that's perfect.' He rubbed the toe of the giant trainer into the pile of the rug. 'So if you were to tell him that something was wrong with someone in his family, his nan say, and that he had to come with you, then he'd do it?'

I shrugged. 'I expect so. If he believed me.'

'You're going to have to make him believe you, innit.' Kyle swivelled on the sofa to face me. His eyes had a narrow, reptilian look. 'Because you know what's going to happen if you don't.'

'Please tell me you're not going to hurt Shane,' I pleaded.

'Like I said, it's about the company he keeps. Like how it might not be such a smart idea. We just want a little chat with him, that's all.' Kyle grinned, then raised two fingers to his own temple and mimed a gun going off.

'When?' I demanded. 'When is this going to happen?'

I was about to throw a tea bag into a mug then changed my mind and yanked a bottle of white wine from the door of the fridge, pouring that into the mug instead. I took a large mouthful of the cold liquid, welcoming the sensation of it slipping down the back of my throat.

Kyle reached into the pocket of his jacket and pulled out what looked like a betting slip. 'You got a pen?'

I found one in my bag and held it out to him, but he indicated that I should keep it and instead handed me the slip of paper. 'Write down your mobile number. The real one: no messing about.'

I did as he asked and handed the paper back to him.

He pushed it into his pocket and got to his feet. 'Sweet. I'll let you know what you've got to do.'

'When?' I repeated. My tongue felt too big for my mouth, and I could barely force out the word.

'You'll just have to wait and see.'

He pulled his cap down over his face, and was gone.

I stood stock still for a few seconds, gripping the mug with both hands in an attempt to stop my trembling.

Once my shaking had lessened, I took a gulp of the wine then reached instinctively for my phone, thankful that I had saved Leo's number when he first offered it to me. When we'd talked in the Salter Building he'd made it clear he viewed me as a friend. And already I needed him to prove it.

I checked the time as I started to type. It was six forty-five: he could still be at work.

*Where are you? Need to see you urgently. I'm at home. B x*

A very long five minutes passed, during which I paced and drank the wine. Then my phone buzzed with a message.

*I'm home too. Give me two minutes*

Sure enough, a few minutes later there was a light knock on the front door of the flat. Leo did a double take when he saw me. I was still wearing my coat and shoes, and had been running my hands through my hair constantly, leaving it a dishevelled mess.

'What's going on?' he demanded. 'Don't tell me... Kyle's been round?'

I nodded. 'Does Ingrid know you're here?'

'She's sleeping. She's had a bad day today. If she wakes up while I'm gone, I'll just tell her I popped up to fix your broadband.'

I waved the bottle of wine in his direction as I topped up my mug.

He shook his head. 'Better not.' He lowered himself onto the sofa and indicated that I should do the same. I pulled off my coat, smoothed down my hair and joined him, recounting the little that Kyle had just told me.

'He obviously intends to harm Shane,' I said helplessly. 'But why go to all this trouble? If he knows so much about Shane he must know where he lives, or works. If he's got some score to settle, why not just jump him in the street?'

Leo picked up one of the pewter candlesticks from the coffee table and turned it over and over in his hands. 'Two reasons,' he said eventually. 'Firstly, if he attacks Shane near his home or work, there are going to be people who see what's going on. Luring him away on false pretences means he – or more likely they – can get him to somewhere where there are no witnesses.'

I nodded. 'Makes sense. And the second reason?'

'You,' Leo stated simply. 'He wants to torment you. To punish you for your past, by involving you in his dealings.'

'You're very good at this, Leo,' I said admiringly. 'Are you sure you're not a criminal yourself?'

He laughed, shaking his head.

'Well, you'd make a very good one. So what the hell do I do now? Because if I don't go along with this, we know what's going to happen.'

'The way I see it, you need to find some way to warn Shane, but without being seen to do so. And it's vital Shane keeps what you tell him to himself. I've done a bit of research, and I did manage to find an address for Kirkwood. Looks like he's living in his mother's flat on the Yorkhill estate in Eltham.'

'I've given him my number so that he can contact me, but I don't have his, not yet. So you can't track him that way, I'm afraid.'

'He'll almost certainly use a burner phone anyway.' Leo sighed. 'You remember what I said about him having a tattoo from the three-one-two gang?'

I nodded.

'Well, it turns out Kayla Jevons has links with them too. I've got a mate who works for the Met and I picked his brains about all this stuff.'

I shot him a worried look.

'All strictly confidential, of course. Off the record. Kayla's dad, Calvin Jevons, is the head of a well-known South London crime syndicate. The three-one-two operate on his patch and are therefore under his control. He uses them as his foot men. So it would be a complete no-no for her to get involved with someone from a rival gang. Which, from what you've said, describes Shane. My guess is they want to teach Shane a lesson for daring to date a Jevons. Or at least scare him off.'

My eyes widened. 'Warring factions,' I muttered. 'It's all a bit Romeo and Juliet.'

'Sort of, but with guns and knives instead of balconies and poison.'

I emptied the last of the wine in my mug. 'Should I tell Shane to disappear for a while?'

'If you do, and Kirkwood's lot realise he's gone to ground, that could come back on you. It might be that his safest option is to break it off with Kayla. But listen, Bryony...' Leo twisted on the sofa so that he was looking at me straight in the face. '... we both know that what you really need to do is go to the police. That's the only way to protect your friend's nephew. You do know that, don't you?'

I had my palms pressed over my nose and mouth, but I nodded my head slowly.

He stood up. 'I'd better get back downstairs. Will you be okay?' He touched me lightly on the shoulder.

I nodded. 'I think so.'

'Text me when you hear from Kyle again. Or if you're worried about anything.' He paused at the door. 'And for God's sake, Bryony, be careful.'

Leo was right. The correct thing was to go to the police. Yet

I feared for Shane if I took that course of action. Would Kyle and his associates stage some sort of retaliation against him?

Even more, I feared for myself. It would be the end for me. Kyle would make public the truth of Reece Parker's accident and I would be heading to prison. I covered my face with my hands again. For the first time in my adult life, I had no idea what I was going to do.

# TWENTY-FIVE
## BRYONY

Diary entries: six years earlier

*2nd September*

*I heard from Robbie again – a long text this time rather than a call. He appeared in the magistrates' court immediately after the incident, but because of the seriousness of the offence, his case was referred directly to the Crown Court. When the case was heard in late August, he entered a guilty plea to causing death by dangerous driving, and driving with an alcohol level above the legal limit. As he saw it, he couldn't possibly plead not guilty because if there were a trial the police would be required to look deeper into what happened on the road that night, and the truth – that it was me who was driving – might come out. He only has to wait another week, and then it's his sentencing hearing. Apparently, he has a very good brief who has assured him that if all goes well for him, he's looking at twenty-four to thirty-six months. Which means he could be out of prison in twelve. And he says he'll be able to handle that better than I ever could, so it's best all round that we stick to the story. I wonder if he's right, but I'm still in such a state of shock that I don't have it in me to contradict him.*

*He's out on police bail until the hearing, and wants to meet up, but I'm not sure that's a good idea. He doesn't know that I've given notice at work and on my flat, and I'm not going to tell him. Not yet anyway. It's such a weird position to be in. I mean, we barely know each other but now we're linked by this huge thing. When I replied to his text, I just said that I would stick by him whatever happens. What else can I do?*

# TWENTY-SIX
## BRYONY

Now

If I slept that night, it was for no more than an hour.

I crawled out of bed at six, my face puffy and my eyes dry. I made myself tea and switched on the radio, as much as anything to drown out my own thoughts. I would have to speak to Shane Quinn myself, I decided. Even though I now accepted that making a confession to the police was inevitable, I didn't believe I could trust Kyle to leave Shane alone. That seemed highly unlikely, whatever course of action I took.

As I arrived at work, it occurred to me that I might be able to intercept him when he drove his grandmother to St Anselm's for an appointment. Hadn't he referred to her as Nanny Quinn? So she was Pauly's mother rather than Dervla and Claire's. When the MRI unit was quiet, I logged onto the patient database and started a search. There were seven female Quinns, most of whom were far too young. The only two in the right age bracket were Prudence Quinn, born in 1939, and Sheila Quinn, born in 1944. Only Sheila was under the care of the podiatry unit, which narrowed it down to one. This had to be Nanny Quinn. I was feeling pretty pleased with myself until I checked for upcoming appointments and saw that her next one was not until the end of January. That was far too long to wait. And I couldn't call at the Quinns' house without Claire somehow finding out. I would have to think of some other way to speak to Shane.

As I walked back from work that evening, I used my phone to look up the nearest police station to Kenley Court. The closest was in Sydenham, but the easiest one to reach on public transport was Gypsy Hill, even though it was half a mile further. Once I was back in the flat, I showered and made myself a double espresso to compensate for my poor sleep the night before. Then I dressed in dark jeans and a navy padded jacket, and tucked my hair – which was always a giveaway – under a baseball cap. Having checked several times that no one was following me, I set off through the dark, drizzly streets. I walked to Kent House and – first checking again that I wasn't being followed – caught the overground to Gypsy Hill.

It was bitterly cold; the sort of cold you can almost taste in the air, and as I walked down the hill towards the police station, I wished I had worn gloves and a scarf. The route took me past pubs, convenience stores and an estate agent. I thought suddenly of Tom Burridge, who still hadn't given me my second set of keys. My reminder to chase him up about it was still on my to-do list. I was just making a mental note to tackle it as soon as I could find the time when I passed Stonebaked, the pizza restaurant where Shane was working.

Like most London pizza places, it experienced an early evening delivery rush, and there was a little cluster of branded scooters outside, like wasps round a pot of honey. The drivers were chatting to each other as they waited; their cold breath hung between them in white clouds. Was Shane one of them? Since they were all wearing crash helmets it was impossible to tell. As I watched, another rider pulled up, this one taller than the others. Flicking down his kickstand and tugging off his helmet, he strode up to the rear entrance of the restaurant. It was Shane, I was certain of it.

A few minutes later he emerged carrying a stack of pizza boxes, which he stored in his scooter's delivery case. As he was about to lift his helmet into position, I stepped out of the shadows.

'Shane!'

He looked startled, and it was clear that he didn't recognise me. I pulled off my baseball cap and my hair tumbled over my shoulders.

'Bryony, right? Hey.' He grinned and the gold tooth glinted under the streetlamp. 'What are you doing here? You live in Gypsy Hill?'

I shook my head. 'Look, Shane. I really need to talk to you about something.'

'Sure, but I'm on deliveries just now.'

'It's pretty urgent.'

The other delivery riders were looking in our direction now, curious.

'Okay, but I've got to get this lot to a place on High View Road. Can you meet me down there? It's not far.' He glanced down at the docket in his hand. 'Number seventeen. I can pretend they took a long time answering the door; that way I can give you a couple of minutes. Only a couple mind: I'm due back to pick up again.'

I nodded and started half walking, half jogging to High View Road. It only took me five minutes, but on his scooter Shane had been far faster and the pizzas were already delivered when I arrived. He was waiting in the shadow of a tall privet hedge, his face obscured by his helmet. Only when he could see that it was me did he remove it.

'What's going on? Why all the secrecy?'

I clenched my hands rhythmically to try and warm my

frozen fingers. 'Am I right in thinking you're seeing a girl called Kayla? Kayla Jevons?'

Fear flashed across his face. 'What's wrong? Has something happened to her?' He fumbled in his jacket pocket for his phone, his eyes scanning the screen.

'As far as I'm aware, she's fine.'

'And the family? Auntie Claire?'

'All fine too. But...' I struggled to frame the next sentence in a way that didn't make me sound completely deranged. 'Someone's making trouble for me and I've just discovered he's mostly doing it to get to you. Someone who's not too happy about you and Kayla being an item.'

Shane curled his lip. 'That'll be one of those three-one-two losers no doubt. Why the fuck are you hanging out with rats like them?'

How to respond to that question? There was no short or easy answer, and Shane's body language was already impatient; he was casting glances at his scooter as though keen to get back on it and return to the restaurant.

'Trust me, I'm not hanging out with them; far from it. You can be one hundred per cent sure about that. Look, there isn't time to explain it all, I just felt I had to let you know that—'

He cut across me. 'People—' he made air quotes around the word '—don't want me and Kayla together. I know, I get it.'

'Shane, it's not just that: they actively wish you harm.' I injected urgency into my voice. 'They're planning to try and, I don't know...' I struggled for the right form of words '... silence you. I think they must be worried about pillow talk between you and Kayla; that you're going to pass on inside information she gives you.'

To my frustration, he just shrugged. 'There are always gonna be people out here on these streets who'd rather you kept your mouth shut,' he drawled. 'That's just the way life is.'

'Couldn't you just stop seeing Kayla?'

His expression darkened. 'Not possible. No way.'

*But it is possible*, I thought. *It's a choice. You can choose not to.* Only the whole world knew that young love didn't work that way.

Shane strode over to his scooter and slung his leg over it. 'Gotta bounce, sorry. If I don't get straight back to pick up my next order, they'll sack me. The gig economy, innit.' He lifted his helmet to position it on his head.

'Shane, just be careful, okay. Be very careful. And for Christ's sake, don't tell anyone I spoke to you. Not even your Auntie Claire.'

'That goes for you too, Bryony.' He hesitated a beat. 'And look, for Christ's sake don't go to the police.' He pronounced it 'polis' in the Irish fashion. 'If the three-one-two think I'm whining to the feds about them then…'

He drew his hand across his neck in a throat-slitting motion. I flinched.

'Listen…' Shane hesitated a beat, then handed me his phone. 'Punch in your digits, then call yourself, so you've got my number. That way you can let me know what you know, and I'll have a chance to do something about it. To defend myself, you know?'

I did as he asked as he was fastening his helmet then handed his phone back. He took it from me with a nod and roared away down High View Road.

Seconds later I was trudging slowly back towards Central Hill, my hands thrust deep into my pockets to keep them warm.

The route back to Gypsy Hill took me directly past the entrance to the police station. And I had fully intended to go in there on my way home and tell them about Kyle's blackmail. I'd decided that even if it meant them digging back into their file on the accident the night of 15th June five years ago, I was prepared to accept the consequences, take the blame. Let it all come out into the open in the hope that the court would be lenient once they'd heard the full story. But after Shane's pain-of-death warning, I no longer dared do it. Not for my sake but for his. How could I ever face Claire if a course of action I took to salve my own conscience led to the death of her nephew? It was an impossible dilemma. For now at least, I decided I would have to keep silent.

I made myself a cup of tea as soon as I got home, and ran a bath, in an attempt to warm myself up. As I was slipping off my bathrobe and stepping into the foamy water, my phone buzzed with a text. I pulled it out of the pocket of my robe, not recognising the number, but already knowing who it belonged to.

Kyle Kirkwood.

# TWENTY-SEVEN
## BRYONY

Now

I froze for a couple of seconds with one foot on the floor, the other in the bath water.

Then, with a rush of irritation, I flung my phone across the room, sending it skidding across the lino and bumping against the closed door. I was cold and exhausted and I was not going to let Kyle Kirkwood into my head. Not for the time being, at least. The phone buzzed with a second message but I continued to ignore it, sinking down into the hot, foamy water and closing my eyes.

Only when I was dry again and dressed in pyjamas did I retrieve my phone and curl up on the sofa with it. The first message was unsigned.

*Wait outside yr place tomorrow 4pm. B alone yeah*

It had to be from Kyle. It certainly sounded like him.
I read the second message.

*Taxi from crown cabs will take u to quinns. Story is ur takin him hospital cus nan ill*

My instinct was to reply and point out the many flaws in this plan. How did he even know Shane would be at the house? His assumption must be that both Quinn parents would be at work, but what it they were not? That was perfectly possible. And if Nanny Quinn had been taken ill, why would I be arriving in a taxi to tell Shane that? Wouldn't one of his parents have already let him know? Or failing that, a member of the medical team caring for her. Shane himself could drive, and there was always public transport. Why would he need collecting, and by me of all people? A long list of questions came to mind. Of course, Shane would be a lot more likely to get in a car if it was me ringing the doorbell rather than Kyle and his sidekicks. But still, to my mind, the story just wasn't credible.

I pressed reply with the intention of pointing all this out but checked myself just in time. What did it matter if the cover story was not believable if Shane himself was in on the deception? And now that I had promised to keep him in the loop, that at least was simple to achieve. I found his number on my phone and dialled it. He did not pick up, but a couple of minutes later he called me back and I put him on speaker while I read out Kyle's texts.

'Will you even be at home tomorrow afternoon?' I asked.

'Yeah, I will. My shifts always start at six.'

'I guess you could just be out.'

'Nah,' said Shane, his tone resigned. 'They'll only come back. Or worse still, they'll go after Kayla. I'm not risking that.'

'So, it looks like you're to get in the cab thinking you're going with me to St Anselm's, but instead they take you God knows where.'

*And what happens to me*, I wondered, feeling suddenly very afraid.

As if I'd just spoken my thoughts out loud, Shane said. 'Look, Bryony, you seriously don't wanna be messing with these people. You get out the vehicle as soon as you can, okay, and just run. Get away.'

'What if I can't?' I demanded. 'And what if they're planning to take us somewhere no one can find us? In fact, Shane, just forget about all of this. I don't want you getting in the cab either. Just make sure you're not at home when we come round.'

'That'll never work,' he said firmly. 'They'll just keep on trying, and I don't want to risk them getting so pissed off they go after Kayla.' He paused. 'I'll tell you what though...' It was clear that, like me, he was thinking through a dozen different scenarios. 'Get one of those tiny GPS trackers, synch it with your phone and put it in the cab, okay? At least if someone knows where we are, that gives us some security. Gives us options.'

He had hung up before I could enquire as to what those options might be. I flicked on the TV and sat in front of a home renovation show, not really watching but unable to face trying to sleep. What I really wanted to do was to go downstairs and confide in Leo, but I couldn't. If I did, I would have to admit to him that I had not been to the police after all. And if I wasn't going to report what was happening now, Leo almost certainly would. No, if I saw him between now and tomorrow afternoon, I would have to pretend that everything was normal.

I was also supposed to be at work all the next day too, but that was the least of my problems.

The following lunchtime, I claimed a dental abscess that required an emergency dental appointment and left Ange covering my shift.

I had found plenty of mini GPS trackers online offering real-time data, but there wasn't time to wait for one to be delivered. Instead, I made a detour to the autocentre on Beckenham

High Street and bought one there. It was a tiny thing that looked like a black plastic matchbox. Once I got home, I followed the instructions to link it with my phone and slipped it into the back pocket of my jeans. At ten to four I put on the jacket and baseball cap I had worn the night before and went onto the street to wait. It was already almost dark.

Four o'clock came, and nothing happened. I considered phoning Kyle's number, then thought better of it. Ten minutes later a black taxi approached, with a yellow 'Crown Cabs' logo on its side. The rear door was opened from within, and I climbed inside to find Kyle himself on the back seat, dressed in his regulation black streetwear. The confined space of the cab was filled with the chemical scent of his aftershave. It hadn't occurred to me that he would be coming too.

'Thought I'd better keep an eye on things,' he said, as though reading my mind. 'Make sure there's no funny business.'

I avoided eye contact as I fastened the seat belt. My heart was pounding so hard in my chest I was sure Kyle would be able to hear it. The driver moved swiftly but smoothly away from the kerb without looking round at me. He was a large, bulky Asian man in a leather jacket, and though he glanced in his rear mirror from time to time, he did not speak or turn his head to look at me. It was clear he knew he wasn't picking up a regular fare. Was he in on it, a member of Kyle's gang? It seemed likely. Someone on the payroll at least. Otherwise how would he know where I was going?

Once again, Kyle deployed his uncanny ability to know what I was thinking. 'Imran here isn't a mind reader. You need to tell the driver where you wanna go,' he said complacently. 'That's how a taxi works, innit.'

Flustered, I told him the address of Dervla's house, and five minutes later we were pulling up outside. 'Go on then,' Kyle told me. 'Go and get your little mate. And remember—' He grabbed my right wrist and his chunky signet ring dug into the flesh '—no messing about. You're taking him with you to the hospital because his nan is sick. Your friend sent you. That's all.'

As I freed my wrist and twisted around to grasp the door handle with that hand, I succeeded in extracting the GPS tracker from my jeans with the other. I dropped it into the door's map pocket at the exact moment I pushed the door open and climbed out onto the pavement. Kyle, who was now glancing down at his phone, definitely hadn't noticed.

I rang the bell and seconds later Shane opened the door, also dressed head to toe in his street black and already wearing his jacket. In the background I could hear the chatter of his younger sisters, who must have just returned from school. In case they overheard, I stuck to the script.

'Your nan's been taken poorly and admitted to hospital. I've got a taxi waiting outside to take us there.'

Shane raised his eyebrows to signal that he understood this piece of play-acting, then called over his shoulder.

'Moll, I've got to go out for a bit, but Mum will be back in an hour. Don't open the door to anyone, okay?'

He pulled the door closed behind him and followed me down the path. This was my chance to warn him that I was not alone, but I decided against it. It was vital that Kyle believed that Shane hadn't had any prior knowledge of my arrival, so I needed his surprise when he saw Kyle to be unrehearsed.

It worked. As we approached and Kyle got out of the back seat, Shane did a genuine double take, and for the first time appeared to be unnerved. I avoided catching his eye as the rear door was held open wordlessly for him. Kyle himself then headed for the front passenger seat. I ducked down to climb into the back next to Shane, but Kyle swivelled round to look at me over his left shoulder.

'Nah,' he said. 'Not you. You ain't coming with us.'

'But—'

He pushed out an arm to stop me. 'You've done what we

needed you to do. Now if you know what's good for you, you'll fuck off out of here.'

I looked helplessly at Shane. He gave me a nod, but his face had turned ashen and I could see that he was now frightened. He must have assumed I would be able to accompany him, like a shield of protection. I gave him one last desperate look, then shut the taxi's door on him. It pulled away from the kerb and headed towards the junction with Perry Hill.

It was only then that I saw it. A black Range Rover with tinted windows so opaque the occupants were not visible. My stomach lurched. Were those Kyle's fellow gangsters, there to offer backup? Despite doing my best to protect Shane, I was in way over my head.

I was suddenly very, very afraid for him.

# TWENTY-EIGHT
## BRYONY

Now

I started walking, dazed, in the direction of Kenley Court.

At least I had managed to plant the tracker, I told myself. That was some sort of insurance. I glanced at the linked app on my phone now and could see that the taxi was heading northeast. Had I just helped deliver my friend's nephew into some sort of terrible trap? I wondered what sort of retribution a rival gang would dole out for simply dating a girl. But then Kayla wasn't just any girl. She was an alleged crime boss's daughter. I realised with an icy jolt of fear that I had been horribly naive in imagining that Kyle's friends only had a bit of a talking-to in mind.

My phone rang. 'Hi, it's Ange. How was the dental surgery?' a familiar voice trilled.

'Painful,' I said, adopting a thick voice as though my face was numb. Since I was experiencing anxiety so acute it resembled an out-of-body experience, this wasn't hard.

'Sounds like you're outside, so are you on your way home now?'

'Yeth.'

'Okay... rest up, and I'll see you in the morning.'

It was after five o'clock by the time I had walked home. I didn't dare phone the police in case it put Shane in even more danger from Kyle's thugs. I would leave it a little longer, I decided, and then try and contact Shane. Suddenly desperately hungry, I found some chips in the freezer and put them in the oven, eating them while they were too hot and burning the roof of my mouth. At least that would lend credence to my cover story about being in pain.

As I ate and cleared up afterwards, I remained glued to the app linked to the mini GPS tracker. It could be configured to show not just a real-time location but a summary of the entire route. So I could now see that the end point had been the Derwent Grove estate in Charlton, some eight miles away to the north-east. According to Google it was a former council estate that had been damaged by fire and fallen into dereliction, and was now earmarked for redevelopment. After reaching Derwent Grove, the taxi had doubled back on itself and was now heading back in my direction. Could Shane be in it?

I tried his number, but it went straight to voicemail. A couple more tries resulted in the same thing. I decided I would try Dervla. I had the excuse that Claire had invited me to her house for lunch.

'Dervla... it's Bryony. Claire said something about coming over for one of your wonderful Sunday roasts, but was it this coming Sunday or the one after? I thought I'd better check.'

'Ah, Bryony... good to hear from you!' Dervla sounded cheerful, which was reassuring. In the background I could hear music and laughter. 'We're away with friends in Southampton this weekend, so the plan is for it to be the one after. And you're very welcome; it goes without saying. It'll be getting pretty close to Christmas, so maybe I'll do a turkey.'

'Lovely,' I said, not wanting to be awkward and remind her

that I didn't eat meat. 'And how is everyone... the family? Are they all okay?'

'Girls are fine... Shane still acting all lovestruck. He's with this new lass so much we barely see him. In fact, his work has just phoned the landline asking where he is. He hasn't shown up for his shift.'

My heart dropped to my stomach. 'Teenagers,' I said feebly. I had crossed to the sitting room window and could see Leo Salvesen walking up the front path. 'Anyway, I'll see you soon, Dervla,' I said quickly before cutting the call. I rapped on the window, making Leo glance up with a look of surprise. He caught sight of me and I gestured wildly for him to come up. Seconds later he was knocking at my door.

'Thank God,' I said as I admitted him, exhaling hard. 'I'm going out of my mind here.'

He looked at me: at my pale face and dishevelled hair. I was shivering, despite the central heating being cranked up high.

'Bryony. What the hell's happened?'

'You'd better sit down.' I pointed to the sofa, and Leo obeyed. And then I told him everything, starting with my abandoned expedition to Gipsy Hill Police Station, then the instructions from Kyle and the taxi ride to Shane's house and finally the Range Rover with blacked out windows that had either been in pursuit or protection.

Leo stared at the ceiling for a second, rubbing his chin with his hand. 'Look, I know it's not exactly helpful saying this now, but you really should have gone to the police.'

'I know,' I groaned. I pressed my knuckles to my forehead. 'I know. And I intended to. But Shane persuaded me it would be dangerous for him if I did. And now...' I made a gesture of helplessness.

'Now you really must do it, Bryony. You've got to tell the cops what's going on.'

'I can't, not now.' I knotted the hem of my top round and round my fingers.

Leo made a scoffing sound to show he did not agree.

'Like it or not, Leo, I'm involved now. I went to the Quinns' house with Kyle. I lured Shane into the cab that took him off to God knows where. I'm no lawyer, but surely that makes me part of it. It's called conspiracy, isn't it? Conspiracy to commit GBH or...' I couldn't bring myself to say the word 'murder' '... whatever this is. I was already facing a charge of perverting the course of justice – on top of the dangerous driving – and now I'll be in even worse trouble.'

I closed my eyes, trying to shake off the dizzying sensation that was swamping me. It was as if I were stranded at the centre of a frozen lake, with crack after crack appearing in the ice around me.

Leo put his hand on my arm. 'I hear you, but I still think it would be better to come clean.'

'Okay. But not until I've at least made sure that Shane's safe. I owe it to Dervla and Pauly, and to Claire.'

'You've got his number?'

'Yes, but he's not picking up his calls.' I stood up and started pacing. 'We need to go to that place where the taxi ended up and check he's not still there. If only one of us had a car.'

'Ingrid has one,' Leo said, and when he saw my expression went on hurriedly. 'And no, before you ask, I'm not going to lend it to you. This is madness, Bryony. You can't just drive over there: these people are way too dangerous.'

I sighed. 'I get it. You don't know me all that well after all: why should you get involved in my mess? But I'm going anyway. I can call an Uber and get it to take me there.'

Leo stood up, sighing heavily. 'No, that's not happening either. What kind of a man would I be if I let you go on your own?' He sighed again, giving me a wry smile. 'You win. I'll go and get the car keys.'

. . .

The Derwent Grove estate had been built in the late 1960s to house evictees from East London's slum clearance. The original red-brick maisonettes were a tangle of burnt-out walls and boarded windows, overgrown with weeds and circled by metal fencing and red plastic hoarding.

We parked Ingrid's little white hatchback in the next street.

'Is your phone off?' Leo asked. He'd instructed me to switch it off before we left Kenley Court, so that my location was obscured.

I nodded. 'Will Ingrid be okay with you taking her car like this?' I asked, as we approached the estate on foot.

'Oh, she won't know,' Leo said airily. 'She's away on a week's respite care.'

I gave him a sideways glance but was more preoccupied with the size of the task that faced us. There were at least half a dozen separate blocks in varying states of disrepair, separated by scrubby grass strewn with splintered piles of wood, mortar and scraps of cladding. 'Where do we even start?' I groaned.

'If our intention is to check that Shane isn't still here, injured or even worse, we might as well start with the building nearest to us and just keep going. Hold on...' Leo darted back to the car and came back holding a torch aloft. 'We're definitely going to need this.'

The scale of the task was immediately apparent when we failed to even get inside the first block. The entrance door was padlocked and chained, and all the ground-floor windows were either boarded or a jigsaw of broken glass shards. I flapped my arms uselessly at my sides. 'Now what?'

'We need to think like Kyle Kirkwood and his buddies. We have to assume he was meeting others here, right?'

I thought about this. Kyle worked out, but he was not a big

man. Shane was taller and possibly carrying a weapon. It would be far too risky to bring him alone. 'Must have been.'

'We need to get into their heads and act as they would. They can't get in here any more easily than we can, and I doubt they're going to waste time checking every single block until they find one with a usable door. So what do they do, if they're here to give someone a duffing up?'

I was now thinking of the black Range Rover following the taxi here. When I first caught sight of it, my assumption had been that Kyle or his puppet masters had arranged to be accompanied by some of their more unsavoury associates. But now I saw that it could just as easily have been the other way round. What was it Shane had said to me? Something about needing the chance to defend himself. Perhaps the car's occupants were on a mission to pull Shane out of whatever was planned for him. This thought should have been reassuring, and yet I felt a cold dread seeping through me. Whoever had been in the Range Rover, more people surely meant more potential violence. More violence, and more bloodshed.

I realised Leo was still looking at me expectantly. 'I think they get as far away from the road as possible.' I pointed to the far western edge of the estate, which was banked by trees. 'Over there maybe?'

'Okay, let's take a look.'

We walked in darkness along an overgrown path to the rear of the furthest block. It was starting to drizzle, but I barely noticed the damp and the cold. Only when we reached the furthest boundary of Derwent Grove did Leo switch on the torch. He swung the beam around. And then I saw it.

A man lying face down on the ground.

There was no doubt that it was the body of a male, dressed in black. The head was partly obscured by a cap which had been knocked askew and a dark pool surrounded it, seeping into the wet mud.

Something ran through me, but I couldn't tell if it was heat or chill. I let out an involuntary gasp.

'Oh, Christ,' Leo said behind me. He switched off the torch so that we wouldn't have to look at the corpse any longer. Because there had been no doubt that Shane was dead.

All I could think about was Claire and the rest of the family. And how I was going to face them if they ever discovered my part in what had happened to him. Even so, something was nagging at my brain.

'Switch it on!' I hissed. 'Switch the torch on again.'

'Are you sure?'

I nodded, and Leo flicked the switch.

'Look!' I pointed to the body's outstretched left hand. Leo moved the beam. Heat rose behind my eyes and I felt a nausea wash over me – so intense that I had to bend double, my hands on my knees. But there was no doubt about what I had seen. A silver signet ring engraved with a spider, glittering red rubies for eyes. Relief washed over me despite the horror of what we were seeing. It was clear now. Shane – or more likely the men who had followed him in the Range Rover – had turned the tables.

They had killed Kyle Kirkwood.

## TWENTY-NINE
### BRYONY

Now

Leo parked Ingrid's car just off Charlton Park Road and we headed on foot to a café we had just passed: an old-school greasy spoon.

The interior was warmed by a fug of steam and frying food. A handful of men in high-vis jackets and work boots were tucking wordlessly into burgers, sausages or eggs, all served with chips and washed down with strong tea. Outside, the weather had worsened and rain was thrumming against the windows. I sat down gratefully at one of the Formica tables, and the violent shivering that had begun while I was in the car started to ease.

'You need tea,' Leo said firmly. 'Sweet tea.'

'You know what's funny?' I said, with a rueful smile. 'I was planning to ask you for supper. But this was definitely not what I had in mind.'

One of the servers brought my tea. I accepted the mug of hot, creosote-coloured liquid gratefully and stirred in three paper sachets of sugar but refused the food menu. My stomach was still turning somersaults.

'This gets worse,' I groaned, once the sweet tea started to take effect. 'I'm in even worse trouble now. Shane is too. That's even assuming he's still in one piece.' I reached into my pocket for my phone and made to switch it on. 'I should send him a text.'

Leo put a hand on my wrist.

'No, wait, Bryony; you need to keep that off for now.'

I put my phone down.

'Okay, let's think about this...' The waitress approached with a laminated menu card and Leo ordered a toasted cheese sandwich. 'If Shane has been hurt in some way, then wait for your friend to let you know... Claire, is it?'

I nodded.

'Surely she'd tell you if the news was bad?'

'She would,' I agreed.

'If he's okay, then he's in at least as much trouble as you are. So it's probably best for now if the two of you don't have any contact.' He pointed at my phone. 'Especially not using that.'

I stared at him, the shock wearing off and the disbelief setting in. 'You're serious?'

'Serious as a heart attack.'

'So... what *should* I do?'

'First and foremost, it's important not to panic.'

The toasted sandwich arrived. After the waitress had retreated behind the counter, Leo continued. 'Okay, I know this is scary, but let's try and think clearly. It didn't look like there were any working cameras at Derwent Grove.' He took a mouthful of the sandwich and went on as though he was talking to himself. 'The car will have been picked up by automatic number plate recognition, but there's nothing we can do about that... we'll just have to hope no one has a reason to look at it.'

'Hold on...' I was trying desperately to keep up with his train of thought. 'I'm confused. So now we're *not* going to the police?'

'Bryony—' Leo glanced around him, but the sound of the rain and the hiss of the coffee machine were muffling his words '—look, I know I've tacitly involved myself by driving you here, but when all's said and done, this is gang-on-gang violence. There's no reason for you to get mixed up in it further if you can avoid it. But meanwhile, I think you should lie low for a few days, just in case.'

I stared at him. 'In case of what, for God's sake?'

'Kyle's been killed. What if his three-one-two buddies come after you?'

I hadn't even thought of that. Not only was I a criminal, but a target too. I was starting to feel as though I was starring in some dark TV drama about London's gangland.

'Is there a family member you could stay with for a few days?'

I shook my head slowly. 'My sister's in New Zealand… there's my dad and stepmum, but I can't go to their house. I wouldn't want to bring…' I hesitated, hardly able to believe what I was saying '… *this* to their door. I can't put them at risk. And they'd think it was odd if I just pitched up in the middle of the week with no warning. They'd know there was something wrong, and they'd ask questions.'

'Fair enough.' Leo took another bite of the sandwich. I wondered how he could possibly eat. 'We need somewhere no one's going to suspect.'

'Exactly.' I took another mouthful of the sweet liquid. 'Maybe a hotel. Would that be traceable?'

'I know,' Leo said suddenly. He slapped his palm on the table making the workmen glance in our direction. 'My cousin Sonja has an Airbnb on the Kent coast, in Ramsgate. It's almost always empty in low season, so there's a good chance you could use it. I can ask her to keep it off the books, so no one need know you're there.'

I shrugged. 'I still need to square it with work.'

'You'll think of something. I'll whizz her off a text and ask.' Leo began to type.

'There's something else,' I said in a low voice, glancing around to make sure no one could hear me. 'We can't just leave... him... there. With the place being derelict it could be days before he's found, or longer. Weeks. And that just doesn't feel right.'

Much as Kyle had tormented me, I did not wish a violent death on anyone. My mind raced back to the night of the accident, to the horror of learning that a young man's life had been snuffed out. I started to shake again.

Leo sighed heavily and pressed his fingers into his eye sockets. 'Agreed. But we have to make sure the tip doesn't come from either of us.'

'You're the IT expert.' I leaned forward, keeping my voice low. 'Surely you can find some way of sending an anonymous email or making an untraceable call?'

'I expect I can figure something out. But one thing at a time...' He pushed back his chair. 'Come on, we shouldn't hang around too long in this postcode.'

*Dear God*, I thought, as we trudged back to the car in the teeming rain. *We're already behaving like a pair of fugitives.*

As he closed the driver's door behind him, Leo's phone bleeped and he checked it. 'Sonja's got back to me... she says the place is going to be unoccupied for the next couple of weeks, until Boxing Day, then a couple from the Midlands have booked it until New Year's Day. She says it's fine to use it as long as it's left exactly as you find it. There's a lockbox outside with the key in it. I've got the code here.' He looked up at me. 'So that's good news, isn't it? She's not going to charge.'

'I suppose so,' I said glumly. I wasn't exactly happy at the idea of having to disappear.

Leo started the engine. 'We'll go back to Kenley Court so you can pick up a few things, then I'll drive you to Ebbsfleet.

The St Pancras to Ramsgate line stops there, and it should only take around half an hour by road.'

'Shouldn't I just get an Uber?'

He shook his head firmly. 'Ride share journeys are traceable. Have you got a tablet? One without cellular service?'

'I think I've got an old one somewhere.'

'Good. Pack that, and once you're connected to the flat's Wi-Fi you can use it for texts and video calls. But keep them to the absolute minimum.'

Fifteen minutes later we were back at the flat and I was standing, frozen, in the middle of my bedroom, unable to think clearly about what I needed. To think at all. Shock had set in, and I was starting to shake violently. I went back into the living room and found the emergency bottle of Scotch, pouring myself a measure and downing it in one. The burn of the alcohol calmed me, and helped focus my mind. I pulled a weekend bag from the cupboard in the hall and tossed in underwear, shoes and a couple of changes of clothes, along with toiletries and make-up and the iPad. I threw away any perishable food in the fridge and stuffed my passport and driving licence into my handbag.

Then I dragged the weekend bag and the contents of my kitchen bin downstairs and deposited the rubbish in the bin store before tapping discreetly on Leo's door.

'Ready?' he asked.

'Ready.'

As we climbed into Ingrid's hatchback again, I turned to face him. 'Thank you for doing this,' I said, placing my hand briefly on his arm. 'I know you didn't want to get involved, but you helped me anyway. I am grateful, I really am. You're one of the good guys.'

I meant it, but I was painfully aware that despite this shared experience, we still barely knew each other. We stopped at a cash point in Beckenham for me to withdraw cash, then embarked on the drive to Ebbsfleet. By this point we were both too drained to speak about the events of the past couple of hours, lapsing into a tense silence.

'Make sure you use the cash to pay for stuff you need,' was all he said eventually as we drew up to the large modern station building. 'And don't contact me; I'll contact you.'

Outside the entrance, Leo helped me get my bag from the car, then abruptly pulled me into a tight hug. I clung to him wordlessly for a few seconds, burying my face in his shoulder.

After he had got back into the car, he gave a brief wave as he pulled away from the kerb, and then I was alone. My life on the run had begun.

## THIRTY

### BRYONY

Then

At the beginning of October that year, I received a visiting order from HMP Rochester.

It almost didn't reach me since by then I'd left my job, and in preparation for emigrating was temporarily based at my father's house. Fortunately, I'd popped back to London to sort out some last-minute visa paperwork and called in at my former flat to pick up my mail.

Of course I did not want to go. No part of me wanted to go. Robbie had taken the blame with good reason: even though I was the one who had been behind the wheel, the accident had ultimately been his fault. He knew that and I knew that.

But still, I felt sorry for him, and since I was leaving the country, I wouldn't need to see him again. I phoned the number on the order and arranged to visit two days later. My flight to Melbourne was in a mere five days, so the window of time left was limited. I would see him and then it would be done. I would be on the other side of the world and Robbie Makepeace would be a regrettable part of my past.

I borrowed my stepmother's hatchback and drove the hour and a half from Sussex, finding a space in the prison car park. The parking limit was two hours, which I assured myself would be ample. It was an exercise in showing my face, that was all. And in my mind, that would take thirty minutes maximum. Remembering to take my copy of the visiting order and the reference number I'd been given, I queued up to be searched and have my ID checked. It was apparent from their body language that most of the other visitors had done this before; some many times before. A few were trailing babies and children in their wake; all of them looked tense or weary or both. Eventually I reached the head of the queue. My details were cross-referenced on a list, my phone taken from me, then I was directed into the visiting hall.

It took me a while to pick out Robbie amongst the other men seated at tables, waiting. They all looked alike with their prison pallor and standard-issue grey tracksuits. His face lit up when he saw me, and he reached out his arms. I hesitated, shrank back.

'It's okay,' he said. 'The rules say we can hug at the beginning and end of a visit.'

Having permitted a stiff embrace, I sat down, examining Robbie's face. His light-brown hair had been cut savagely short, which didn't suit him and his pale blue eyes – always his best feature in my opinion – were bloodshot and had the sort of dark circles underneath them that indicated poor quality sleep.

'How are you?' I asked, genuinely moved to show concern. 'How are you coping?'

'Oh, you know, it's not so bad.' He attempted a smile. 'I'm in a double, but it does at least have its own shower. I can apply to be transferred to a single at some point, but my cell mate's quite a decent guy. We get along all right.'

'That's good,' I said with artificial brightness. 'And is there... are you finding stuff to do?'

'There's vocational training, and you can get day release if there's a specific course you want to do. And I'm hoping to sign up to teach the inmates some basic coding.'

'That's good,' I repeated weakly.

'And there's a gym.'

'Even better.'

He leaned forward so that the tips of our fingers touched. I was taken back suddenly to the night we had slept together. To the stares, the intensity, the premature 'I love you'. 'It is so bloody good to see you, Bryony,' he said. 'I know that if I've got you, I can get through this.'

*You've got to tell him. You've got to tell him you're moving to Australia.*

'The thing is,' Robbie went on, and there was an urgency in his voice, 'I know what happened that night was terrible, and I'm completely prepared to take the blame for it. But in a weird way it's brought us so much closer, don't you think? Going through an experience like that... it can only bind you. Because only you and I know the truth.'

He was smiling as he said this, as though we really were partners, and there was something faintly chilling about that smile. I was suddenly desperate to move things on.

'Robbie, there's something you need to know.'

And I told him that I'd been offered a job at Monash Medical Centre, which came with an Australian work visa. That I was leaving in a few days.

'Oh God,' was all he managed to say. His pallor intensified. 'I don't believe this is happening.'

'But I can write to you here, can't I?' I said desperately. 'And the visa is only for two years. I'll be back long before you get released.'

He relaxed a fraction. 'So you'll be here waiting for me when I get out?'

'Of course!' I assured him, because what else could I do? 'Absolutely. And I'll write to you once I'm settled. Like you say, we're in this together. I'll always be here for you.'

Little did I know how my words would come back to haunt me.

## THIRTY-ONE
BRYONY

Now

My train arrived in Ramsgate at nine forty-five. It was still raining steadily, and after the fifteen-minute walk from the station to Sonja's Airbnb, I was drenched.

My temporary home was a basement flat in a Georgian townhouse a couple of blocks inland from East Cliff. I let myself in and took in my surroundings. The rooms were decorated in shades of olive green and sludgy beige, making the place feel a little dark, but it was clean and comfortable. There was a small log burner, which I immediately lit, sinking to my knees in front of it for a few minutes and soaking in the warmth. Outside, a storm lashed against the front of the house. The sea was only a few hundred yards away and the wind whipped off it, rattling the windows.

The urge to switch on my phone again was strong, but I resisted, despite being curious to know whether Shane had been in touch. Leo was right: it was best that Kyle's criminal associates had no means of working out where I was. Instead, I unpacked my few belongings. Having refused food at the greasy spoon café, I was now ravenously hungry. I found a jar of biscuits next to the tray of tea and coffee, and there was a packet of crisps with the complimentary bottle of wine. These were no doubt meant for the couple who had booked the place after Christmas but I opened them anyway, making a mental note to replace them.

I poured a glass of wine and started working my way through the crisps. Only when the edge had been taken off my hunger did I fetch the iPad from the bedroom and connect it to the Wi-Fi. There were routine checking-in messages from my stepmother Gayle, and from my friend Holly. Nothing urgent, and nothing from Claire. As Leo had pointed out, if something terrible had happened to Shane she would have phoned me. But still, I feared for him. He could be lying somewhere undiscovered, as Kyle Kirkwood had been. Now that the shock of discovering Kyle's body was wearing off, I was wondering if we should have searched the entire Derwent Grove estate in case Shane was also still there. At the time Leo and I had been simply too shocked to think.

I had to accept the fact that I could not go back and undo this. I poured myself a second glass of wine, then ate three of the biscuits with a cup of tea, before heading to bed.

As I rearranged the pillows, the iPad chirruped with a message.

*All okay? L x*

I typed a two-word reply, before switching out the light.

*All okay*

The following morning, my first task was to explain my absence from work. Hardly ideal, given that I had only just faked the need for dental surgery.

I could claim my face was still in pain, but most people would expect it to have settled down within another twenty-four hours and I might be gone longer than that. I settled on flu, not only because it could easily be expected to drag on for longer than a week but also because I already had the beginnings of a sore throat. Since I was supposed to be keeping my phone switched off, I had to find another way to make the call. The only colleagues whose details I had stored in my contacts were Rochelle and Craig. Rochelle and I were closer, and for that reason she was more likely to be suspicious of any sudden absence. I opened the video call app on my iPad and changed the settings to audio only, before selecting Craig's number.

'No worries,' he said cheerfully, in his sing-song Belfast accent once I'd told my story.

'I'll be back in as soon as I can,' I said, exaggerating my hoarse whisper.

'Don't rush: we don't want you bringing flu in here.'

I attempted a laugh, which turned into a genuine cough.

'You stay in bed and just rest up, hun.'

Feeling guilty, I hung up. As I brewed coffee in Sonja's tiny but immaculate kitchen, I contemplated the empty hours ahead. It should have been fun and liberating to have an unexpected day off, but it wasn't. I could not relax, could not push the image of Kyle's dead body from my mind. After the coffee and a couple more of the biscuits, I set off towards East Cliff.

The previous day's storm had passed, but it was cloudy with a bitterly cold wind, and I wished I'd had the foresight to pack a hat. I took the steps down from the promenade to the beach and walked for a while on sand that was brown and damp rather than soft and golden. The cafés and amusement arcades were all closed for the winter, and apart from a couple of dog walkers,

I was completely alone. I headed west to the marina before doubling back towards the town centre. Apart from the few smarter boutiques at the beach end, the high street was a depressing parade of boarded up retail units, betting shops and discount stores. Christmas lights were strung across the street, and I decided the whole place would be a lot more cheerful after dark.

There was nothing to tempt me to join the few Christmas shoppers that were about, but I did buy a woollen bobble hat in a pound shop before going to the supermarket and spending some of my cash on groceries. Snow had started falling, and although it didn't settle the flakes stung my cheeks as they were blown by the wind. I had bought a replacement for the bottle of wine I had consumed the night before, plus another couple to tide me over and was tempted to open one of them as soon as I had trudged back to the apartment. But it was not even midday, so instead I curled up on the sofa and opened a search engine on the iPad and typed in *'Dead body found Charlton London'*.

The only result that came up was from April of the previous year. I tried *'Dead body found South East London'*. The most recent news item was from two weeks earlier and concerned the body of a woman found in a park in Blackheath. I hesitated for a moment, then typed in 'Kyle Kirkwood'.

The results were the same as I had found previously: Snapchat and Facebook accounts and an appearance in court for affray. Nothing more recent, and nothing under the news section. Just to be on the safe side, I deleted my search history. I took a deep breath and paced the tiny sitting room, then went back into the kitchen and opened a bottle of red wine. I poured a generous glass and took a few gulps, but still my heart was beating unnaturally fast. Surely the absence of news could only mean one thing – that Kyle remained undiscovered on that patch of muddy wasteland. Despite my thick sweater I was shivering, so took the wine with me to the sitting room and lit the log burner.

I picked up the iPad and composed a message to Leo. I balked at referring directly to human remains, instead typing: *Did you report K's location?* I stared at the screen for several minutes, but there was no reply.

I could at least check on Shane Quinn, I decided. I opened his social media accounts, but there were no new posts. Scrolling back to a post where Kayla Jevons was tagged, I clicked the link to her account. And to my relief, there was a selfie of her with Shane, eating a huge plate of chicken wings. The time stamp said '*13 hours ago*'. I closed my eyes and relief washed over me.

Once I had started to think rationally, my relief was all too short-lived. Yes, it appeared that Shane was safe and sound for now. But if he and his fellow gang members were indeed responsible for Kyle's death, then he would surely not remain safe for long. There would be recriminations; some sort of street justice handed out. I did not want to risk upsetting Claire, but I did wonder – and not for the first time – whether I should speak to Dervla and Pauly, in addition to trying to speak to the police. And when was that going to happen? I tried calling Leo. Nothing. I searched the news websites again, looking for reports of Kyle's death. Nothing.

Deciding I needed to break out of this anxiety spiral, I made myself a sandwich, poured another glass of wine and settled in front of the TV. It had a linked Netflix account, so I scrolled through the menu until I found a Christmas romcom set in New York. A high-powered business executive was in the process of falling for the carpenter who was fixing her kitchen when the combination of wine and heat from the log burner overcame me, and I drifted off to sleep.

I was woken by a long ring on the flat's doorbell. And then a voice I did not recognise.

'Bryony – are you in there?'

## THIRTY-TWO

### BRYONY

Now

I had definitely not been mistaken. There it was again.

'Bryony?'

But how? Nobody was supposed to know where I was. My heart pounding, I dragged myself up from the sofa, knocking my glass and splashing wine over the side table and onto the carpet as I did so.

'Who is it?' I called from the hallway.

'It's Sonja. Sonja Salvesen.'

'One second!'

I darted into the kitchen and grabbed a cloth, dabbing frantically at the spilled wine before opening the front door. A tall, Nordic-looking woman with a round face and blonde hair worn in a bob stood there smiling at me. A small child in yellow wellies and a navy duffel coat peered at me shyly from behind his mother's legs.

'Hi,' I said, brushing a hand over my tousled hair. 'Sorry, I wasn't expecting anyone.'

'I just thought I'd pop round and see how you were getting on.'

'Of course... come in.'

It felt a little strange telling Sonja to come into her own property, especially as I wasn't paying to be there, but she did not seem fazed. We stood slightly awkwardly in the kitchen, and I moved to boil the kettle, as much to have something to do as because I wanted a drink. I wondered if Sonja could smell the wine fumes.

'Tea? Coffee?' I said brightly.

Sonja shook her head. 'Not for me, thanks. Artie and I are on our way home from a playdate and he's ready to crash, so we should get home. You know how it is with toddlers.'

I didn't but nodded anyway.

'We were passing the flat, so I just thought I'd call in and check you were okay. From what Leo said, you'd been... you've been having a bit of a difficult time.'

I wondered exactly what Leo had told her. From the head cocked on one side and the sympathetic look, Sonja probably believed that I was embroiled in some sort of abusive situation with a domestic partner. I chose my words carefully.

'Nothing that a bit of time away won't fix. It's incredibly kind of you to let me stay, and I'm very grateful to Leo for arranging it.'

'He's one of the good guys, my cousin. And he has a lot to put up with.'

I turned away from the kettle and looked at her face. 'You mean with Ingrid?'

'Exactly. He's a bit of a saint where she's concerned, poor man.'

I thought of the sour-faced Ingrid, who was clearly not easy to live with. She had reason to be grateful to Leo's good nature, and now so did I.

Artie started squirming behind his mother's back, pulling on the hem of her coat. 'I'd better get this little man home for a nap.' Sonja hoisted her son onto her hip and headed for the door. 'Like I said, I just wanted to make sure you were doing okay. And if you need anything, my number is in the house manual on the bookshelf next to the fireplace.'

'Thank you: that's very kind.' I summoned a reassuring smile as I closed the front door behind her. 'And don't worry; I'll take good care of the place.'

I was about to rewind the movie to the place where I had fallen asleep when the iPad buzzed with an incoming FaceTime call: '*Leo calling*'.

Such was my haste to speak to him that I accidentally pressed the 'Reject' button and had to call him back.

'Christ, Bryony, it's good to see you!' he said as soon as his face appeared on the screen. He was wearing a sweatshirt, and I recognised the living room of his flat in the background. 'Is everything okay? You look okay.'

I reassured him that I was fine.

'And you haven't had anyone come to the flat?'

'Not unless you count your cousin.'

I told him that I had met Sonja and her son. 'And I keep checking the news, but there's nothing about...' I suddenly found myself considering the possibility that our call could be hacked '... about what we found.'

'I haven't seen anything either. And no one's made any enquiries about Ingrid's car, but I guess it's still early days on that front. It feels like a lifetime ago, but it's only been twenty-four hours. Hard to believe.'

I let out a groan. Only a day, yet I felt as though I'd been on the run for weeks. 'And did you tell the police about... the thing.'

Leo nodded. 'Yeah, I used a VPN and a guerrilla email

service to send an anonymous tip-off. I decided that was preferable to phoning.' He picked up a TV remote and started tapping it distractedly on the edge of the coffee table.

'So now they know, how long do I need to be here? I've got work to get back to, remember. And I can't keep my phone off forever: someone will raise the alarm.'

'It should be a couple of days more at least. Or until we have more information.' Leo checked his watch. 'Listen, I've got to be somewhere, but let's aim to speak again tomorrow.'

'*I've got to be somewhere*'. Or with someone. It would be the petite brunette dietician, I decided, as I switched the movie to 'play'.


I used to think there was something romantic about the seaside in winter. It definitely featured in my escape fantasies.

Working in a clinical service in an overstretched hospital is unrelentingly stressful, and there were times when faced with a waiting room full of acutely ill patients that I imagined myself walking on a deserted beach, alone apart from the seagulls. The reality, however, was proving different. Ramsgate was no doubt very appealing in summer, but the following morning as I trudged through the slush on litter-strewn streets with fellow shoppers keeping their heads low to avoid the wind and the gaudy Christmas decorations unlit, it felt very bleak. I wished instead that I was in the bright, overheated St Anselm's imaging department, drinking coffee and exchanging jokey banter with my co-workers.

There was a multiplex cinema on the northern edge of town, and I weighed up going to see a film, but the prospect of sitting in an empty theatre on a Friday morning was too dispiriting. Not even the popcorn or the oversized bags of chocolate tempted me. I went for a walk along the promenade in the drizzle, abandoning it after an hour to return to the Airbnb and repeatedly refresh the news headlines. Not being able to use my phone was growing ever more frustrating, and I tried to take mental stock of who might be trying to speak to me. It occurred to me that I ought to cover my tracks with work before someone from the department attempted to check up on me and my flu. I messaged Craig and said I was feeling a little better and hoped to be back next week.

Then there was Claire. I had messaged her on Monday to get news of the pregnancy, and she had told me she was waiting for an appointment for a scan on the early pregnancy unit. 'I'll call you,' I had told her. But it was now Friday, and I had not. I decided that I would FaceTime her with the iPad, first disguising the background so that she couldn't tell I wasn't in my flat. I sat on the bed and heaped all the pillows behind my head so that all she could see was my face and an expanse of white cotton.

She answered on the second ring.

'What's going on? Have you had your scan?' I asked. I was relieved to see that she had more colour in her face than when I last saw her.

'I thought I sent you a text about that? Sorry; I had so many people messaging me about it.'

'You may have done,' I said quickly. 'I've been laid up in bed and had my phone switched off most of the time.' This was more or less true.

She grinned. 'Well, the scan was on Tuesday. And they found a heartbeat.'

'Oh, Claire, I'm so happy for you! To be honest, I was a bit scared to ask.'

'It's okay, I get it…' She peered at the screen. 'So how come you're not at work?'

'Like I said, I've been off sick. Flu. That's why I haven't called round; didn't want you catching this bug.'

*That and the fact I'm a fugitive in Kent.*

We talked for a few minutes longer, and Claire eventually said, 'Don't forget, Sunday lunch with the family next weekend.'

'Family all okay?' I asked, thinking she would surely mention it now if there were a problem with her nephew.

'Yeah, they're all grand. Couldn't be better.'

'Listen, I don't know if I'll be able to come that day,' I prevaricated. 'I'm not sure I'll be completely better.'

The last thing I needed was to face Shane Quinn across a dining table and pretend that nothing was wrong.

'Of course you will – it's over a week away. And we've got so much to celebrate. Say you'll come!' she wheedled.

'All right then.' Perhaps Shane would be out. I would have to hope so.

As I ended the call, I saw the journal app which was installed on my iPad as well as my phone. I spent a productive twenty minutes writing an entry in my diary in which I didn't describe what I'd done – which in Ramsgate was very little, and pre-Ramsgate was too horrifying – but rather how I felt. I wrote about my fear and my paranoia and my anger.

*Overwhelmed with the unfairness*, I wrote. *None of this is my fault. Robbie and I both know that the accident wasn't my fault, despite me being at the wheel. And yet here I am paying the price.*

I was aware that this was self-pitying but I didn't care. No one but me was going to read it after all.

> *I'm just desperate to get back to my flat. Kyle is dead, and yes that's another huge nightmare, but at least he's not going to be showing up there uninvited at all hours of the day and night. At least I'll be safe from him when I'm there.*

Eventually I closed down the journal app, feeling a little

better, a little calmer. I sat still for a couple of moments, taking some long, deep breaths, then went back to the news sites. And, finally, there it was.

BODY OF A YOUNG MAN FOUND IN SOUTH EAST LONDON

## THIRTY-THREE
### BRYONY

Now

My heart thumping, I read on, but the news item was only a couple of lines long and there was little detail.

> The unnamed victim was found on the derelict Derwent Grove council estate in Charlton, South East London. Local police have opened an investigation into the circumstances around the man's death.

Whether or not it was due to Leo's tip-off, at least they had now found Kyle. Was he 'unnamed' because the police didn't want to release his identity, or because they didn't yet know who he was? It was unclear.

Having been calm, my pulse was now racing again. I thought about opening another bottle of wine, but I already had the beginnings of a headache and more wine was not the answer. Instead I searched through Sonja's kitchen cupboards until I found a selection of herbal teas.

As I was brewing myself some camomile, I sent a message to Leo.

*Can you talk now?*

He replied a couple of minutes later.

*In a meeting. Give me an hour*

I had no desire to watch any more romcoms, so I set about shampooing the patch of carpet I had splashed with red wine the day before. By now I was on a roll, so I mopped the kitchen floor and cleaned out the kitchen cupboards, before emptying the grate in the wood burner.

Eventually the iPad registered an incoming audio call. I switched it to speaker mode as I continued arranging fresh firewood in the burner.

'I've just snuck out from the IT department,' Leo told me. 'I'm now on the canteen terrace with the smokers.'

I could picture it with clarity, and I felt a rush of homesickness for London and the hospital.

'There was something in the news about them finding the body,' I said, kneeling down and striking a match. I watched with satisfaction as the firelighter caught and started licking at the wood.

'Yes, I saw that.'

'But they didn't mention Kyle's name. Do you think they know who it is?'

Leo was speaking quietly, trying not to be overheard. 'They must do, because I gave his name in the anonymous email. If they haven't published it, it's probably because the next of kin haven't been told yet.'

'And no one's said anything to you about the car?'

'Not a thing.'

I closed the door of the stove and leaned back on my heels as the flames became a roaring mass of gold and orange. 'I'm going to come back,' I told him. 'I don't care if it means going straight to the police, I can't live like this. I'll end up with a drink problem.'

Leo gave a short laugh. 'Let's hope it doesn't come to that. But listen, I've taken some advice, and I don't think that you should speak to the police after all.'

I frowned at the screen. 'What do you mean – you've taken advice?'

'I've got a close mate from uni who's a criminal defence lawyer; a guy called Steve Adkins. I told him about your situation – anonymously, of course – and his view is that you were coerced into going with Kyle to fetch Shane. In legal terms it means you were acting under duress, which exonerates you from any criminal liability. And you said Kirkwood made you get out of the cab before it headed to Derwent Grove, didn't you?'

'He did.' I could feel my cheeks turning pink in the glow of the fire. 'Before Shane even got into it.'

'Right. And what happened after that was completely out of your control. You don't bear any responsibility.'

I thought about this. 'But surely I should still tell them what I know? I'm a witness, even if I'm not a suspect.'

'True. But if you do, there's a good chance Shane Quinn will end up serving a prison sentence. Is that what you want?'

I pictured the amiable teenager driving his grandmother to her hospital appointments. 'No. No, I don't.'

'Well, there we are then. I know it's hard, Bryony, and I know I'm contradicting my own advice, but it's best you stay silent.'

'I'm still coming back,' I said stubbornly, adding, 'Not that I'm not grateful to you and Sonja.'

'I can't stop you. I'd even...' I sensed his hesitation. 'I'd be glad to see you, okay? But as a compromise, why not hang on until next week? Just a couple more days. I'm still concerned for your safety. Kyle's gang could still make trouble for you.'

'Okay,' I agreed, getting to my feet. 'Just til after the weekend.'

I set my alarm for six on Monday morning. After packing my few belongings and giving the flat a quick clean, I headed through the raw December dark to the station.

I was at St Pancras before eight, and back in Beckenham an hour later, after barely making a connection at Three Bridges. I only just had time to drop my bag at Kenley Court before heading to work, but I spent a few seconds looking around the place with a feeling of deep gratitude. It was good to be home. And now that Kyle Kirkwood was gone, there was no reason that my flat couldn't go back to being a place of safety and sanctuary again.

At the Monday staff meeting I was greeted with a degree of nonchalance, but then I had to remind myself that as far as my colleagues were concerned, I had only been off for a couple of days with a nasty virus. As had plenty of other people working at the hospital. They had no idea that in reality I had been through something far worse. There were pine garlands and fairy lights everywhere, and the sound system in the staff room was playing Slade's 'Merry Christmas Everybody'. People were discussing their plans for the festive season. For the first time in weeks, I felt a sense of peace.

There was still the issue of Sunday lunch at the Quinns' house to resolve. Of course I wanted to see Claire's extended family, but after the events of the last week I wasn't sure I could be in the same room with Shane without giving something away. Or at the very least acting strangely.

I tried making subtle enquiries with Claire about who would be there.

'Maggie's lot and Nanny Quinn. Oh, and Miss Ember, of course.'

I was about to ask about Shane, when she volunteered. 'Dervla's girls will probably be around but not Shane. He'll be off with the new girlfriend's family.'

Relief surged through me. 'Tell Dervla to let me know if I can bring anything.'

'So, you'll be there?' Claire asked hopefully.

'I'll be there.'

# THIRTY-FOUR
## BRYONY

Now

I decided I was ready to extend the Christmas celebrations to my own flat.

On Saturday morning, after a blessedly uneventful week at work, I took the bus to a place on the South Circular called 'The Christmas Forest'. I selected a small but perfectly formed tree, had it wrapped in netting, and brought it back to Kenley Court in a black cab.

'Here – let me help you with that.' I looked up as I was struggling to extricate the tree from the back of the taxi, and into the eyes of Leo Salvesen.

'Look, I'm sorry I haven't been in touch this week,' he said in a low voice as we dragged the tree up the front steps and into the ground-floor foyer. 'It's not that I haven't wanted to, it's just that given...' he hesitated, glancing towards the front door of his own flat '... given everything that happened last Wednesday, I thought it safer if we kept some distance from each other.'

'It's fine.' I straightened the tree and brushed needles from my coat sleeve. 'I get it.'

'Ingrid's back,' Leo went on. 'She knows I've used the car. I invented an essential errand, but I'm not entirely sure she bought my story. She's a bit suspicious.'

'It's fine,' I repeated, though the truth was I had missed our co-conspirators' discussions. I started dragging the tree up to the top floor. 'I'll see you around, okay?'

I spent a pleasant couple of hours setting up the tree and hanging some silver and gold baubles, before checking my news feeds again. Nothing. So I felt relatively relaxed the next morning when I set off for the Quinn household, carrying a large potted poinsettia for Dervla.

'Come and see our tree!' Aoife bounced up to me as soon as I arrived and led me into the living room. In the corner of the room stood a much larger tree than mine; every inch covered in mismatched and home-made decorations and swathed with bushy tinsel. Underneath its branches there was a growing pile of presents. 'Me and Molly did all of it.'

'That looks wonderful,' I told her, as she hooked one arm through the crook of my elbow and flung the other out with a jubilant flourish. I meant it. It was a proper family Christmas tree, for what would be a proper family Christmas. And soon Claire's baby would be joining their ranks. I was struck suddenly by an uncomfortable sense of life passing me by. I had left for Australia as a twenty-something, and now I was entering my mid-thirties. I had heard other women speak of the same faint sense of panic I was now feeling. What was I doing wasting my life on the likes of Andreas Koros? Not to mention getting caught up in inter-gang drama. In the New Year, I decided, I would return to the dating apps with a renewed purpose. I would screen out the deep-sea fishermen and mountain climbers and go on some dates with men who were serious about finding a life partner.

The festive atmosphere continued into our lunch. Dervla had roasted a turkey crown and Pauly's mother, Granny Quinn, was there, a short rotund woman with a steel-grey perm and a thick Irish accent. Claire had a better colour in her face, and claimed she was feeling stronger, though she complained about the non-alcoholic wine Dervla had provided. 'Tastes like disinfectant,' she said, pulling a face. 'Mind you, everything tastes like disinfectant at the moment.'

Miss Ember's contribution was a box of crackers, and most of the assembled company gamely put on their paper hats.

'Will Miss Ember be coming on Christmas Day?' I whispered to Maggie.

'Of course. Every year,' Maggie replied calmly. 'Poor old duck has no family, so it's a given.'

'She doesn't even have the excuse that she eats like a bird,' I observed, as Miss Ember added two more roast potatoes and three pigs in blankets to her plate. 'You'll need to make sure the turkey's big enough.'

After a bowl of sherry trifle had been passed round ('I draw the line at Christmas pudding,' Dervla announced), we went into the living room for tea and coffee. A key turned in the front door and there were voices in the hall.

'Ah, that'll be Shane,' Pauly told me. 'He said he might try and pop round.'

I felt the blood draining from my face. *Just don't look at him*, I told myself. *Don't make eye contact and it'll be all right.*

Moreover, Shane was not alone. He ushered in a slim, pretty girl with a lot of artfully waved dark hair and the sort of make-up that would have taken me over an hour to perfect.

'Everyone, this is Kayla.'

Kayla Jevons. Daughter of South London gang supremo Calvin Jevons, whose lackeys had been intent on causing serious harm to her boyfriend, and who had counted Kyle Kirkwood as one of his foot soldiers. What did she know about any of this? An image flashed through my mind: the dead body lying motionless in the mud. The blood rushed back into my face, and I felt my cheeks turn from ashen to flaming pink.

'Granny Quinn!' Shane enveloped his grandmother in a bear hug before asking me easily, 'You all right there, Bryony? And how's yourself, Miss Ember?'

Claire was looking at me oddly. 'Are you okay, Bry?'

'Bit warm in here,' I muttered. 'I'll get some water.'

I almost ran into the kitchen and filled a glass under the tap. The door opened and Shane came in.

'Shane! We shouldn't be speaking!' I hissed. I glanced over his shoulder to make sure Kayla hadn't followed him.

'I just wanted to check that you were, you know *really* all right.'

'I'm fine,' I assured him. 'But what about you? What happened to you? I didn't think it was safe to call you or text you after...'

'Nothing much happened. The car took me to this rundown place, and there was a bunch of guys waiting there, but before they could do anything, my mates showed up in another car, grabbed me and we got the hell out of there.'

*The black Range Rover.*

'Thanks to you giving me the heads up I was fine. I owe you one.' He grinned, showing the gold tooth.

'But Shane,' I lowered my voice, 'someone was killed. It's been in the news. They found a body there.'

He shrugged. 'I don't know anything about that. Didn't happen when I was there.'

He was still smiling but the expression in his eyes was hard and unyielding. The message was clear: this subject was closed as far as he was concerned.

'And you and Kayla... everything okay there?' I asked.

'It's sweet now. I've met her old man, and he's cool with me seeing her. Just as long as I stay away from certain people, you know?'

I nodded, although I was still a little confused by this turnaround.

'Anyways...' he slapped the countertop '... gotta head out. Me and Kayla only dropped in to say hi.'

I followed him back into the living room, and after a prolonged round of goodbyes, he and Kayla left.

'Shane's doing ever so well,' Dervla said as the front door closed, and there was a trace of smugness in her voice. 'Really getting things back on track. He's not delivering the pizzas anymore. Kayla's dad has given him a job as a manager in one of his warehouses.'

'Really?' I asked, keeping my eyes fixed on my coffee. *Talk about keeping your friends close and your enemies closer.*

'We've met them: the Jevons. Really nice family,' Pauly said with the same smugness.

'Ever so nice,' Dervla repeated. 'They've got a villa in Spain, and they've said we can borrow it.'

'Amazing,' I said weakly. 'What does he do for a living?'

Dervla flapped a hand. 'Oh, he's in business,' she said vaguely.

So she had not made the link between the Jevons family and the gang her son had been entangled with. I could only assume that as the head of a crime syndicate, it served Calvin Jevons's purpose to have the veneer of respectability, to appear outwardly to be an upstanding member of society. Wasn't Al Capone known to have donated money to local causes?

I thought about this turn of events as I waited for my bus back to Beckenham that evening. I fervently hoped that this really was Shane giving up the gang life, and not just some sinister manipulation by the opposing faction. For now, at least, he seemed to have got things back on track. And I, too, felt as though I had been given my life back.

There were changes ahead, and I fully intended them to be changes for the better.

## THIRTY-FIVE
### BRYONY

Now

The first change came only a couple of days later when I received a rare phone call from my father.

'I've got a big surprise for you,' he announced, and there was an unusual note of excitement in his voice.

'You know I hate surprises.'

'You'll like this one. Your sister Flora's coming over for Christmas.'

'But she never comes at Christmas,' I protested. 'And anyway, that's next week.'

'Well, she is this year. She got some last-minute deal on flights that was too good to turn down.'

'Are they all coming?'

'Evan can't leave the farm over Christmas and New Year, but she's bringing the children. Not quite sure where we're going to put them all, but I dare say we'll manage.'

'That's fantastic news!' I was already calculating that I would not only have to go out and buy four extra Christmas presents but also arrange to hire a car to get to Sussex and back on Christmas Day when the trains weren't running. The arrival of Flora with my niece and nephews meant that there was no possibility of staying at my father and stepmother's house overnight, since there were only two guest rooms. The boys would share the larger room and my niece Lily would have the small one, leaving Flora on the sofa bed in the study. But still, it would be something a little different, and a lot more fun than Christmas Day alone with my father and Gayle. That was something I hadn't done since the year before I left for Australia, and I wasn't looking forward to repeating it.

I rented the car for two days, driving to Sussex and back on both Christmas and Boxing Day. The empty roads meant I could be there in just over an hour, and I was quite happy to retreat to my own space in the flat after a day spent with nine- and seven-year-old boys and a five-year-old girl. Not that it wasn't lovely to see Jack, Isaac and Lily, who I hadn't set eyes on since Lily was a toddler and I was living in Melbourne. Just as I'd hoped, it turned out to be an enjoyable Christmas. Our father was a lot more relaxed around his grandchildren than he had been when Flora and I were small, and although Gayle was not a very maternal woman, she was happy to spend her time in the kitchen churning out a seemingly endless supply of delicious food.

'I thought I'd come up to London for a day next week,' Flora said to me as we were washing up after a Boxing Day lunch of leftover turkey curry. 'I need to do some shopping, and I'd really love to see your new flat. Gayle says she'll mind the kids for a few hours.'

'I'd love that.' I grabbed her hand in a mock handshake. 'It's a deal.'


My lightness of heart continued when I returned home. I was free of Kyle's constant threats and the feeling of being watched.

Free to get on with the life I had envisaged for myself when I bought the flat.

I was working between Christmas and New Year, but I arranged to finish work early one day that week. I met Flora for a cocktail at Selfridges, then the two of us and all her bags of shopping caught a cab back to Kenley Court.

'This is nice,' Flora said, surveying the building from the outside. 'Really nice, Bry. You've done well. Can't wait to see inside.'

As if on cue, the front door opened and Leo emerged onto the front steps, dressed in cycling gear.

'Hi, Bryony. Good Christmas?' There was an awkward silence during which he and I did not quite make eye contact.

Flora looked from me to Leo and then back again.

'Aren't you going to introduce me?'

'Yes, sorry. Flora, this is my neighbour, Leo.'

'Hi, Leo, nice to meet you.' She extended a hand. 'I'm Bryony's big sister.'

'Ah, the one from New Zealand?'

'That's right.' Once again, Flora looked at both of us, trying to ascertain exactly what the dynamic was between us. 'So how long have you lived here, Leo?'

'I bought the flat about five years ago. I work at St Anselm's, like Bryony does, and I was renting in the area, so it made sense.'

Flora had a look on her face that I recognised all too well. 'So you moved here alone?'

'I did. I'm not on my own now though. My sister, Ingrid, is staying with me for a bit while she deals with some health problems.' I could sense Flora trying to catch my eye in an attempt to make me join in this conversation, but I ignored her. 'If you ladies will excuse me, I need to get my bike out of the store.'

'He seems nice,' Flora commented as we hauled her shopping bags up to the top floor. 'And single too.'

'You did grill him a bit, Flo.' I looked askance at her as I unlocked my front door.

'Well, there was such a weird vibe between the two of you I was just trying to work out what was going on. He is quite attractive, in a nerdy way.'

'I suppose so.'

'Come on, Bry, don't tell me you haven't noticed!' Flora had dropped her bags and was taking in her surroundings. 'Cute single guy living downstairs, it's like the plot of a romcom.'

'If you're trying to encourage me to pursue him, forget it,' I said repressively. 'We're just friends. And I think he's seeing someone. So not really single.'

Flora had picked up one of my velvet cushions and was stroking it admiringly. 'Not married though,' she countered, as though we were having one of our interminable teenage arguments. 'So actually technically single.'

We stared each other down over the top of the cushion, then both of us broke into giggles.

'Look...' I started, then hesitated. There was no way on earth that I was about to tell my sister about the Kyle Kirkwood nightmare, which was why Leo and I had become close in the first place. That in turn would mean divulging the real reason behind my move to Australia. It was too complicated to explain on a fun girls' day. Besides, I had no desire to burden Flora with any of it, not when she was about to fly back to the other side of the world and was unable to offer any meaningful support.

'Yes, okay, I do like Leo and he's been... really helpful since we moved in. But he's not currently a free agent, so there's no point really looking at him that way. I'm not about to get mixed up in a love triangle. Not at this stage in my life.'

I took the cushion from Flora, replaced it on the sofa and went over to the kitchen corner to boil the kettle.

'Are you looking to settle down then? How long has it been since Joel? It's been a while, right?'

This was the first time we had discussed my personal life, partly because the chaos of Flora's over-excited children made it impossible, and partly because my sister knew I didn't like talking about it in front of our father and Gayle.

'It's been about a year now,' I said, pouring boiling water into the teapot. 'And yes, it would be nice to find someone special. It just hasn't happened yet.'

Flora came over and put her arm round my shoulders. 'Next year,' she said, pulling me into a hug. 'I have a feeling next year is going to be your year.'

## THIRTY-SIX
### BRYONY

Then

In the end my time in Australia wasn't two years; it was five. After moving in with Joel, I successfully applied to have my visa extended. I can't claim that I gave Robbie Makepeace no thought during that time. The truth is I tried not to think about him, but for many months my sleep was filled with nightmarish anxiety dreams of that terrible night in the car.

For a short time, I continued to mail perfunctory letters to HMP Rochester, and his arrived frequently in return, filled with lyrical passages about how he and I were joined forever by the events of that June night, and how we would see each other as soon as his sentence was served. But the letters inevitably became a source of friction between Joel and I, and when we moved from our first apartment in St Kilda to a house in Auburn, I did not give Robbie the new address. After I'd been away for nearly four years I heard via Claire, who was Facebook friends with Charlie – one of the group we had met in the Alibi – that he had been released on licence and returned to Scotland where his mother's side of the family lived.

Joel and I had met at a games night held at a bar in Port Melbourne called the Tipsy Cow. Evenings like these were very popular among the city's under thirties, and I had already been to a couple with colleagues at Monash during my first year in Melbourne. They were loud and fun, and featured games I already knew (Pictionary, Bananagram) and ones I'd never heard of, like Unstable Unicorns. On the night in question, I found myself seated next to a sun-bleached, tanned surfer type during a game of Cards Against Humanity, and stole glances at him all evening. He was startlingly attractive, and I was quietly thrilled when we ended up having a drink together after the game. Although he looked like the archetypal Aussie lifeguard, Joel held a master's degree in indigenous archaeology and worked as a curator of cultural heritage at Melbourne University.

We started dating and quickly became exclusive, moving in together towards the end of my second year at Monash. Encouraged by Joel, I applied to extend my visa by a further three years, and we moved from our apartment to a small house with a garden. We even acquired a dog called Squirrel; a small hairy creature adopted from the local shelter. Our weekends were spent at the beach, or combing flea markets for bargains, or working our way through Melbourne's endless supply of ethnic restaurants. We talked about buying a place of our own and spent hours scouring online property sites. Life could not have been sweeter.

And yet when Joel proposed to me on Valentine's Day of my fifth year in the country, I was unsure. Accepting would mean applying for the Prospective Marriage visa, and marrying within fifteen months of it being issued. Once married, I would be entitled to apply for permanent residency. Joel wanted children, but I was all too conscious that if we ever had them, I would never be able to leave the country without risking losing custody and even contact. Much as I loved Australia, I had never intended to live there forever. Some invisible force, some unspoken tie, was pulling me back to London. After a lot of soul-searching, I turned down Joel's proposal. With his male pride fatally damaged, our relationship started to unravel. Within a couple of months it was over.

Joel retained custody of Squirrel and I moved out of the house in Auburn and into employee accommodation on the Monash site. For those last few months I abandoned my social life and worked all the hours I could to save up some money. Then I read about, and applied for the job at St Anselm's. Three weeks later I was on a flight to Heathrow. Enough time had passed since my entanglement with Robbie, I decided. That was in the past.

# THIRTY-SEVEN
## BRYONY

Now

'What we need,' Rochelle said a couple of days later, 'is a proper, no-holds barred New Year's Eve celebration.'

The two of us were sitting on low chairs in the imaging department's break room. Rochelle tossed her polystyrene cup in the direction of the bin and missed. Over my short time at St Anselm's, the two of us had become friends, and I enjoyed her company. Unlike Claire she was a single girl up for anything.

'Going out on New Year's Eve is so hard though,' I sighed, 'Everywhere's so full, and places grossly overcharge, plus public transport is a nightmare...'

Rochelle shot me a stern look. 'All right, New Year grinch!'

'It's not that I don't want to go out. But it has to be worth the effort.'

'Challenge accepted!' We were due back in the CT suite, so Rochelle stood up and gave me a hand to pull me up from my chair. 'I'm going to put some effort into this, and I'm going to find somewhere for us to go.'

Sure enough, on the morning of New Year's Eve, she

bounced into work looking pleased with herself. 'You might have thought you were destined to be a New Year's loser, but you're not.' She gave my ponytail a playful flick. 'I've found us somewhere to go tonight.'

Rochelle's cousin, it turned out, had a good friend who was having a house party in Brockley. 'She told me to bring someone, so I'm bringing you, Bryony!'

I was unsure about seeing in the New Year surrounded by a group of strangers, but reminded myself that I was trying to embrace the new and the different. So after my shift had ended, I went back to the flat and changed into a sequinned dress and heels. After re-styling my hair and applying make-up that said 'party', I caught an overpriced Uber to the address that Rochelle had given me.

I could hear the music some distance before I was dropped outside the three-storey Edwardian house on one of the streets leading from Hilly Fields. The front steps were lit by fairy lights, and other partygoers were making their way up them when I arrived. Inside was dimly lit and throbbing with electronic dance music and bifold doors were flung wide open to reveal more fairy lights and a fire pit. I squeezed through the throng, simultaneously tugging down my short dress and looking out for Rochelle.

I found her eventually, but it was one of those parties where the noise level made it impossible to have a conversation, and interactions had to be mimed. There was nothing for it but to help myself to a drink from a side table littered with an assortment of bottles that people had brought. I helped myself from a plastic cup full of warm white wine, praying that it hadn't been spiked, and made my way to the dance floor. I reasoned that if I couldn't talk then I may as well dance, and Rochelle was already waving her arms over her head and singing out loud to 'Show me Love'.

I was soon wholeheartedly enjoying myself, my inhibitions

washed away by several more lukewarm cups of wine. After what must have been several hours but seemed merely minutes, someone had turned down the sound system to make way for Big Ben's chimes, and we were all drunkenly singing 'Auld Lang Syne' and embracing people whose names we didn't even know.

'Hey! Bryony!'

Suddenly a familiar face loomed in front of me – a face that I could neither accurately place or name. A face with a nice smile and dimples.

'It's Tom. Tom Burridge.'

I must have looked blank.

'From the agency that sold you the flat,' he shouted.

*Oh yes, Tom the estate agent.*

He said something that I think was 'Did you have a good Christmas?' but it was drowned out by the music, so I just nodded.

'And how's it going with the flat? Must be about three months now. Are you settling in okay?'

He seemed fairly sober, or at least less drunk than I was.

'Yes, it's great,' I mouthed over Haddaway's 'What is Love'. 'It's all worked out just fine.'

In that joyful moment I had once again forgotten being stalked and blackmailed and coerced into wrongdoing.

Tom leaned in close to my ear so that I could hear him. 'I feel really bad: I never did drop your spare keys round. I meant to, but we've been crazy busy.'

'Don't worry about it.' My words were lost in the noise but I shook my head to show that it didn't matter. 'I've had a spare set cut.'

'I'll get them to you as soon as I can, I promise. I've got your details so I'll be in touch.'

He mimed phoning me.

I gave him a thumbs up, and then he was lost in the crowd.

## THIRTY-EIGHT
### BRYONY

Now

It had been unexpectedly pleasing to bump into Tom in a normal social setting, and over the next couple of weeks I secretly hoped I might hear from him. But nothing happened, and I eventually put him from my mind.

It was time to carry out my resolution and return to using dating apps. According to my co-worker Craig, the new app to use was Align – designed to get users away from the rapid-swipe culture – and the navigation ensured that once you clicked on a profile, you could not move on from it until you had scrolled through and absorbed all the biographical data that person had chosen to share. The idea was that you would no longer be able to reject a potential match just because you didn't like their sunglasses or their pet dog.

*It's so frustrating at first,* I wrote in my diary. *I came very close to deleting the stupid thing. But then as I've spent time using it, I've actually started to see the point. In taking the time to read about people, you're going against the disposable dating culture that we all claim to hate so much, where you move onto someone new in a few seconds. You're made to read about a person's likes and dislikes and really get a feel for who they are. If you then decide they're not for you, you still have the option to select 'no, thanks', but only after you've given them a chance. If someone is interested in you, then you receive an alert and the option to look at them but the same rule applies: you can only navigate away from their profile once you've read all there is to read, and looked at all their photos. Yes, it's time consuming, even a little pointless if your initial impression that you're not interested holds true, but if you really want to find 'the one' then surely that's time well invested?*

The Align app became strangely addictive, and I spent all my lunchtimes and a lot of my evenings reading painstakingly through dozens of profiles. Despite this new format, it remained a numbers game and after reading everything there was to read there were very few options. There were far more women than men on the app, presumably because they were more willing to play a long game. Of the men I did honour with a 'yes', some did not match with me and a couple proved dull when we started to talk.

And then I found Mike. Mike had a lovely open face and a warm smile. He was nice-looking, but not intimidatingly so, with sandy hair and hazel eyes. Like me, he had grown up in Sussex and travelled in Australia. Like me, he worked in the health sector, as a hospital-based physiotherapist. He was interested in wine, liked dogs and dancing and enjoyed board games played strictly for fun. He was even a few inches taller than me, and lived a short distance away in Forest Hill. In short, he was perfect.

We exchanged phone numbers, and within only a few days were messaging each other constantly. I grew to expect a 'good morning' text from him when I woke up, various updates and words of encouragement during the working day, and then flirty messages during the evening wind-down periods, followed by a 'good night'. The connection was strong, and instant. 'I really feel like we already know each other so well,' I told Rochelle when she commented on my constant texting during a break at work. 'It's like he just gets me.'

She was a little sceptical.

'Remember what happened with Dr Koros,' she cautioned. 'That was all hot and heavy, but it turned out you were being catfished. Just be careful.'

Rochelle was wrong, of course, but her warning hit home. This endless messaging was risky, and should be cut short. You could never be sure until you were face to face with someone.

*We should talk on the phone xx*, I texted that evening, to test the waters.

*Let's go one better. Let's meet up, soon as possible xx*

That had to be a good sign, surely, if he wanted to go straight to a face-to-face meeting. Feeling excited, I suggested a drink in a couple of days' time at a bar called Paper Tiger, which was roughly halfway between our two homes.

*Fab. I'll be there xx*

I felt a cold rush of panic when I remembered waiting first in a pub and then a restaurant for a fake Andreas who had no intention of being there. It was natural to be gun-shy, I told myself, but there was no reason the same thing was going to happen again. This felt very different. It felt like a real connection. Like the start of something.

Even so, I was very wary. As I was about to get dressed (just a white t-shirt and plain trousers; I wasn't prepared to make a huge effort this time), I fired off a text.

*You are going to show up? Promise me! xx*

I felt quite weak with relief when he replied with a photo. It was a grinning selfie taken standing in front of a window. He was wearing a blue chambray shirt and holding up a bunch of pink roses with a florists' card that read *'For Bryony, love M x'*. He was real. It was happening. I let out a long, slow breath and applied my lipstick before putting it in my bag with other essentials like keys, phone and compact mirror. Because keeping tabs on a large bag in a busy bar is always a pain, I had switched to a small green crossbody bag that only just had space for them all. It was so over-full that my door keys were scratching my phone screen, so I removed them and dropped them into the pocket of my overcoat.

As I was climbing into my Uber a few minutes later, I received another text.

*Already here – choose a cocktail! xx*

He had attached a screenshot of the drinks menu. *You see*, I told the imaginary doubters. *He's there already. He is real.*

I texted back that I would have a negroni. As I was walking up to the entrance to Paper Tiger, my phone buzzed with yet another text.

*Just running to the bathroom: have left our drinks on the bar xx*

Sure enough, as I came in through the front door I could see two stools set up with the drinks in front of them. Next to them was the bouquet of pink roses.

'Are you Bryony?' the bartender asked with a smile. He held out the flowers. 'These are for you.'

I took them from him and climbed onto one of the high stools. And as in his selfie, there was the card reading *'For Bryony, love M x'*.

'Your date said to tell you he'll be back in just a

second... This is also for you.' He indicated the lowball glass filled with amber liquid and topped with an orange slice. Mike's drink looked like gin or vodka with either tonic or soda water.

I took a sip, and felt the warm burn of the gin at the back of my throat. It felt good. It tasted good. A little bitter, perhaps, but that would be the Campari. The thought that Mike would be standing in front of me in no more than a couple of minutes prompted a flurry of butterflies in my stomach. I was ridiculously nervous, probably because I so badly wanted – needed – this to work out. I could feel myself shaking. I took a gulp of the negroni, then another.

Soon I had drunk almost all of it, but there was still no Mike.

'Can I get you anything else?' the barman asked. He was polishing glasses with a white cloth. It was still early and the place was quiet.

I shook my head. 'How long ago did he go to the restroom?'

'Not long. Only about a minute or so before you arrived.'

'Oh. Okay.' I took another swig of my drink and closed my eyes, grimacing.

'Worried he's done a runner through the bathroom window?'

'Something like that.'

'Don't worry; maybe he just had to take a phone call or something. Look – he left his jacket.' He pointed to the back of the stool next to mine.

I opened my eyes to look where he was pointing, but the room swam around me. The truth was, I was starting to feel distinctly unwell. I was sweating, and nausea surged through me. 'Could I please have a glass of water?'

The barman poured me some, eyeing me closely as he did so. 'Are you okay? You've gone very pale.'

I wanted to get off the stool, but I was afraid that if I did so I would pass out. I was overwhelmed with acute dizziness, and a sense of being out of my own body.

'Sorry, need to get some fresh air,' I mumbled and slid off the stool, staggering in the direction of the door. Fortunately, I was still wearing the crossbody bag and somehow had the presence of mind to grab my coat. My legs felt as though they belonged to someone else, and I could no longer remember where I was, or why.

I must have made it outside, because I felt a rush of cold air, but I could no longer see properly and there was a ringing in my ears. I managed to thrust one arm awkwardly into my coat before lurching forward, bending double and vomiting violently. Whether into the gutter or over the pavement I couldn't tell, but I felt the sour liquid splash up against my face.

'It's okay,' I heard a disembodied voice say somewhere. 'I've got this. She's with me.'

The voice was somehow familiar. *I know him*, I thought, in a pinpoint moment of clarity. Could it be Leo, come to my rescue again? Or could he have somehow caused this? The thought swirled in my head that Leo had IT skills, and Leo could have easily set up a fake Align account. Could also have been behind the fake Andreas messages.

But then the clarity gave way to confusion and I was no longer sure what I had heard. A vehicle slowed to a halt somewhere nearby. A door was opened, and I was pushed roughly inside, tipping face-forward onto what smelt like a leather car seat. I think I tried to move, but it was hopeless: I could not, nor could I cry out. It was as though I was paralysed. The car was moving now and I was being suffocated by the leather, unable to move my face. I passed out.

I could have been out cold for minutes, or it could have been hours; I had no way of telling.

When I did eventually come round, I was no longer in the car. My head was pounding and my mouth was dry, but the paralysis and the sense of disembodiment had receded. I still felt sick, and I was desperately thirsty. It was very dark, and I was in some sort of confined space, on a hard, cold surface. My arms wouldn't move, but this time it was because they were tied behind my back. I smelled vomit, then remembered it was my own.

Suddenly there was light, not from overhead, but from a torch. It took me several seconds to work out what I was seeing. I let out a groan of horror, before collapsing onto the ground again.

'Oh God. It's you.'

# PART TWO

# THIRTY-NINE
## ROBBIE

Then

The first thing I noticed about her was her hair.

She has this incredible head of tawny hair, so long, thick and lustrous that it almost has a life of its own. It's a head-turning feature. It turned mine.

I was at a bar called Alibi with a few of my mates from work: Charlie and Dev and Brett. We were all working at the same cyber security company in Moorgate called Citadel Security Group; all IT geeks. Our clients were big corporations who needed bespoke solutions to keep their data safe. It was the very early days of cybercriminals using generative AI, and our team's job was to find ways to use it against them. Brett was leaving to go to a rival firm so we were having a drinks do near where he lived. Usual thing: plenty of lagers, bunch of techie work chat. So far so standard.

And then I saw her.

She was out with a plump, dark-haired girl, but I barely noticed the friend. All I could see was the tall, stunning woman with the amazing hair. They moved from the bar to a table right next to us, and as is often the case in a rowdy bar with all-male groups and all-female ones, we all started talking. Turned out the brunette had a boyfriend. She left after a couple of drinks, but as I said, I wasn't interested in her anyway. I smiled at the other one and introduced myself.

In addition to the hair, she had straight dark brows and a curvy mouth with a very pronounced cupid's bow. Her skin was very tanned, and although the brown colour was clearly out of a bottle, in the dim light of the bar it gave her a golden glow all of her own. She told me her name, and after a bit of subtle probing I discovered that she had recently come out of a long-term relationship and was finding dating life hard. So far, so relatable. I asked for her number and she gave it to me. Yes, it really was that easy.

After that night in the bar, I couldn't get her out of my head.

Straight away I did a Google search – standard, right? – but there wasn't a whole lot to find. There were some stunning photos of her on her social media, all of which I immediately screenshotted and saved into a special album on my phone. As I looked at them – frequently – I imagined what it would be like to go out with her. To live with her.

Everyone says you're meant to leave it at least twenty-four hours between meeting a female and asking her out. That's supposed to be the rule. I made it to about eighteen hours. Then I texted her and suggested we go for dinner. To my delight she was instantly receptive. She even seemed quite chuffed to hear from me. Okay, she just wanted to go for a pizza when I had somewhere fancy and French in mind: somewhere with candles and thick tablecloths and proper waiters. But at least she wanted to meet up. That had to be a positive. Had to mean she liked me. I asked Charlie, who has more experience of these things. He's had several girlfriends: I've barely even had one, unless you count that girl from accounts that I went on two dates with.

'Are you kidding, mate?' was his response. 'Gives you her number straight off the bat and wants to meet up for dinner? Course she like you: it's obvious.'

This was encouraging, but when the night of our date approached, I consulted Charlie again. I wasn't sure which topics of conversation made girls most interested in the opposite sex. I'd had little contact with them at secondary school, and when I got to university, my only interaction with the opposite sex other than discussing our computer science coursework was at drunken house parties where you couldn't hold a conversation over the music.

'They like pets,' Charlie told me without hesitation.

'But I don't have a pet. I never had a pet growing up either. My mum has a dog now she's widowed, but I can't stand the thing.'

'Just lie. Pretend you like dogs. Dogs and travel. Chicks like guys who are into travelling. And mention soccer. She probably won't know anything about it, but it reassures them that you're normal if you're into footie.'

I made a mental note of all this. 'And when it comes to texts, I've been signing them with two kisses. When d'you think I should progress to three kisses?'

Charlie made a scoffing noise. 'I've never sent a bird three kisses.'

My face must have fallen because he went on quickly. 'But hey, they love all that stuff, don't they? Why not ramp up to three after you've seen her, and you're sure she wants to meet up again. Sound fair?'

'Sounds completely fair,' I agreed.

'Word of advice, though, mate, don't go in too quickly asking for the next date, if there is one. Don't scare her off.'

'How soon?'

'Leave it at least a week, okay? Promise me?'
'Promise.'


The pizza night went pretty well. We got on brilliantly, and if I felt as though there were lapses in the conversation, I mentally referred back to Charlie's list. Dogs, travel, football. I even threw in a few mentions of going to the gym, because that seemed like safe, common ground. The travel stuff went down particularly well, because her sister lives overseas and she's keen to try and spend some time visiting her and exploring that part of the world.

We parted agreeing to meet again 'sometime soon', as she put it. I left it four days before contacting her. So not quite a week, but near enough. When I spoke to her, she didn't initially seem keen, saying she was tired and over-worked. It felt like a body blow.

'Oh, come on,' I wheedled. 'Surely it would do you good to get out for a bit. We could meet in the pub, or even just go for a walk. It's light til really late now.'

How magnificent would that be, I thought, to be seen out walking in the park with *her* as my date. Heads would turn; other men would think how lucky I was.

'Honestly, I'm too knackered. But tell you what, why don't you come round here for a quick drink?'

So I ended up going inside her flat, which in many ways was even better. There was a bottle of wine open and I accepted a glass, even though I don't much care for wine. The suggestion was that we 'chill' on the sofa and listen to some music, but she was having trouble hooking her phone up to her Bluetooth speaker. After watching her get very frustrated for a couple of minutes, I told her I was sure I could sort out the problem for her.

'I guess techy stuff is your bread and butter,' she said with a little laugh.

'Exactly. Hand me your phone and I'll sort it out in the time it takes you to make me a cup of coffee.'

I didn't want coffee, but I did want her out of the room. While she was gone I installed an app on her phone, hiding it in the 'Utilities' tile. It's a product marketed commercially as a parental control tool, but referred to on the street and the dark web as 'stalkerware'. With this installed, I could read all her messages, record her screen activity, track her location and use the microphone and camera to spy on what she was doing.

Not that I had any intention of doing anything so sinister. Of course not. I was no stalker, I was just someone who was looking out for her. Beautiful women who naturally attract attention are at risk out there alone in a huge city. Who knew what situations she could get into?

When all was said and done, I was just trying to protect her. To keep her safe.

# FORTY
## BRYONY

Now

*I need my phone.*

That was my first, purely instinctive thought. My crossbody bag was on the ground just in front of me and I scrabbled at the strap with my fingers, trying to pull it towards me.

'Oh no, I don't think so. I'll hang on to that.'

It was snatched from my grasp. The torch light was out now, but I could sense him behind me and smell the familiar notes of his aftershave. It was there every time I breathed in. A scent I knew so well.

'Now,' he said in a wheedling tone, 'if you're a very, very good girl and promise not to scream, I'll put the light on.'

I said nothing, too confused and frightened to respond.

'Can you do that for me?'

I nodded, although I wasn't sure whether I wanted it. There was a certain safety in darkness. It meant I didn't have to look at his face.

A harsh strip light was flicked on, and although it took a few seconds for my brain to process the information, I could see where I was. I was on the concrete floor of the bike store at Kenley Court. Why on earth had he brought me here of all places? Brought me to my own place of residence? Try as I might, I couldn't get any of this to make sense.

'Want some water?' He thrust a plastic bottle of mineral water in my direction.

I shrugged helplessly, indicating that my arms were tied.

'Oh yeah,' He bent over me and, with difficulty, untied the length of nylon rope round my wrists. 'Only temporary, mind. Just while you have a bit of a comfort break.'

I gulped down the water, so desperate to slake my thirst that it ran down my chin and neck.

'Better use the facilities while you can,'

With a mock courtly flourish, he pointed to the door in the corner. I staggered towards it and tugged open the door. Inside was a very basic toilet cubicle, which must have been there for the use of the caretaker and maintenance staff. I emptied my bladder and splashed water over my hands and face. When I emerged, I was handed a protein bar. I was still nauseous and didn't really want it.

'Well, go on then,' he said with a trace of irritation.

'Can I eat it later?' I assumed there would be a later. It seemed obvious that I was to be kept here.'

He brandished the rope. 'You won't be able to. Shame, but that's how it goes.'

'How what goes?' I demanded, tearing the wrapper off the bar. 'Why am I here?'

He observed me for a few seconds as I chewed on the bar. It tasted like sweetened dust. 'You're here because you owe me.'

My wrists were grabbed roughly and the rope was knotted around them.

'How do you work that out?' I asked as he thrust me down onto the floor in a seated position. There were a couple of cardboard boxes in a corner, and he broke them up, flattened them and put this makeshift mattress on the floor beside me. I looked him in the face properly now, taking in its familiar contours. The closely trimmed goatee beard, the slightly overlapping teeth. He was dressed in his street uniform of black padded jacket and black cap, the spider signet ring glinting on his finger.

'Come on, don't pretend you've forgotten already. I saved your life, innit.'

And with that, Kyle Kirkwood flicked off the light and left me, locking the door behind him.

The pounding in my head started to recede after I had drunk the water, but rest was impossible.

*How?* my wired brain was demanding. How is he here, now? How is he still alive?

I replayed the mental video tape of that night at Derwent Grove. What had we really seen? Leo's torch beam had picked out a man's body. A man dressed in black, lying face down and wearing a spider signet ring. But if the spider ring was a 312 insignia, then other members of the gang could wear the same thing. When the body's discovery had been reported in the news, we were only too ready to brush past the fact that the man's identity had not been revealed. Quite happy to jump to conclusions. And that conclusion was that we had seen the end of Kyle Kirkwood.

We had not.

My secondary question was how he had managed to procure a key to the bike store. In my time at Kenley Court I had discovered that they were handed out sparingly. Had Kyle stolen one, or was he conspiring with someone who lived in the building? Leo had one, because he kept his bike there.

Leo's bike. Surely he would come down here to fetch it in the morning, to cycle to work? The thought made my heart leap. Then just as quickly it sank, as I remembered he was away. We had arrived at work together the previous week, and he had told me he was attending a medical IT systems conference in Harrogate and would be gone until the weekend. Theresa then. She had a key, but as far as I knew she did not own a bike, so the chance of her coming down here seemed small. Somebody would, though, before long.

I consoled myself with this thought as I curled up on my makeshift cardboard mattress. Kyle couldn't keep me locked up in the bike store without discovery; it simply wasn't sufficiently private. My overcoat was still with me, half on and half off as it had been when I staggered out of the bar. I managed to shrug it around me as I lay on my side in the foetal position. I was cold and uncomfortable, but the effects of whatever drug had been used to spike my negroni were still in my system, dulling my senses despite my terror for my life.

Eventually that and sheer exhaustion brought a dreamless sleep.

# FORTY-ONE
## ROBBIE

Then

It was another week before we went out again.

Which was fine, because now I didn't have to spend the intervening days wondering what she was up to. Thanks to the app I had installed, a daily report of her activity was sent to my own phone. Yes, that meant that I would be aware if she was going out with anybody else. But also I knew that she was okay.

Not that she didn't have some sloppy security habits. She kept a record in the Notes app of all her login details and passwords: email, iCloud, banking, the lot. I made sure I kept a copy of it securely for her, even printed it out to be doubly sure. I was doing it in her own best interest. And no, I didn't read her emails or texts or listen in to her conversations. That would have been an invasion of her privacy. But I looked at her photos, including some racy ones she had sent to her ex. And that did get me thinking about sleeping with her. The more I looked at them the more I thought about it until it was pretty much all I thought about.

Eventually we would sleep together, and then we would

move in together, eventually getting engaged. But first things first. Another date was the next step; this time a double date. Sensing that she was unsure about the pace at which things were progressing, I suggested we go out for a drink with Dev and his girlfriend, Erica. More people: less pressure. The four of us went bowling, which she seemed to thoroughly enjoy, then Dev and Erica went home leaving us to have a drink on our own at the Bricklayers Arms.

We had a good chat, and she seemed relaxed, happy even. So I suggested going back to her flat with her. If she was prepared to put on red lacy lingerie for this guy Aaron, then why not for me? That photo had imprinted itself on my brain, making my pulse race.

She pulled a regretful face, turning down the corners of her mouth. 'Sorry, I've got an early shift. Another time, though, okay?'

This was good, surely? She hadn't ruled out the possibility entirely, even though earlier that evening I'd confessed to her that I'd never been in a long-term relationship. I left the pub determined that there would be another time, and that it would be soon.

I could see from her phone calendar that she had nothing on that Saturday. I could also tell from some online links she'd followed that she was interested in a new restaurant that had just opened in Peckham. One that everyone was raving about on their social media.

After phoning and pestering the manager at least five times, I succeeded in booking a table there. I then casually dropped it into conversation, making out that I'd originally been meeting a friend there, but that they had cancelled. She was only too happy to try it out and met me there looking spectacular in a cream off-the-shoulder dress. She wanted something called a

Pornstar Martini, which sounded disgusting to me, but from the way she winced when she first sipped it, was pretty strong. I quickly ordered her a second, then a bottle of wine with our food, which I barely touched myself.

There was something important that I wanted to broach with her over dinner. My former colleague Brett had invited me to his wedding in Kent, and I so desperately wanted to go to it with *her* as my partner. Would she come with me?

'Sure,' she said expansively. 'Why not? It'll be fun. I love a wedding.'

I wondered if it was the alcohol talking, because she was a bit tipsy at this point, but still, a yes is a yes. That's what Charlie drummed home to me when I told him about it later.

'She's into you, mate,' he declared, giving me a fist bump. 'Got to be.'

'Are you sure?'

'Sure. If a bird wants to go to an event as your plus one, that's a great sign. Shows she's keen, trust me.'

Now that we were officially a couple, it was definitely time for us to seal the deal. I had barely drunk anything for fear of not being able to perform, but I acted merry so that she didn't think it was a calculated move on my part. It's best if these things are spontaneous, right? I offered to share the taxi after dinner, and she snogged me drunkenly on the back seat. When we neared her flat, she told the driver not to stop, but to keep going to my address. So that was it. The condoms were ready in my nightstand drawer. The deal was sealed.

The cliché about great sex is that the earth moves. And now I get it, I truly do. Talk about an out-of-body experience, it was amazing. I was nervous; of course I was, but it's not like I was a virgin. I had a girlfriend, Bianca, when I was in the sixth form, and a couple of times during my uni days there were post-party one-night stands with a couple of girls who were drunk enough.

It was a close, humid night, and we were both sweating

profusely, but that only heightened the experience. It was incredibly passionate, incredibly intense, and she was everything I had imagined she would be, and more. It was so mind-blowing to see her lying there in my bed that I just couldn't help staring at her the entire time.

'I love you,' I whispered into her ear as I collapsed on the sheet next to her.

She didn't say it back, but she was feeling it too. I could tell.

## FORTY-TWO
### BRYONY

Now

I had no idea what time it was when I woke, nor when Kyle returned sometime later.

The bike store was a windowless subterranean cube, so it was impossible to tell. I was given a bottle of a sports drink and another energy bar and released to use the toilet again. From the tiny slit of window at the top of the toilet cubicle I could just about discern daylight. My best guess was that it was probably late morning.

'Where did you get the key to this place from? I demanded when he returned.

'Nicked it off the old girl on the first floor.' He must have meant Theresa rather than Lida. To him fifty was old. 'Followed her to Tesco and took it out of her bag.'

'How did you know she'd have a copy?'

He just tapped the side of his nose.

'So why are you doing this, Kyle? What's it all about?'

'Obvious, innit.'

'Not to me, it's not.' I rubbed my wrists and walked up and down on the spot to ease the stiffness in my legs.

'I saved your life, and I needed you to do something for me in return, but you messed up. You told Shane Quinn what was going on. And someone got cheffed. You know...' He mimed throat slitting.

I struggled to keep the emotion from my voice. Kyle was almost certainly armed, and I was completely at his mercy. 'I didn't agree to lure Shane away because I owed you my life. I did it because you were blackmailing me. You were threatening to go to the police and tell them...' My mouth was suddenly dry, and I stumbled over the words. 'Tell them it was me who was driving the car.'

'Oh yeah,' he grinned; an ugly, joyless grin. 'Let's not forget the little matter of you killing my cousin.'

I looked away.

'What is it they say? A life for a life. In the Bible, innit.'

An icy chill swept along the length of my spine. So he did mean to murder me.

'Is that what you want? You want me dead?' It came out as a croak.

But he was shaking his head, a look of satisfaction on his face. 'Nah. Not now. Not yet anyways.'

'What then?'

He tilted his head to one side. 'You know what, Ms Pearson? When I met you I thought you were a bit of a looker. A bit of class. But you thought you were too good for me, though, didn't you? A bit above me.'

'No, I...' My reply petered out. I was genuinely confused. I remembered Claire asking if Kyle's frequent visits were because he had a thing for me, and telling her that no, they were not.

'And as it goes, I always knew.' He was closer now, taking a strand of my hair and winding it between his fingers. 'I always knew I could get close to you eventually, if I wanted to. Once I'd seen if you could be useful to me.'

So that was it. This was the revenge he'd planned to exact all along. Oh yes, he meant to hurt me, but it was a different kind of physical assault he had in mind. I felt a swell of sudden heart-stopping, lung-burning panic.

As if he were reading my mind, Kyle parted his lips in a sneer, suddenly releasing my lock of hair as though it repulsed him. 'Nah, that ain't going to happen. Fuck no! You may be good-looking but you're really not my type, darling, sorry. I go for something a little bit more exotic. A bit more street. You know: tatts, piercings.'

So he wasn't planning on raping me. That took us back to maiming or killing. Cold comfort.

'What then?' I demanded. I decided acting as though I was afraid would not serve me, and I managed to inject some anger into my voice. 'What the hell am I doing here, in my own building?'

'There's something planned for you, and you'll find out in a bit what it is, don't you worry. You're about to find yourself somewhere a lot more comfy.'

I stared at him, my brain struggling to de-code what he was saying.

'Now be a good girl and hold out your hands.'

He tied my wrists; in front of my body this time instead of behind my back, then turned out the light and left again.

I sat there in the dark forcibly slowing my breathing and trying to engage my rational brain.

I couldn't afford to wallow in emotion; I had to think logically. Kyle almost certainly intended to come back for me when it was dark, which I calculated gave me a window of roughly four to six hours. So when might someone next come down to the bike store? Theresa did not cycle, nor did Ingrid, and old Lida on the first floor definitely did not. When the light had been switched on, I spotted just two bikes chained up in the racks. One I recognised as Leo's, but he was away. The other one, by default, must belong to Chu Hin Wong, the astrophysicist who lived on the ground floor. I had never seen him using it.

Waiting for someone to unlock the bike store was probably futile, but the other reason people came down to the basement was to put their recycling and refuse in the dumpsters. Sure enough, a couple of hours later I heard footsteps at the far end of the passageway.

'Hello?' I shouted. 'Hello? Can you help me?'

There was a rustling sound then the footsteps receded. I was behind a steel security door, and my voice was weak from thirst and exhaustion. Whoever it was simply couldn't have heard me. Despite my determination to remain rational, I could feel myself giving way to tears of despair.

It didn't help that it was cold – very cold – with an icy draft blowing in under the doorframe. I attempted to pull my coat closed, which was difficult with my hands tied. As I wrestled with the folds of material I heard a faint sound. The jangle of metal on metal. And with a sudden jolt of memory it came back to me. My door keys. I had taken them out of the crossbody bag so they wouldn't scratch my phone, and put them in my overcoat pocket. And on that same key ring was a key to the bike store, added to the bunch when I had coffee with Theresa in her flat.

Not only were my hands tied at the wrist, but they were stiff from cold and inactivity. Even so I managed to twist my arms to the side just far enough to allow me to reach my fingertips into the top of the pocket. I could just about touch the keys, but couldn't get enough purchase on them to pull them clear. After what felt like hours of wriggling and twisting but was probably only minutes, I managed to lean back and raise my knee to push the pocket a little closer to my grasping fingers. I pulled out the keys with a rush of triumph.

I still had no idea what time it was or how soon Kyle would return, but I knew I had to act quickly. Inserting the key in the lock with my hands tied was almost as difficult as retrieving them from my pocket, especially as I could barely see. I kicked open the door to the toilet, which let in a little daylight. This allowed me to identify a wooden pallet propped against the wall in the corner of the store. I manoeuvred it awkwardly up to the door with my tied hands, and standing on it could just reach the lock without being able to fully raise my arms. The key slipped in, it turned, the door swung open. I was free.

I needed to get my hands untied and I needed to get to a phone, so that I could call the police. Giddy with exhilaration, I stumbled round the side of Kenley Court to the front entrance. Thank God it hadn't occurred to Kyle to tie my legs too. Once I had unlocked the building door, I hesitated at the Salvesens' flat. If Leo was away, then only Ingrid would be in. I didn't much fancy explaining my predicament to her. I tried Chu Hin's flat but there was no reply.

Staggering up to the first floor, I hammered on Theresa's door, but there was no reply there either. Lida's door opened a crack.

'What's going on out there?' she demanded tetchily.

I couldn't face enlisting her help, which meant I had no choice but to carry on up to the top floor and my own flat. I no longer had my phone, but my iPad was still there: I could use it to contact someone. And the instinct to return to the sanctuary of my own flat was overwhelmingly strong.

Like a hunted animal, I slammed the door shut behind me. I locked it immediately to protect myself, still struggling with the cord round my wrists. The first thing that struck me was how warm the flat was. At first, I thought it was just the contrast with the bone-chilling cold of my basement prison, but then I realised that the central heating was on. This was odd, since it was programmed to come on after I normally returned from work. Was it a lot later than I had imagined? But no, it wasn't even completely dark outside and it was January. It couldn't be later than four o'clock.

And then I saw them. A large bunch of pink roses in a vase on the table. Exactly the same as the roses that I had left on the bar at Paper Tiger. My legs turned to putty and my tongue stuck to the roof of my mouth. Because in that instant, visceral instinct told me that I was not alone in the flat. That there was someone else already here. This knowledge came a fraction of a second before I took in a man's jacket hanging on the hatstand in the hall, and the small black backpack propped against the wall beneath it. Kyle. Blood pounding in my ears, I forced my jelly-like limbs to the far end of the hall. The door to my bedroom was ajar, and lamplight streamed through the gap.

That must have been what he meant. He was intending to bring me upstairs to the flat that I was so proud of. The very place he'd cased himself so many times. Now I thought about it, it was obvious. And I'd just completely played into his hands. By moving myself from one location to the other, all I had done was make things easier for him. The light blurred in front of my eyes and I felt my legs start to tremble. I was still clutching the keys with my tethered hands and I knew I had to turn round, unlock the front door again and flee. Somewhere, anywhere. I'd even bang on the front door of the grumpy Lida, or the sour-faced Ingrid if I had to.

Before I'd even had the chance to move, there was a sudden blur of movement and the keys were snatched from my hands. I inhaled so sharply that I felt as though I was about to pass out. Through the open bedroom door I could see that my precious vintage bedside lamps were on, and there was an ice bucket with a bottle of champagne and two glasses on the nightstand.

'Welcome home,' said Robbie Makepeace.

## FORTY-THREE
### ROBBIE

Then

Okay, it's time. I have to talk about Brett's wedding. It can't be avoided.

It was my idea that we would stay somewhere nearby overnight: some plush manor house hotel with a four-poster bed, for a prolonged session of lovemaking. But she insisted she had to get back to London afterwards, which is why I ended up hiring a car.

Even so, it all started out so well. She looked incredible in a pale-green dress and a straw hat. Everyone was looking at her, which was amazing.

'Can I introduce you to my girlfriend?' I said, when one of Brett's brothers came to speak to me. At this, she pressed her lips together as though she hadn't liked my choice of words.

'Did I say something wrong?' I asked after he'd gone.

'It's fine.' She smiled at me and laid her hand briefly on my arm. 'We'll talk later.'

The thing about weddings is that they serve nonstop champagne. I'm not really any more of a fan of it than I am of wine, but there's always someone at your elbow with a bottle, and by the evening portion of the reception I'd had quite a bit.

She decided she wanted to go home, and wasn't happy once we reached the car park and it became clear I was not exactly sober.

'If you knew you were going to be driving, why on earth didn't you stick to soft drinks?'

'I'm sorry, I guess I didn't really notice how much I had.' I waved a hand. 'You know how it is at these do's.'

'Give me the keys. I'll drive.'

'You can't. I only got the standard insurance, which just covers me.' She tried to take the car keys from me but I pulled them from her reach. ''Sokay, I feel fine. I'll be good to drive.'

'No way, it's far too dangerous.' The keys were firmly extracted from my closed fist. 'It's only a short journey, and there won't be any traffic; it'll be fine.' The straw hat was removed and tossed on the back seat.

And it should have been fine, it really should. Okay, there was a brief summer shower, but she was right about there not being any traffic. I tried to make conversation, but she said she needed to concentrate. I settled on looking at her profile instead. So beautiful. And then my mind went back to the night we had become lovers and I felt a crazy surge of desire. My reaction was purely instinctive; I reached for her, kissed her and started to caress her thigh. She was enjoying it, I could tell.

And then came the sudden, unmistakeable bang.

'What the hell was that? You made me hit something.'

I straightened up. 'Probably just a deer. One of those muntjac things.'

She hesitated, slowed right down.

'It's fine, keep going.'

But only a couple of miles later came an unmistakeable

sound from behind us: a police car siren. And then blue lights visible in the rear-view mirror. I've often asked myself how things would have turned out if that squad car hadn't happened to have been on patrol in the area and seen the accident. We'll never know.

I suddenly felt quite sober, my mind clearly focussed. 'Pull over!' I said urgently. 'Pull over, now!'

Before we'd even come to a halt I had my seatbelt off and my car door open, and I was running around to the driver's door and manoeuvring her awkwardly over the gear stick and onto the passenger seat I had just vacated. 'For God's sake, don't tell them you were driving,' I hissed as the patrol car pulled in behind us, lights still revolving. 'You're not insured, remember. I don't want you getting into trouble, or the car hire people imposing some sort of penalty.'

'Robbie! You're over the limit!'

'I'm fine now. It'll be fine.'

But even as I was saying this, the officer had approached and asked for my driving licence. By which time, of course, it was far too late. Because it had not been a deer. It was a pedestrian.


What happened next is still a blur. I remember the look of terror on her face, and her weeping silently, dabbing at her face with the sleeve of the green dress. I remember being breathalysed, and being informed I was at nearly twice the legal blood alcohol limit.

At this point she tried to attract the attention of one of the police officers and it looked as though she was about to say something, to come clean. I managed to catch her eye and shook my head. They took the car keys from me and made us both get into the back of the patrol car. As the doors were closed on us and the policemen were conferring about which station to take us to, I mouthed, 'It's okay, trust me.' If we had been violent offenders we would have been transported in separate vehicles, but rather than wait for a second patrol car to arrive, the police instead instructed us not to speak for the whole journey. I tried turning and looking at her, but she kept her head turned away and stared out of the window into the rain, still crying.

At Biggin Hill Police Station she was taken off to an interview room and I was put in a cell and left there. They wouldn't be able to 'process' me, as they put it, until I was fully sober. I think I must have slept for a while, probably because of the alcohol still in my blood, and after waking very early the following morning, my memory became sharper. There was a plastic tray with tea and cold toast, then I was breathalysed again, and a short time later a police doctor took a sample of my blood. I learned later that if they planned to charge you with a serious driving offence they needed to double check what other substances might be in your system.

Then I was taken to an interview room and joined by a duty solicitor, a man whose shirt barely buttoned over his beer belly and who had terrible body odour. He had trouble meeting my eye, and I soon learned why. The female detective sergeant who came in to conduct the interview told me with professional detachment that the man who had been hit had died soon after arriving at hospital.

I felt a plummeting sensation in my innards, and let out a gasp of shock.

'Perhaps you could give my client a few minutes to process this,' the solicitor offered.

I looked down at my hands for a few seconds. 'No, it's all right,' I whispered. The truth was I feared any delay would lead to me falling apart altogether. At this point I had no idea what she had said in her statement; I just had to guess. I said that it had been raining and dark, and that I hadn't seen the person walking along the side of the road. This was true after all. That I'd felt fine to drive, otherwise I wouldn't have done so. That my girlfriend wasn't insured on the vehicle so I didn't deem it appropriate for her to drive instead. That I'd never been in trouble with the law, not even a parking ticket. This was also true.

After I had completed the interview, I made a formal statement with the help of the solicitor, and was taken to the front desk, where the custody sergeant charged me with causing death by dangerous driving, contrary to Section 1 of the Road Traffic Act 1988. Police bail was granted, and the details of my court appearance confirmed. I think the solicitor said something about legal representation but my brain was simply no longer able to process anything further. What I do know is that at no point did I think of retracting my statement and telling them what had really happened on the road. That it was not me who had been driving. No, there was no way in the world I was going to do that. I had made it my mission to protect her at all costs, and if that meant going to prison, then go to prison I would.

I stumbled out onto the street unshaved and in my crumpled suit, my newly returned phone and wallet in a plastic bag. Somehow I found my way onto a bus to New Addington, where there was a stop on the tram network.

'Jesus!' my flatmate Pete said when I eventually got home. I wondered briefly what he was doing home, then remembered it was Sunday morning. 'You look absolutely wrecked. That must have been quite the wedding reception.'

'It was,' I said, forcing a grin. For some reason I couldn't tell him what had really happened to me.

'And you spent the whole night away... don't tell me, there was a woman involved,' He gave a suggestive chuckle.

'Yes,' I said, heading to the bathroom. 'There was a woman involved.'

He grunted and went back to reading the news on his phone. I did not tell him that this weekend was meant to mark the start of a wonderful life together for that woman and me. And that now it might never happen.

## FORTY-FOUR

### BRYONY

Now

'Welcome,' Robbie repeated, ushering me into my own bedroom. In my own flat. Which he was inside.

So bizarre was this set of circumstances that I did not even react, my tongue still feeling too big for my mouth. I stood there numbly while he untied the cord from round my wrists, tutting disapprovingly. Was he objecting to the fact that I had been restrained, or to the poor job Kyle had made of it, allowing me to reach my own keys from my coat pocket and escape from the basement? It was abundantly clear that Robbie and Kyle were working together. How? The prison connection: it had to be. Reece Parker.

I was shivering violently now, from the hours of cold and the shock.

'You'll soon warm up,' Robbie said cheerfully. 'I got here in plenty of time so I could get the heating on and make the place nice and toasty.'

His Scots accent was very pronounced as he said this last word. 'I thought you were in Scotland,' I said, confused.

'I was, but I'm not now. Obviously.' He smiled, and started removing my overcoat. Still stunned, I let him.

'How did you get in here?' I asked. I had definitely locked the front door when I left the previous evening.

'You've a spare set of keys, hidden under the left-hand planter outside the main door,' he said complacently, again speaking as though this was obvious. But the only person I had told about the keys, in case of emergencies, was Claire. Perhaps the hiding place was too obvious, and anyone intending to break in would look there. I could not go back in time and unmake this mistake, so I forced my mind to focus on something else.

'You're Mike,' I said heavily. 'Of course you are.'

With the gift of hindsight, it seemed obvious. The photo he had sent proving that he was real had been anything but. 'Mike' had been standing in a window lit by sunshine, but it was January, and already dark at the time he texted it to me. In the photo, the note attached to the flowers was typed; but the one on the flowers in the bar was handwritten. Tiny things. Vital clues.

Robbie was opening the bottle of champagne on the nightstand. He pulled the cork from the bottle with a flourish, as though we were on a date.

'Here.' He held out a filled glass towards me. I did not take it.

'I bought us steaks,' Robbie was saying, 'And some French fries and spinach. I know you like spinach.' He spoke as though we were an old married couple.

'You shouldn't be here.' My voice sounded odd – flat – to my own ears. 'You can't be here.'

But how to make him go? I asked myself helplessly. I was locked in, and he had my keys. I did not have my phone. Where was my phone?

My question was soon answered. There was an aggressive

hammering at the front door and Robbie went to answer it, admitting Kyle.

'She here?' Kyle demanded, then saw me in the bedroom doorway and looked visibly relieved. 'Thank fuck for that.'

'You screwed up,' Robbie told him, like a teacher admonishing a pupil whose work was sub-standard. 'That might have to affect your payment.'

'Not if you want this, it won't,' Kyle snarled, holding up my green bag. 'Her phone's in here, innit.'

Robbie reached for the bag, but Kyle snatched it out of his reach. 'Payment first. Then you get this.'

Robbie pulled a phone from his pocket and used it to make some sort of money transfer. This must have satisfied Kyle, because he tossed Robbie the bag with a grunt.

'Kyle!' I cried as he turned towards the front door. 'Kyle! Don't do this! For God's sake, you can't leave me with him!' I tried to go after him but he ignored me and slammed the front door behind him. Quick as a flash, Robbie locked the door again and pushed the keys into the pocket of his jeans.

'From what he told me, you thought he was dead.' He spoke with what almost sounded like amusement.

I didn't reply, instead going to the door and hammering on it. It relieved my frustration, but my efforts were futile. The entrance to my flat was tucked away at the back of the building, which had been a strong part of its appeal. All the flats had heavy fire doors, and if my neighbours were shut away behind their own, they would not be able to hear me.

Perhaps I could call from the window and attract the attention of someone passing on the street. I ran to the living room window, but all the catches were locked and the keys nowhere in sight. A glimpse of St Anselm's was just visible from where I was standing. How I wished I was there, surrounded by people I knew and trusted.

The lack of ventilation and the cranked up central heating

combined to make a stupefying stuffiness. I knew that the double-glazed panes would be tough to break, but started trying to identify an object that was both heavy and sharp enough to do so.

Robbie followed me into the room and, ignoring my frantic searching, held up his phone screen. 'Here; you might want to take a look at this.'

It was a brief news article, identifying the body that had been found on the Derwent Estate just before Christmas as Lawrence Hitchman, aged twenty-four. It had clearly not made the headlines, because I had missed it.

'Looks like he wore an identical signet ring to Kyle's,' Robbie was saying, as calmly as though we were discussing the weather. 'A lot of Kyle's gangland mates wear the same jewellery and clothes, so I suppose it was a natural assumption on your part. But as you realised yesterday, it wasn't Kyle.'

He'd put his own phone away and was looking at the screen of mine. 'Plenty of people keen to know where you are,' he said thoughtfully. 'Especially your colleagues, who are worried that you didn't show up today or phone in.' He gave a little shrug and started typing. 'Better put their minds at rest.'

'How can you get into my phone?' I demanded.

'Your passcode is zero-seven-zero-five-nine-one,' he said with a smile. 'Batshit idea to use your birthdate; you know that, don't you?

'I've told everyone you've got a nasty dose of this gastric flu that's raging round London at the moment, and that they're not to call round in case they catch it. That should keep them away for a few days at least. Oh wait, what's the name of the guy downstairs, the one who's a bit sweet on you? Your white knight.'

I kept silent. Leo felt like my only hope simply because he was the closest person – or at least would be once he returned from his course – and therefore the most likely to work out something had happened to me.

'Leo, isn't it?' Robbie was saying. 'I'd better message him too, hadn't I? We don't need him poking his nose in.'

I watched helplessly as he typed. Then he switched off my phone and placed it in the locking drawer in my antique bureau before pushing the key into his jeans pocket with his other hand. I could force that drawer open, I decided. It was made of thin rosewood and relatively flimsy. I could find a knife or a screwdriver and force it open. I looked away quickly, before he could work out my train of thought.

But Robbie was already in the kitchen, opening the fridge.

'Now, dinner!' he said brightly, starting to season the steaks that I would never eat. I watched him, my mind struggling to process the chasm between his reality and mine. I veered towards breaking down into screaming and shouting, attacking him even, but pulled myself back from the brink.

This would soon be over, I told myself bracingly, and then Robbie Makepeace would be on his way back to prison.

Someone would come. It was the faintest of hopes, but it was all I had.

# FORTY-FIVE
## ROBBIE

Then

My phone battery was flat by the time I had got back from Biggin Hill, so I had no idea if she'd tried to reach me.

I put it to charge while I showered and changed my clothes, and then checked. There was nothing, but I told myself this was hardly surprising. She was suffering the aftereffects of shock; we both were. So it took a little while before I remembered the stalkerware app I had installed on her phone. If she had spoken to anyone about what happened, I was in a position to find out.

Since we left the wedding reception, she had only received one message. It was from Claire, the friend she had been with when we first met at Alibi.

*Have you done it yet? xx*

If that referred to me, then perhaps she was asking if we had slept together. As I was thinking about all the implications, she sent a reply.

*I can't. Not now*

*Why, what's happened?*

*I'll call you.*

I watched on the app in real time as the call was placed, then inserted my headphones and listened in via her microphone. Any qualms I might have had about doing so disappeared when I heard her. For the first few minutes of the call, all she could do was sob, as her friend desperately tried to discover what was wrong.

The impact on me was visceral. Of course I was doing the right thing by protecting her. If I'd had any doubts before, they were dissipated by how desperate she sounded. Even so, she stuck to the version of events we had presented to the police. I knew she and Claire were pretty close, but still she didn't tell her what had really happened. The call was brought to an end quite quickly by Claire telling her she would come round straightaway. I was never privy to what they discussed, because either she switched off her phone at that point or the battery went flat.

The next couple of days were taken up by meeting with my brief – not the one with body odour, one recommended by a friend of Dev's – and preparing to be swallowed up by the British legal system. Once I had a better idea of what was going to happen, I felt calmer. I phoned her using a burner phone, in case our communications were being monitored. She assured me that she was all right, and that her concern was all for me, which made my heart swell. I told her I was fine, and that everything would continue to be so as long as we stuck to the story that I was driving. Anyway, I pointed out to her, even if I did change my statement now, I could face a charge of perverting the course of justice, which would potentially carry a longer sentence. 'I'm here to support you,' she said as we ended the call. 'Whatever you need.'

I felt a surge of joy. So she did have feelings for me, or why would she say that? It almost made the hell of facing prison worthwhile.

After my case had been heard in Woolwich Crown Court, I made contact with her again. I sent her a long text bringing her up to date. I told her I was about to be sentenced, and assured her I had a great brief who was confident that with my unblemished record I wouldn't do more than twelve months, possibly less. That it was far better it was me and not her that was facing this.

*I'd really like to meet up with you*, I wrote at the end of the text. *Because soon I won't be able to. Do say you haven't given up on me xxx*

Her reply didn't mention us meeting and yet it gave me so much hope. Because it showed she was committed.

*I'll be here to support you whatever happens x*

It was that commitment that got me through the nightmare that followed.

Eight years. An eight-year sentence. My brief reminded me that the guidelines permitted up to life, but admitted that even so it was harsh for a first offence and he had been expecting something less. You never knew what line an individual judge would take, he told me apologetically. But I knew I would be all right. I knew I would get through the time better than most of the men at HMP Rochester, because I had her waiting for me on the outside.

THE GOOD NEIGHBOUR 233

As soon as the initial shock of being locked up had started to wear off and I was beginning to get my bearings, I sent her a visiting order. And she came straight away, greeting me with a warm embrace.

Of course she was full of concern for me, which was touching, and I was able to reassure her that I was coping. I told her about the gym, and that I was hoping to be allowed to teach some basic coding skills.

'I know that if I've got you, I can get through this,' I murmured, as our fingers touched. The lightest touch, but it was like water in a desert. She leaned in and her curtain of hair grazed my face. I could smell her.

'The thing is,' I went on, 'I know what happened that night was terrible, but in a weird way it's brought us so much closer, don't you think? Going through an experience like that... it can only bind you. Because only you and I know the truth.'

A shadow passed across her face. 'Robbie... there's something you need to know.'

I stared at her, my throat constricted. I could tell from the tone of her voice that it was nothing good.

'I've been offered a new job. It comes with lots of opportunities for training and career development, so I'd be mad not to take it.'

'Of course.' I smiled, and tried to take her hand, but she pulled it back and rested it on her lap. 'Where is it?'

'That's the thing. It's at Monash Medical Centre.'

'And that is?'

'In Melbourne.'

'Melbourne in Australia?'

'Yes. I leave at the weekend.'

The shock was a body blow. For a few seconds I couldn't speak at all. 'Oh God.'

I felt bile rising at the back of my throat. 'I don't believe this is happening.'

'I can write to you. And the visa is only for two years. I'll be back long before you get released.'

Relief washed over me. My first thought had been that her plan was to emigrate for good. 'So you'll be here waiting for me when I get out?'

'Of course!' She gave me a beaming smile. 'Absolutely. And I'll write to you once I'm settled. Like you say, we're in this together. I'll always be here for you.'


She did eventually write, after what felt like an eternity. It had taken her a while to find a permanent address, she explained, but she'd just moved into a small unit; apparently the word Australians use to refer to self-contained flats.

It was a brief letter, with a few words about her job and the weather. I wrote back immediately, of course. After that first letter, she started using the 'Email a Prisoner' service. As a prison inmate I was not allowed access to personal computers or internet access for security reasons, but relatives and friends can send emails which are printed off for the prisoner to read. No doubt she found sourcing airmail writing paper and stamps too much of a chore in the digital age, but the printed communications felt a lot less personal.

They dwindled in frequency over the next couple of years, but then to my delight I received one which said, 'My change of address is below'. My heart leapt at this. She was coming back to the UK. But it was another Melbourne address. When I queried it, she eventually replied that she had extended her visa for work reasons. Soon after that, she stopped writing altogether, and eventually my own letter was returned with 'Not known at this address'. She had moved again without telling me.

The days of me being able to look at her phone were long gone, but I did not let that deter me. There are always ways and means. I may have had no access to the internet for personal use, but there were other cons who had illicit smartphones smuggled in. I paid to get a few minutes online and took a look at her Instagram account. Not only did she have an Australian boyfriend, but they were living together in a pretty little house with a white picket fence. They even had a dog. They were living the exact life she and I were supposed to have had. The life I was serving time for.

I remembered the last words she said to me as if they were engraved on my heart. *I'll always be here for you.*

But the thing you need to know about Bryony Ann Pearson is that she's a liar.

# FORTY-SIX
## BRYONY

Now

Robbie continued preparing dinner for two as though we were on a date.

He was not a natural cook, and I hated seeing him fumbling his way around my kitchen, banging drawers and cupboard doors as he searched for the correct utensil. I was almost tempted to jump in and help him, but I did not.

*We're just going to eat dinner together. I'll be able to talk to him, make him see sense. Then he'll let me go.*

I sat in front of the plate of overcooked steak, burnt chips and watery spinach, pushing them around the plate. I think I managed half a glass of Bordeaux, but only after watching Robbie like a hawk as he uncorked the bottle and poured it. I wasn't going to risk being drugged again.

By contrast, there was something almost childlike about the relish with which Robbie approached the meal, beaming at me between mouthfuls. He'd gained weight since I last saw him; his face doughy and pale, but he still had those ice-blue eyes.

'Come on, eat up!' he wheedled. 'The steak's a bit well-done, but it tastes fine with a spot of mustard and horseradish.'

'I'm a vegetarian,' I said flatly.

He slapped his forehead. 'Of course! Sorry, I forgot. Well, never mind, we can do something veggie next time. Or something with cheese? Now we're living together, you can show me some of your favourite recipes.'

'Robbie, we're not living together.' I kept my delivery as unemotional as I could.

He looked around in surprise, as though someone had just told him the earth was flat. 'Of course we are. I don't know what else you'd call this.'

I opened my mouth to object but he went on hurriedly, twisting the stem of his glass through his fingers. 'Of course, I know we would have wound up living together much sooner if it hadn't been for the accident. But no matter, we're here now.' He shoved another slice of the grey steak into his mouth.

I modulated my tone, kept it reasonable. 'No, we would not have ended up living together, because I never wanted that. I didn't love you.'

'Of course you did,' he said fiercely. 'We were lovers.'

I did not argue: it was futile. There was no point trying to shake him from his delusion; the most disturbing feature of which was that he didn't believe what he was saying any more than I did. I could see it lurking there behind his eyes: a distrust, a fury. What he felt for me was not love, but something altogether darker.

I insisted on clearing up, because it was easier to have a task to complete than be stuck inside my own head. I moved slowly, though, dropping with exhaustion.

'Right, time for bed,' Robbie said briskly. I turned my back on him and headed into my bedroom, undressing quickly and pulling on a large t-shirt. Robbie followed me.

'Where are you going to sleep?' I demanded as I climbed under the duvet.

'In here with you, of course.' He removed his shoes and socks and went round to the other side of the bed. Just as quickly I leapt out again. Christ, this is like one of those 1970s theatrical farces, I thought.

'I'm not sleeping with you!' I hissed at him.

He looked at me sadly for a second, then shrugged and got out of the bed again.

'All right, because I'm a gentleman I'll go on the sofa.'

He left the room and I sank back gratefully into my own familiar-smelling bed. Despite my churning fear, sleep overwhelmed me within seconds.

When I woke some hours later, I instantly sensed that I was no longer alone. Robbie was lying next to me, on top of the duvet but with the throw from the sofa covering him. He was deeply asleep, snoring faintly.

Recoiling in distaste, I got up and tiptoed round to his side of the bed. I lifted the corner of the woollen throw. He was still wearing his jeans, the lump where the keys were stowed clearly visible in the pocket. It seemed unlikely I could extract them without him noticing, and even if I managed it, I was pretty sure I wouldn't be able to unlock the front door without him hearing. On the other hand, surely it was at least worth a try. Anything was worth a try.

I reached out two fingers gingerly, but just as they brushed the fabric of his jeans, he rolled over abruptly, so that the pocket with the keys was out of reach beneath his left hip. I watched him for a few seconds, feeling anger and revulsion yes, but mostly pity. Then I crept into the living room.

Outside on the street there were still a few pedestrians about; shift workers and late- night drinkers. I tapped on the glass as loudly as I dared, and gestured frantically as a couple of men walking past looked up at me curiously. But their interest was fleeting and they continued walking without giving me another glance. From their vantage point, with my face two storeys up in a darkened room, they could probably barely see me.

Now wide awake, I turned my attention to the drawer of the antique bureau that had once belonged to my father's mother. Taking a short-bladed paring knife from the kitchen drawer, I inserted it in the lock itself and jiggled at the delicate brass cylinder. Nothing happened. I then inserted it in the top edge of the drawer and prised it free, splintering the wood around the lock. I was able to tug the drawer free and retrieve my phone.

Unsurprisingly the battery was flat, but I kept a spare charger in one of the kitchen drawers. Once the screen sparked into life I held it up to my face. Nothing happened. No face recognition. Robbie must have disabled it once he'd got into my phone. Instead, I was invited to enter my six-figure passcode. I typed in 070591. The digits on the keypad jiggled to show that the code was incorrect. He'd changed it. Of course he had. There were notifications on the screen of messages that I had received. Messages that he would reply to, pretending to be me. He could keep people at bay that way for weeks, maybe even months.

I stared at the screen for several seconds, then looked out of the window at the dawn sky growing silvery pale over the roofs of the hospital.

I was completely trapped.

There was a spare duvet in the cupboard in the hallway. I dragged it out and curled up in a foetal position on the sofa with the duvet over me.

Eventually exhaustion overcame me and I dozed for a few

hours. The flat was silent when I woke, but I could hear the distant sounds of traffic and voices on the street as people went about their daily business. Not rushing to work, but strolling with takeaway cups of coffee in hand, paper bags of fresh produce from the farmers' market two streets away. It was Saturday, I realised.

With the perspective of a new day, I felt a little more resilient, a little more optimistic. *Someone will come*, I kept saying in my head. *Someone will come. They have to.*

The clock on the oven told me that it was already almost midday. As I filled the water reservoir in the espresso machine and switched it on, it occurred to me that my monthly coffee pod subscription was due to be delivered soon. And the delivery driver the company used knew me by sight and often brought the package to my front door rather than leaving it in the entrance hall. It arrived on the 25th of each month and today was the 22nd. Could I hold out that long?

Robbie must have heard me moving about, because he appeared in the kitchen, still fully dressed.

'Morning!' he said cheerfully, as though we were a regular couple enjoying a regular weekend breakfast. I did not offer him coffee, but he took a mug from the cupboard as though I had.

'We're getting a bit low on milk,' he observed after opening the fridge.

I hoped he might see this as reason to leave the flat, but he went on cheerfully. 'Never mind, I'm okay with black. There's cheese and bread we can make into sandwiches, and you've got plenty of pasta we can use for supper. No more meat, of course. Can't believe I forgot that.'

I remained silent.

'Is that okay with you, babe?' he asked earnestly.

*Babe?* I felt as though I were appearing in some twisted, black-mirrored romcom. Impressing on myself that for now, at least, it was best I played along with him, I shrugged.

'Sure.'

The rest of the day dragged in a way I had never known time drag before. Whenever I glanced at a clock to see how much time had passed it was only five or ten minutes later rather than the hour it felt like. I went into the bedroom and emptied my wardrobe and chest of drawers, folding and re-organising all my clothes, while Robbie switched on the TV and watched the Champions League.

After it had gone dark and we had eaten pasta in bleak silence, Robbie suggested we watch a movie together.

'You've got microwave popcorn,' he announced excitedly, going through my cupboards. 'Perfect!'

While the corn was cooking he handed me the remote. 'You choose... whatever you fancy.'

Flicking swiftly past anything violent or criminal, I settled on a romcom I had been wanting to watch, grimacing inwardly at the exquisite irony of my choice. But the movie was entertaining and with my beleaguered brain desperately needing diversion, I eventually became engrossed in the plot. After an hour or so I was almost enjoying it, even reaching for the popcorn bowl and helping myself.

'See!' said Robbie triumphantly. 'This is fun. We *do* have fun together.'

I gave him a long look, but said nothing.

As the credits rolled, the unmistakeable sound of voices was audible, coming from the first-floor landing. In a flash it came to me. Every last Saturday in the month, Theresa hosted a book club in her flat, inviting a few ladies of a similar age round for wine and chat. The voices on the stairs must belong to her departing guests.

Immediately I was off the sofa, racing to the front door and hammering on it with my curled fists. 'Theresa!' I shouted. 'Theresa, can you hear me?!'

My voice broke into sobs as Robbie grasped me by the shoulders and dragged me away from the door.

'Come on, babe,' he said, adopting the same wheedling tone he had used when he wanted me to eat the steak. 'Let's not do this. We've had a lovely evening; let's not spoil things.'

I looked straight at him; the pale blue eyes now sunk in the fleshy face I'd once found attractive. 'You're the one doing this.' I could barely muster the energy to feel angry, 'Not me.' In the distance, I could hear the footsteps of Theresa's friends retreating.

Robbie led me by my wrist back into the living room. 'You don't want me to get Kyle's rope out again, do you?' He spoke as though he were reprimanding a wayward child. 'Come on, let's go to bed.'

Once again, I refused to share my bed with him, and once again Robbie capitulated and went to lie on the sofa. I was woken from a deep sleep sometime later by the sound of a voice speaking softly.

'This feels lovely, doesn't it? Oh, my darling…'

The word 'darling' had a distinct Scots roll of the 'r'.

'If you only knew how I've longed for this…the thought of being with you was the only thing keeping me going.'

This time, not only was Robbie on the bed with me, but he was underneath the duvet, his right arm resting on my shoulder as he stroked my hair and ran his fingers through it.

'Jesus!' I sat up, pushing his arm away. I considered the odds if it came to a show of force. Robbie was taller than me, but not in the best shape. I was smaller, but probably fitter. In that moment I decided that I would fight him if I had to. I had little to lose.

But Robbie merely mumbled, 'You don't understand.'

I waited for him to move, but he continued to stare at me

pitifully. In a repeat of the previous night, I extricated myself from the bed and retreated to the living room to sleep on the sofa that Robbie had vacated: the whole thing like some terrible bedroom farce.

*Someone will come*, I repeated like a mantra as I stared at the living room ceiling. *Tomorrow, someone will come.*

# FORTY-SEVEN
## ROBBIE

One year earlier

After spending the first four years of my sentence at Her Majesty's pleasure, I was released on licence.

I returned to my mother's house in Dumfries. In my mind this was never more than a temporary measure. She lived alone; I her only son. (I say she was alone, but after refusing me any sort of pet as a child she now had a ratty little Yorkshire terrier). It was always going to be awkward, given her desperation to hide the truth of my life from her genteel neighbours in Moffat.

How would I define my relationship with my mother? That's a tricky one. She referred to herself as a widow – again, the obsession with respectability – but the truth was my father had cleared off when I was two, never to be seen again. Perhaps he found someone else; even had another family. My mother would never talk about him, so I had no information to go on. For as long as I could remember, it was just me and her. At school the other pupils laughingly referred to me as Norman Bates, implying that we were like the mother and son in the movie *Psycho*, but the truth was we were never close. She behaved as though she were the landlady of a lodging house and me one of her guests. She took care of me efficiently but impersonally. Once I overheard her saying to one of her friends that she would rather have had a daughter. That it would be easier. So much for the mother and son bond.

And there was no male presence to help me navigate the world and teach me how to relate to the opposite sex. I remained terrified of girls. That is, until I met Bianca Gardyne. I suppose you could call her my first love. She joined the school in the sixth form: tall, blonde, sporty and popular. All the girls liked Bianca. All the boys fancied her. And it was me who she asked out on a date. Beautiful, tragic Bianca who was destined to lose her life on a school field trip, sending my life into freefall. I'd intended to leave my mother's house as soon as I could, and after Bianca's death I resolved to leave Scotland too, applying only to English universities. I never intended to return, but after prison, there I was.

When I first arrived back in Dumfries, I kept my head down while I weighed up my options.

At this point it was almost two years since I'd had any contact with Bryony. But now I was at least free to use the internet, and I intended to make the most of that freedom. My mother had offered me the use of her old and underpowered laptop, but I refused. It relied on an ancient operating system, but more importantly I did not want her reading my search history. I got into the habit of using the grand Victorian Ewart Library in the town centre, just until I could buy a laptop of my own. I had my phone back now, too, returned to me with the possessions on my person when I arrived at HMP Rochester. Of course, that model was now several years out of date, but it still worked fine.

As I said, I was weighing my options. I could always email

Bryony, or contact her on social media, but what could I possibly say? That she had betrayed me, and lied to me. That she had promised she would be here for me when I was released from serving a prison sentence for a crime *she* committed, but instead had fucked off to the other side of the world. Not only that, but she was living with another man, very likely to be married to him before long, from the saccharine photos of the pair on Instagram.

No, there was no point in making contact, because I was pretty sure of the response I would get. But information is power, is it not? And that was the power I now had. Because attached to a draft email on my own account was a copy of the document Bryony had carelessly kept in the Notes app. The one with all her login details. I even had a hard copy somewhere amongst the boxes of my stuff that had been languishing in my mother's garage for the past four years. She was using an Australian SIM card these days which prevented me employing the secretly installed stalkerware, but I could still access her iCloud. I had both her ID and password.

If I used them, Bryony would quickly receive an alert that someone had signed into her iCloud account and be urged to change her password. I had to act fast. The time difference was in my favour. If I accessed her information during the afternoon in Scotland, I would almost certainly have a window of several hours while she was asleep and unaware of the data breach.

I looked through her photo albums, but there was nothing there that I couldn't view on social media. Besides, I didn't particularly relish witnessing the images of her new life and her new love. I went through her emails, but apart from the occasional message to her father and stepmother she only really used it to contact retailers about online orders. Frustrated and running out of time, I was about to give up and sign out again when I saw some .ipa file extensions which contained the content from a journal app synched to the cloud. Someone without my training in IT probably wouldn't have spotted them.

My heart rate quickened as I opened the files. There was a lot of data there, more than I could read in one sitting. I pulled out the USB stick I had brought for the purpose and used it to copy the files. The library's computer room offered a printing service, but I was squeamish about the uptight bespectacled librarian being able to read what I was printing. Instead I went to a scruffy internet café and print shop on Queensberry Street and paid for a hard copy of all the files. The alternative was to install the relevant extension software on my mother's laptop and read it on there, but I didn't want her breathing down my neck, literally or metaphorically. The cost of printing the pages took quite a chunk of my limited funds, but it was worth it. Oh yes, it was well worth it.

Once my mother was ensconced in front of her favourite TV detective drama, I helped myself to a glass of her precious single malt and began to read.

Bryony made diary entries sporadically every few days or so, occasionally leaving gaps of a few weeks. I remembered the date that we had met at Alibi, and found the corresponding entry: 7th May, four-and-a half-years ago. Bryony's own birthday.

At first she said good things about me. She used words like 'nice' and 'attractive' and 'normal'. I felt a little rush of pleasure reading them. 'See!' I wanted to shout. 'There *was* something there between us. We *did* have a connection.' But then she just started bending the truth, making stuff up. Nonsense like implying we weren't really dating. If we weren't dating, then what the hell were we doing? And all those vicious exaggerations about when we slept together. Calling me sweaty, for example. It was hot, and we were engaged in physical activity. It's not wrong or odd to sweat in that situation. I read on, feeling a cold, panicky sensation, a churning in my guts.

'Are you all right in there, Robert?' my mother called. 'Would you like a cup of tea with a wee piece of shortbread on your saucer?'

'I'm fine,' I shouted through the closed bedroom door. 'Just doing some jobhunting.' I was supposed to be looking for work, but with a criminal record no one in IT will hire you. They're too scared of hacking and data breaches.

It got worse. The bit that hurt me the most – worse even than the spiteful incel comment – was what she wrote about my inviting her to Brett's wedding. Displaying the most horrible cynicism, Bryony confided in her journal that she would dump me after the wedding; worse still, using her attendance as an opportunity to meet other men. More lambs to the slaughter in the giddy whirl of Bryony Pearson's love life. I thought back to the text that her friend Claire sent her that evening: *Have you done it yet? xx*

I had naively assumed she was referring to the two of us having sex, but now I knew what Bryony had confided in her friend, it was clear Claire was asking if she had ended things. Bryony claimed she felt bad about me having to serve time when it was her her who hit the guy on the road, but did she really? It now appeared to have been all too convenient that I was locked away in prison while she continued to further her career and pursue a romantic life. Convenient as hell. She'd had no intention of sticking by me, wasting no time at all in fucking off to the other side of the world.

*I'll always be here for you.*

That had been the biggest lie of all. But Bryony Pearson was about to find out that ultimately, one way or another, all of us are punished for what we have done. And that includes her.

## FORTY-EIGHT
### BRYONY

Now

I woke to Robbie scrutinising the contents of my kitchen cupboards.

Sunday morning. I was supposed to be having a roast with the Quinn family. And the birdlike Miss Ember. At the thought of this haven of family normality, my chin quivered and tears pricked behind my eyes.

'I'm going to have to get us some more groceries,' he said with an exasperated sigh, as though the lack of supplies were my fault. 'And I'll pick up some milk while I'm out. I know you like a milky coffee.'

He put on the jacket that was hanging up in the hallway and went to the front door, reaching in the pocket of his jeans for the front door keys. I thought about rushing him then, as he undid the locks, somehow getting past him and onto the landing. But if I failed, he would tie my wrists again, and once that happened I would no longer have the chance to look for the second set of keys. Because it had occurred to me as I lay awake on the sofa in the small hours that there were two sets of keys in the flat. My original set that Robbie had snatched from me and stowed in his jeans pocket, and the set that I had had cut and hidden under the planter: the ones he had used to gain entry. Those keys had to be here somewhere.

So I watched him go, without saying anything, then began searching. I looked in all the kitchen cupboards and drawers, the cupboard in the hall, the dresser and wardrobe in my bedroom and the cabinet in the bathroom. Nothing. Feeling disheartened, I returned to the bedroom and took out a set of clean clothes, then ran a hot shower, first bolting the door to keep Robbie out. The face that stared back at me in the bathroom mirror had chalky skin smeared with dirt and three-day old mascara making black rings round red-rimmed eyes. *Who are you?* I asked the woman in the mirror. I no longer recognised myself; not just my reflection, but my entire existence. I'd always been the level-headed, ambitious, grounded girl. How the hell did I wind up here, in this nightmare situation?

If I couldn't get out of the place then I could at least feel clean while I was in it, I told myself firmly. I washed my face before stepping into the shower and lathering my hair with shampoo.

Then I heard it. Footsteps approaching the front door.

I switched off the shower tap so that I could listen. There was a sharp slapping sound as something was pushed through the letterbox.

'Wait!' I scrabbled for a towel, slipping on the shower tray in my haste and banging my knee on the tiles. My fingers fumbled for the bolt on the bathroom door, and I ran into the hallway.

'Wait!' I hammered on the front door, but whoever I had heard was now retreating down the staircase, out of earshot. Then I saw the package that had been pushed through the letterbox. It hadn't come from the postman, because he left the mail in the front hall. It was a manila envelope with handwriting on the outside. 'FOR BRYONY PEARSON', it said and then, '*Sorry I was so late getting these to you, Tom.*'

Tom? Who the hell was Tom?

And then it came to me: he was the nice-looking estate agent I had bumped into at the New Year's Eve party. My hands trembling, I ripped the envelope and pulled out a set of keys. A set of keys for my own front door.

I stumbled back into the bedroom, dropped the towel and pulled on my fresh clothes, my hands shaking so much I could hardly lace my trainers. Taking nothing with me – I couldn't use my phone anyway, now that Robbie had blocked my access – I unlocked the front door. I started down the stairs with the keys still in my hand, taking them two at a time. At the exact same moment, the front door slammed as someone came into the building.

What happened next was swift and vicious.

Robbie dropped the shopping and rugby tackled me on the flight of stairs between the first and second floors, knocking me to the ground and winding me. I cried out in pain and heard a rustling behind Lida's front door as she attached the security chain and pulled the door open a crack.

'Lida!' I shouted, but she swiftly closed it again and retreated. Robbie pressed his left hand hard over my mouth to prevent me making any further sound, and with his right bent my arm behind me and up my back. I struggled, but the idea that he was out of shape proved illusory. Using the threat of a broken arm he marched me back up the stairs and into the flat, locking the door behind us.

'Where the hell did you get these from?' he demanded, wresting a set of keys from my hand for the second time in two days.

'Someone put them through the door.'

Robbie's eyes narrowed. 'Someone? Who?'

'It doesn't matter, he's gone now.'

'He? Oh, I see... another one of your men, was it?' he spat. 'Because there's always someone with you, isn't there?'

I tried to wriggle free from his grasp to get back to the front door, but he yanked my arm up higher so that I could not move without excruciating pain. The length of cord that Kyle had used was still on the kitchen counter, and he grabbed it with his free hand and tied my wrists behind my back. Only then did he lock the front door, tossing the keys onto the kitchen counter. The set from his jeans pocket joined them, followed by a third pulled from his inside jacket pocket. So that was where my spares had been. Turning the flat upside down had been a waste of time.

'You won't be needing any of those,' he said. 'Not anymore.'

He looked me up and down, as if trying to make a decision about something. 'Nope,' he said, shaking his head. 'Tying the wrists alone isn't enough. Kyle tried it and look what happened: you got out.'

I was forced down onto one of the dining chairs and my ankles were tied, then my wrists retied behind the back of the chair, fully immobilising me.

'Better,' he observed.

*Someone will come*, I kept saying inside my head. *Someone will come.*

Now that I was safely restrained, Robbie unlocked the door again and went to fetch the shopping he had dropped in the stairwell. 'We don't want people wondering who it belongs to,' he mused, as he came back into the flat and re-locked the door. He started unpacking a loaf of bread, a carton of milk, some apples, a plastic-sealed piece of cheddar and a packet of Twix bars. With a sense of dazed disbelief, I watched as he unloaded my dishwasher then filled a bowl with hot soapy water and wiped down my kitchen surfaces.

'It's a shame that things have ended up like this,' he said once he'd finished, opening a Twix and offering me half. I shook my head furiously. 'For a while there it felt like we were getting our relationship back on track.'

'There is no relationship,' I said coldly. 'There never was.'

He looked at me, astonished. 'Of course there was! We went out. We slept together. We attended a wedding as a couple. What else would you call it?'

'Robbie!' My voice was shrill with frustration. 'Yes, we went on a few dates. We even slept together. That's nothing unusual in twenty-first-century dating. But it was never going to go anywhere. I liked you, but that was all. It wasn't love.'

'I went to prison for you, Bryony!' He was shouting too now. 'I served four years for you even though it was you who was guilty. I did it because I thought we had something special. You even came to see me: you said you'd stick by me. Why else would you do that if we didn't have something real?'

It was my turn to become angry. 'No!' I roared. 'No, Robbie! I felt sorry for you when you went to prison, but not because I was guilty. You went to prison because of an accident that was *your* fault.'

His face became pale, his pupils so large his eyes looked black all of a sudden. 'What do you mean, the crash was my fault?'

'Robbie, we both know what happened! I ran the car off the road because of what you did.'

Suddenly I was back there again, hands gripping the steering wheel as he drunkenly attempted to press his mouth on mine. His hand between my legs, pulling up the hem of the green dress, his fingers digging into the flesh of my thighs, going higher. I had been concentrating hard on the road, but the probing fingers that had threatened to penetrate me made me look away for one split second, sending the car drifting to the left. A memory I had worked hard to suppress all these years surfacing now more vividly than ever.

'It was your fault that guy died, not mine!' I shrieked, finally losing the control I'd fought to hold on to. 'Yes, I felt badly for you because I'm a decent human being with empathy, but it was right that you were sent down rather than me.'

'So why not just tell the police the truth?'

I could see it all so vividly. Robbie pushing me into the passenger seat, getting behind the wheel. 'Because you had already told them the lie. And because, I admit it, I was scared.'

We stared at each other for a few seconds, then he broke eye contact and turned away.

'So what's the plan, Robbie? Tell me,' I said, my voice quiet now, rage burned out. 'What are you going to do now? You're crazy if you think you can keep this up forever.'

'Oh, that's right,' he sneered, stepping closer to me. In his hand he held a short knife that he had been using to cut up an apple. He thrust it near to my face. 'Women like you think that men like me are crazy. That we're pathetic. That's what Bianca thought of me, and she ended up regretting it. Oh yes,' he spat, and his saliva landed on my face. 'She paid for it. Big time.'

'Who's Bianca?' I asked, hoping to get him to move the knife away.

'Girl I went out with when I was eighteen. Only it turned out she was only going out with me as a dare, a little joke with her friends. She started texting me, and she was sharing the messages I sent her behind my back. She asked me to meet her one night, and like an idiot I showed up, only to find she was there with her mates. Some of them filmed the whole thing and shared it on Snapchat. Everyone saw it, not just the rest of the sixth form but the whole school.'

He adopted a sneering expression. 'So when we were away on a Duke of Edinburgh Award field trip, I got her alone and confronted her. The little witch was only too happy to admit she'd been stringing me along from the get-go; she thought it was hilarious.' His pupils were so enlarged now his blue eyes were almost black. 'She was still laughing when I picked up a rock and hit her on the side of the head, then pushed her into the River Esk.'

I felt a lurch of dread. 'You killed her?'

He shrugged, apparently unconcerned. 'Was it me, or was it the river? Official cause of death was drowning. Yes, she'd had a bash to the skull, but her body had been dragged over so many rocks on the river bed it was impossible to tell that one of her injuries had been inflicted before she fell.'

There was a terrible silence for a few seconds during which I felt the blood drain from my face.

'I proved to Bianca that I was not the idiot she took me for, and now I'm proving to *you* that I'm not the loser you think I am. I installed surveillance on your phone years ago. I hacked into your iCloud and you didn't even notice. I read all your deluded swooning in your diary over men like the Cypriot doctor.' With the next sentence he made small jabbing movements with each word. 'You're the crazy one. Not me.'

So many small clues snapped into place in my mind, like pieces in a jigsaw. I drew in a long breath, shaking my head. 'Robbie. Think about what you're doing. You're out on licence, so you're going to serve the rest of the eight years, plus whatever you get for kidnapping. Which I imagine carries a pretty stiff sentence.'

He ignored this.

'The police will get to know the truth, you know.'

He put the knife back on the counter and turned to look at me again. There was a strange expression on his face that I could not quite read. A mixture of triumph and weariness, sadness even. 'You know none of this has been how I thought it would be. It doesn't feel how I thought it would feel.' There were tears welling in his eyes.

'What do you mean?' I asked, but he ignored the question.

'Anyhow, it's all there on my phone,' he went on. 'A copy of your journal where you admit you were driving and lied about it. As you've said yourself, perverting the course of justice is a serious offence in its own right.'

I gave a bitter little laugh. 'So, now *you're* planning on turning *me* into the police, is that what you're saying? How the hell is that going to work?'

But he was shaking his head. 'You're right, Bryony; who did what is pretty much irrelevant now. I'd rather end it all than go back to prison. So that's what I'm going to do. I'm going to end it for both of us and that way...'

His face wore an expression of terrifying certainty.

'... you and I will be together forever.'

## FORTY-NINE
### ROBBIE

One year earlier

The desire to make Bryony Pearson pay ate away at me for months.

But there was precious little I could do about it from ten thousand miles away. It wasn't as though I could fly out to Australia: I couldn't afford the flight. I was picking up a few bits of basic IT work here and there, small cash in hand jobs where people didn't bother with a DBS check. But I wasn't earning anywhere near enough to fly to the other side of the world, and my mother certainly wouldn't have sanctioned a loan for such a frivolous endeavour.

Then several things changed. Firstly, in the spring after my release, I saw from my surveillance of her social media that Bryony no longer appeared to be living in the twee little love nest with Surfer Guy. Secondly, I discovered to my shock that despite my logging into her iCloud, she had still not bothered to change her password. An omission that's pretty typical of women like her. So one evening when I was bored, I checked through her emails and saw that she was applying for jobs. But not jobs in Australia. Jobs in London. She was planning to return. The thought made my spine tingle. A couple of months later she secured the job at St Anselm's in her old South London neighbourhood. Her flight was booked for September.

None of this would have been much help to me, stuck in Scotland. I couldn't afford London, not without a proper salary. I was still in touch with Dev and Charlie, but they were both married now and I could tell their small-minded wives would not look kindly on an ex-convict sleeping on their sofa. But then something else of significance happened. My mother had a stroke, her health compromised by the stress and anxiety of her son being in prison. She was admitted to the stroke unit at the Western General but a few days later had a second, more serious, stroke and died.

It was a shock, of course, but also an opportunity. Within a week of the funeral I had given away her annoying rat of a dog to one of her neighbours and put her house on the market, instructing the agent to price it low for a quick sale. Even at a reduced price, the handsome sandstone villa eventually fetched a very decent amount and left me with several hundred thousand pounds as my inheritance. That was the upside of being an only child, I thought, as the 'For Sale' board was hammered onto a post by the front gate. I arranged for a house clearance company to come and empty the place, then used my mother's debit card to remove all the cash from her current account and booked myself on a train from Dumfries to Euston.

I already knew that Bryony was buying a flat in Beckenham. On her return to the UK she had started using the SIM card for her former UK mobile, conveniently cloning the data from this old phone onto whatever new handset she had acquired. And because she was too ditsy to check these things, the stalkerware was still installed alongside all her other apps. So I was aware when she made the offer just after arriving in the country, meanwhile based at her father's house in Sussex while the purchase went through.

I rented a furnished studio flat in Tulse Hill, close enough to be able to keep tabs on her, but not so close that I would bump into her in the grocery store. I found a bit of freelance coding work, but I now had enough of a financial cushion not to need to worry about that too much. Which left me free to keep an eye on Ms Bryony Pearson.

Keen to move all aspects of my life onto a more normal footing, I reached out to Charlie, and to Dev and to Brett. Although they all claimed sympathy for my situation, promises to meet up never materialised. I was effectively ostracised. However, there was one person who was keen to meet up with me after my release. Mr Clifford Godley.

What is there to say about Cliff?

A career criminal of the old school, he'd been a regular of the prison system since the age of seventeen. He even claimed to have known the Kray twins, although by my reckoning he'd still have been a child when they were sentenced to life. When I came to share a cell with him, he was in his early sixties, but looked older. His offending went from handling stolen goods, through burglary to a couple of armed robberies. Having him as a cell mate turned out to be a piece of luck in the end, although we got off to a rocky start. A softly spoken avuncular man, he reminded me of Ronnie Barker's character in *Porridge*. Like I said, an old-school criminal, who believed in employing good manners until he had a reason not to.

Everyone in HMP Rochester respected Cliff, and if you had his protection, others would leave you alone. He took a kindly interest in showing me the ropes when I first arrived, green and scared. Until, that was, he discovered the details of my conviction. Because, by a freakish coincidence, his nephew

Lee Sweeney was close friends with a man called Kyle. And this Kyle was the cousin of Reece Parker, the man who I was alleged to have mown down.

I had fully intended to keep the truth to myself. But to avoid being stabbed in the shower with a weapon improvised from a razor blade or something stolen from the metal workshop, I shared the facts with Cliff. I told him that it was not me who had been driving the car, but the girl I was with. I avoided telling Cliff her name, or anything about her, so that he couldn't pass it on to the victim's relatives. Because it's important to remember, at that point in time, I didn't know the truth about Bryony Pearson. I was still loyal to her, still wanted to protect her.

I was worried that Cliff might think I was lying to shift the blame, but he must have been able to tell that I was sincere. And once he was sure that it was not me who had killed Reece Parker, Cliff took me under his wing. Until he was released three years into my sentence, I enjoyed a relatively stress-free existence. Once he had left I was moved to a single cell, and by then my fellow inmates had come to understand that I was no kind of threat. Or perhaps they thought Cliff would have my back even from the outside. Either way, I was largely ignored.

And now that I was out, I had been summoned, and Cliff Godley was not someone you ignored. I'd given him my old mobile number, I number I kept once I was released, and he sent me a text with an address, a day and a time. I caught a Central line train out to Epping, and while it was rattling its way through the far eastern suburbs, I caught up with what was currently happening on Bryony's phone. When I saw that she had now agreed completion on Kenley Court for early November and was busily making her moving plans, I felt a little quickening of excitement.

Cliff lived in a neat late-50s semi-detached on the north

side of Epping town centre, a fifteen-minute walk from the tube station. It had a pretty front garden either side of a crazy-paved path lined with bright pink and orange begonias. I arrived at three thirty, exactly as instructed, and there he was at the front door, in slippers and a knitted cardigan, welcoming me in.

'Robbie, old son, good to see you. Come in, come in!'

A small woman with iron grey curls appeared in the doorway behind him, wiping her hands on her apron. 'This is Doreen, my better half. Cup of tea for the lad, Dore, there's a good girl.'

He ushered me into a cosy sitting room decorated in a style not dissimilar to my mother's house. There was a carriage clock ticking on the mantel above the electric fire; the kind presented to employees on their retirement, which seemed ironic. Cliff saw me looking at it and smiled, as though in on the joke.

'Everyone gets to retire in the end, son, even cons.'

'Even you, Cliff?'

'Even me.'

I looked at him more closely. He'd put on some weight since we were inside, but even so he looked old and tired. 'You're not tempted to take on any more jobs then, Cliff?'

'Can't say I'm not tempted, son. Would be nice to take on just one more, something that would pay enough to buy a nice little apartment on the Costa del Sol. That's Dore's big dream.'

On cue, Doreen came into the room with a tray of tea and chocolate biscuits, which she placed on the coffee table before retreating.

'But I don't know... I can't be sleeping in a cell bunk with my lumbago. Not at my age. Nah, time to give it all up. How about you, son... you managing to keep your nose clean?'

I told him that I was. That I had somewhere decent to live and was finding some work, deliberately not mentioning that I had just inherited a sizeable sum of money. You didn't discuss that kind of thing with the criminal fraternity, not if you had any sense.

Cliff took a swig of tea and bit into one of the biscuits before leaning down to stroke a fluffy grey cat that was stretched out in front of the fire. 'Good for you, son. You deserve it, especially since you were wrongfully convicted.'

I drank my tea. 'So, what can I do for you, Cliff?' I knew he wanted something. This wasn't just a social call: that wasn't how his kind operated.

'That bird who was driving the car that killed Lee's mate's cousin, your ex-girlfriend... you never did tell me her name.'

I shook my head. 'No, I didn't.'

'Protecting her honour, that's to be commended. But the thing is, son, the lad's family are understandably still cut up about it. And I've told them I'll help them out by passing on the information.'

I felt an involuntary shiver run through my body. 'Her information, you mean?'

'That's right.' Cliff broke off a piece of chocolate biscuit with a satisfying snap. The carriage clock ticked. The cat let out a low rumbling purr. We could have been discussing goings on at the local bowls club.

'And it's the man's cousin who wants to know?'

'That's right, son; he does.' He munched the biscuit, adding, 'I expect he just wants a bit of a chat with her, you know.'

We both knew this was not true, but I went along with it. By this time, there was no loyalty to Bryony, no protectiveness. She had betrayed me in so many different ways. Nor was I finished with her myself, but that didn't mean I wasn't going to hand her off to the criminal fraternity. Let them do their worst; it could only make things more interesting for me, as I sat back and surveyed her life. In that moment I felt like some God-like puppet master, pulling all the strings.

'Of course,' I said easily. He handed me a lined pad and a pen and I wrote down her full name and the address of the flat she was about to move into.

'Anything for you, Cliff.'

# FIFTY

## BRYONY

Now

I was frozen with shock.

The cord tethering me to the chair prevented much movement, but even if I had been free, I would not have been able to move. I could barely even breathe, my chest so tight that I was struggling to suck air into my lungs.

All my mental energy had been focussed on finding a way to escape. I had not thought further than that, not cast my mind forward to what Robbie's endgame might be. He had turned away from me now and was putting the food away in the fridge, food we were no longer going to need.

Knowing my only chance was to keep calm, I tried to engage him in conversation, but having acted the role of the model boyfriend for the past two days he was suddenly mute and withdrawn. He released me from the chair just long enough to use the bathroom, keeping the knife in his hand to discourage me from any sudden moves. Then I was tied up again. Outside, dark was falling on a bleak, grey January afternoon.

'What are you going to do with us?' I asked, as Robbie made

himself a cheese sandwich in silence. He had offered me one, but I could not force food past the knot in my stomach. 'I'd quite like to have an idea of my fate, if that's all right with you.'

'You don't need to know that,' he said flatly. 'Just that I had it all planned, in the event that...' He let the sentence trail off.

'In the event that... what?' I spat. 'That I turned down the chance to become your girlfriend?' I was already failing in my attempt to remain calm.

'Like I say, I have a plan for every eventuality.'

Of course he did. If nothing else, Robbie had already demonstrated a prodigious ability to plan. He was sitting at the table now with his sandwich in front of him and my phone in his hand, tapping away rapidly. No doubt answering the latest concerned enquiries from my nearest and dearest. There would be more and more of them as more time elapsed. In fact, that was my only chance, I realised. To somehow delay events long enough for somebody to come to the flat. I tried to calculate who that might be. Leo was due back from his course some time over the weekend; it could be him. Then there was the coffee delivery man, who might arrive in the morning. Or perhaps Theresa had heard raised voices and would come and investigate. Perhaps I could attract her attention now?

'Theresa!' I bellowed at the top of my lungs, making Robbie jump. 'Theresa! Are you there!'

'Oh no, you don't!' Robbie was instantly on his feet, grabbing for a tea towel and forcing it into my mouth, tying it in place so that only muffled sounds came out. 'We're not playing that game!'

Once I had fallen silent, he took the throw from the sofa and draped it over my shoulders. 'You should try and sleep now; we've got to be up very early.' His voice was matter of fact, as though we were setting off on a holiday. 'I've told Kyle to be here at four a.m.'

'Kyle?'

'Yes. I've offered him another five grand if he'll act as driver again. And I'll need his help getting you into the car. Much like before.'

I stared at him, fear enveloping me like a chilly veil. Abruptly he switched off the light and left the room. I heard the shower running in the bathroom. Shrugging off the throw with my elbows, I kicked hard at the ankle restraint until it was sufficiently loosened for me to plant the soles of my feet on the floor. I was now able to tip forward into a semi-standing position, albeit still attached to the chair and with my hands behind my back. Then, by using a combination of nose-scrunching, chewing and gurning, I managed to remove the tea towel from between my jaws.

With a strange crab-like gait I made it to the kitchen counter. The sets of keys that Robbie had tossed there were visible, the metal glinting in the light from the window. Picking them up with my hands was an impossibility since they were still tied behind my back, but I worked out that I could just about grab the leather keyring of my original set with my teeth. Quite how I would then use the keys I had not worked out, but this felt like a start.

As I balanced there with keys between my teeth and a chair attached to my back, like a strange circus performer, Robbie came back into the room. His hair was wet from the shower and he was dressed only in a t-shirt and jogging bottoms.

'Oh no you don't!'

With one savage blow he knocked me to the floor. Unable to break my fall with my hands, I landed face first to a hideous crunching of bone. Blood spurted from my nose and my mouth. I had bitten into my tongue.

'Why don't you just kill me now?' I said thickly through the blood. 'Just get it over with.'

With a strange echoing cry, he snatched one of my pewter

candlesticks and held it aloft. In the thin grey light from the window I could see that once again there were tears in his eyes.

A split second of silence was followed by the scuffle of footsteps, someone calling my name. And then, with an earth-shattering, splintering crash, the front door was broken open.

# FIFTY-ONE
## ROBBIE

Four months earlier

Once Bryony had moved into her new flat, I decided to exploit my role as puppet master. I was going to have some fun with it.

Although I could keep up with her daily life pretty effectively via the stalkerware app, it was more entertaining to do some on-the-ground stalking. After all, we're always being told we need to minimise our digital life and engage with the real world. So I followed Bryony in the street. I followed her from her flat to the hospital a few times. I followed her when she went to meet her friends. I found out more about those friends and the lives they led. But this quickly felt a little empty. I needed more.

I turned to her journal entries again, and discovered that she had a ridiculously puerile crush on some Greek god of a doctor at the hospital. So far, so predictable. Depressingly predictable. But there was no reason not to exploit the situation, and by swooning like some silly schoolgirl over the guy she was really just asking for it. I bought a burner phone and started messaging her as Dr Andreas Koros. She was only too keen to play along, and desperate to meet up with him. Sadly, 'Dr Koros' could not attend their planned assignations. From her later text messages it became clear that she did eventually go on a date with the real Dr Koros, but that it led nowhere. I really enjoyed this little piece of irony. Something was going on with her downstairs neighbour, too, but from the few messages they exchanged it was hard to decipher the exact nature of their relationship. It didn't seem to be romantic. Was it linked to her later switching off her phone and disappearing from the grid for a few days before Christmas? Possibly. In my idle moments I tried to figure out what exactly the connection was between her and Leo Salvesen.

But all this was irrelevant games playing, and after a few months back in London I inevitably wanted more. I wanted to get close to Bryony again. I wanted to be with her as a partner. As a lover. I'd once thought that was about to happen, and I was robbed of the experience.

It quickly became obvious that to get as close as I wanted, I would need help. And so once again, I caught a Central line train and returned to Epping, only this time it was at my own instigation. Cliff was surprised and, I sensed, a little annoyed at me turning up at his house uninvited.

'Robbie, lad... did we have an arrangement I've forgotten?' he asked, once Doreen had let me in. He looked worse than when I'd last seen him: paler and puffier.

'No, I was just...' I could hardly claim to have just been passing. 'No, I needed to pick your brains about something.' I handed Doreen a bunch of flowers I'd bought on the high street, and she disappeared to put them in water.

Cliff sank back into his leather recliner chair and muted the racing he was watching on TV. The fire was switched off this time, and there was no fluffy cat stretched out in front of it. 'Go on then, let's have it.'

'That friend of your nephew Lee, the one whose cousin was killed – Kevin, was it?'

Ever the criminal with a criminal's mindsight, Cliff narrowed his eyes. 'Who wants to know?'

'I do,' I said simply. 'I need his name, and an address and a way of contacting him.'

'Why?' he demanded.

I shrugged helplessly. 'Look, Cliff, it's a long story—'

'Something to do with that bird, no doubt.'

I did not confirm or deny this.

'Not sure I can do that, son. This Kyle's had a few run-ins with the law himself, and I've got to think of his privacy. I don't want to go upsetting Lee, either.'

'I'll make it worth your while.'

Cliff threw back his head and laughed at this. 'Yeah, right! And the rest.'

At this I reached in my backpack and pulled out my cheque book. I had brought it along as a prop really; it was an old one I'd had since long before I went to prison. I, like most people my age, never used cheques anymore. But Cliff was old school and he and Doreen probably did.

'That apartment in Spain you've got your heart set on... would this help with the down payment?' I wrote out a cheque for ten thousand pounds.

Cliff looked first stunned, then wary. 'This rubber?'

I shook my head.

'Where did an ex-con like you get this sort of cash?'

'My mum died,' I said simply. If in doubt tell the truth.

'I see. My condolences.' He looked at the cheque for a long time. 'Tell you what, I'll let our Doreen take this down to the building society and pay it in. If it's legit and doesn't bounce, I'll give you the information you need.'

I was about to ask how I could be sure I'd hear from him, but thought better of it. You didn't question men like Cliff.

'Fair enough,' I said, standing up. 'I'll wait to hear from you.'

Three days later I received a brief text message from Cliff. As usual there were no niceties.

*Kyle Kirkwood. Lee reckons still based with his mum 205, Hazlett House, Welling Way, Eltham*

Then there was a mobile number. Bingo.
Smiling with satisfaction, I texted back '*Enjoy Spain*'.

Dealing with Kyle Kirkwood proved to be trickier.

To begin with he didn't answer texts at all, and when I tried to phone him he either cut the call or yelled abuse at me down the line. I had to contact Cliff again and get him to ask his nephew to try and reason with his friend. Eventually, Kyle agreed to meet with me. Maybe curiosity overcame him, or maybe it was just the money. Because of course he wanted paying, and he must have heard via Lee Sweeney that I was good for the cash.

We arranged to meet at a ten-pin bowling alley in Bromley. His choice not mine. I couldn't help but be aware of the irony that the last time I'd been bowling I'd been on a double date with Bryony. It was a horrendous place, all pink and purple neon lighting and needlessly loud music. As if it wasn't hard enough to hear someone speak over the rumble and clatter of the bowling balls hurtling down the lanes. But maybe that was the point.

Kyle Kirkwood was an odd-looking man, dressed in his gangster's uniform of black athleisure wear, signet ring as big as a gull's egg on his left hand. His head seemed too small for his body, his eyes too close together, and he had a sculpted chinstrap of a beard. On the other hand, he was bulky with gym-honed muscle, and no doubt strong. Which would suit my purposes very well.

'I want twenty grand, innit,' he said before we had even taken our seats on the plastic banquettes in the refreshments 'zone'.

'Okay...' I said slowly. This was more than I had planned on parting with, though obviously I had enough in the bank. On the other hand, Kyle Kirkwood did not seem the sort of man you could haggle with.

'You've got it, yeah?'

'I have, but—'

'And this is to do with Bryony Pearson?'

'It is.'

He pulled a vape and puffed on it, despite a sign on the wall saying they were prohibited.

'Tell me what you know about her.'

He filled me in, although some of it was hard to follow. It did help complete the picture of what the hell had happened to Bryony in that period when her phone went dark. Something to do with her helping her friend's nephew double-cross him, which had led to him almost being killed, and one of his mates being fatally stabbed.

'Anyway, what d'you want me to do to her?' he grunted after he'd finished his rather rambling tale.

'I don't want you to do anything to her,' I retorted hotly. 'Well, I do,' I continued. 'But it doesn't involve hurting her. You'll need a car of some sort. You can get your hands on one I take it?'

'It'll cost extra. Extra expense, innit.'

'No,' I said flatly and firmly. 'For twenty grand I expect you to be able to come up with a vehicle.'

I laid out the plan for him, one that I could not possibly execute on my own. I would go into Paper Tiger, buy the drinks, tell the barman the flowers were for Bryony, then go into the gents toilet. Everything would be as it seemed, except that while the barman's back was turned I would tip Rohypnol into whatever drink she had ordered. I would then leave the bar via the back exit or fire door, and lurk somewhere with a view of the front entrance. When she realised that 'Mike' was not coming, Bryony would leave, by now under the influence of the Rohypnol. I would give a signal to Kyle, who would be waiting in his car a little further up the street. He would pull up and bundle Bryony into the car.

'Take her straight to Kenley Court and put her in the locking store in the basement.'

I knew all about this from Bryony's journal, where she had talked about how her neighbour Theresa had been to some meeting and secured them both a key to the store.

'You'll need to get hold of the neighbour's copy of the key,' I instructed Kyle as he vaped impassively in my face. 'It's probably in her handbag somewhere. Again, for twenty grand I expect you to figure that out for yourself. Leave Bryony overnight to sleep off the drugs, then move her up to her flat. Only that will have to wait til three or four in the morning, once you're sure all the neighbours are in bed and asleep. We can't risk you being seen.'

'And when she's back in her flat – then what?'

'Then you'll get the second part of your fee. If you give me your bank details I'll transfer the first half now.'

Kyle held out his phone and showed me the peer-to-peer money app he favoured, then AirDropped his account details to my phone. I transferred ten thousand pounds to the account, and saved his details.

'I'll text you details of the time and location,' I told him.

'Sweet.' He stood up and left.

It was as simple as that.

. . .

A week or so later, it all went pretty much to plan.

I stole photos from some random guy's social media and used them to create Mike. I even used my middle name knowing full well that Bryony would never have taken the trouble to discover that I was Robert Michael Makepeace. Oh, how I enjoyed that little detail. I knew her so well by now, after reading her innermost thoughts, that I could tailor his profile to match what she needed. What she imagined she needed, at least. And from my access to her phone, I was aware that she was now using the Align dating app. It was simple enough to set up a profile matching the parameters she herself set in her search criteria. Sure enough, we were quickly matched, and started chatting.

I was pretty sure that following her experience of being catfished she would be wary about meeting up. It was just as well I had experience of using AI and could – quite literally – manipulate the situation. Using one of the stolen photos, I created an image of 'Mike' holding a bouquet of flowers with a personalised note addressed to her. Buying real flowers that were as identical as I could find, and leaving them on the bar for her was intended to allay her fears, both about her date showing up, and him being a real person. Which of course he was not. It was me who ordered the drinks and told the barman who they were for, but he didn't know who I really was, nor did he care. Like I said, almost everything went to plan.

Kirkwood completed his part of the evening as well as could be expected. The only thing he screwed up was restraining her so inefficiently that she managed to get out of the bike store a little early. Something that didn't matter in the end, because she did the most foolish thing possible and headed to her own flat, where I was ready and waiting for her. I was a little surprised to hear her key in the lock, but I didn't let that show. As I said, I was ready for her anyway. And since my reflexes were far faster than hers at this point, I succeeded in taking her set of keys off her before she had the chance to resist.

But what did not go to plan was how I felt seeing Bryony in the flesh after all this time. It was not how I thought I would feel. I was floored by how beautiful she was, even after spending nearly twenty-four hours locked up. And instead of feeling angry and vengeful, my heart sang. *Yes*, said the voice inside my head: *yes, yes, yes! We were meant to be together*.

This was how things were supposed to be all along.

# FIFTY-TWO
## BRYONY

Now

From the hallway, light flooded into the room, which was a sudden blur of sound and movement.

There were male voices; voices I recognised. Someone was pulling the chair upright, untying the cords on my wrists and ankles. Someone else switched on a light. Shane Quinn was standing there with Claire's husband, Ryan Byrne, and behind them Leo Salvesen. In their attempt to take in the scene and work out what sort of condition I was in, they failed to prevent Robbie from racing into the hallway. He tugged his jacket from the hatstand, sending it crashing to the floor, grabbed his backpack and hurtled through the open front door.

'Go after him!' Ryan bellowed, and Shane ran in the same direction, vaulting the fallen hatstand. As Leo helped me onto the sofa and poured me a glass of water, Ryan was talking into his phone.

'Police please, and an ambulance... yes, the patient is conscious and breathing... an incident of kidnapping and false imprisonment... Kenley Court, Beckenham.'

'It's okay, I don't need an ambulance,' I mumbled. 'I'm fine.'

'You are not fine,' Leo said firmly. 'Let the medics check you over at least.'

'I'll have something stronger,' I mouthed thickly through my swollen tongue when he offered me more water, and he fetched a shot of whisky. As we waited for the police to arrive, Ryan explained that Claire had received a strange text from me, crying off attending the family Sunday lunch.

'It addressed her as "Clare" without an "i", and that's not a mistake you would ever make. And there was something about the syntax that didn't feel right. I told her to phone you and despite calling several times, you didn't pick up.' He gave my shoulder a squeeze. 'So we decided I would come over, and bring Shane as back up.'

'Claire suggested they call in on me and ask if I knew what was going on,' Leo interjected. 'I'd only been back from Harrogate a couple of hours so I had no idea, but I volunteered to come up here with them...' His voice trailed off and he pointed back in the direction that Robbie had fled, his expression confused. 'But that wasn't Kyle, was it?'

I shook my head, but found that I was unable to say any more. Shane burst back in through the door. 'He got away,' he gasped, bending forward with his hands on his knees to catch his breath. 'Christ alone knows how, because he'd no shoes on. He must have hidden in a side alley somewhere. I looked, but no luck.'

The sound of a police siren carried up from the street below, and blue lights blinked against the living room walls. Once the police officers were in the room I had no choice but to try and explain the events of the past few days, but it proved almost impossible for me to order my thoughts. My attempt was interrupted by a team of paramedics, who examined me and took my blood pressure and heart rate. They wanted me to go to hospital once the police had taken my statement. My first instinct was to refuse, but in the end my radiography training told me that I probably needed an X-ray of my nose.

Before the paramedics took me downstairs, Leo found my phone in the kitchen and helped me re-set the password and Face ID so that I could use it again. 'Get some rest as soon as you can,' he said as he followed us down to the front door of the building. 'I'll text you later.'

He kept his hand protectively on the small of my back, as though reluctant to let me out of his sight. 'I'm all right,' I assured him, although it was the adrenaline speaking. 'I'll be fine.'

Ryan and Shane followed the ambulance, and sat in the A&E waiting room until I had been scanned by my colleague Marat. I could tell that he was alarmed at my injuries, but he maintained his professional demeanour throughout as he confirmed that there was no break in my nose but a lot of bruising and a nasty laceration on my tongue. He discreetly summoned Bianca, one of my favourite nurses in the department, and she quietly and efficiently cleaned up my face.

'You must come back to ours,' Ryan said once I was cleared to leave. 'Or to Dervla and Pauly's.'

But I shook my head firmly. 'It's not safe. Robbie will know your addresses.'

'How about Miss Ember's then?' Shane said with a grin. 'No one would ever look there. And she'd never squeal on you.'

I tried to imagine spending a night with the tiny, silent woman. I could not, but Shane's suggestion at least made me smile for the first time in days. Which hurt my face. In the end we settled on the flat belonging to Claire's Aunt Geraldine; a garrulous but motherly woman in her late sixties. She lived in a secure block filled with neighbours she had known for years, and plenty of security cameras. Ryan and Shane drove me there from the hospital, and left me in Geraldine's care, which involved the running of a hot bath and the making of Horlicks. This, Geraldine told me, was a panacea for all ills.

I collapsed into her soft, lavender-scented spare bed, overwhelmed by physical and nervous exhaustion and yet, despite the Horlicks, quite unable to sleep. Rising from the bed, I went to the window and stared out, across the roofs of South East London. Robbie was out there somewhere, lurking like a cornered animal. I knew deep in my gut that I hadn't heard the last of him. That he had something planned for me. I climbed back into bed, but almost immediately got up again; looked out of the window, paced.

'Is that you, Bryony?' Geraldine called out.

Anxious not to disturb her I kept quiet, but she appeared at the bedroom door anyway, swathed in a quilted floral housecoat.

'God love you; it must be so hard to switch off your mind after what's happened,' she murmured. 'How about if I bring my knitting in here for a bit?'

I feared she would ask me endless questions, but instead Geraldine sat there in silence, working away on what looked like a huge maroon sweater. The click-click of her knitting needles was instantly soothing. Eventually I drifted into a deep sleep.

Two days later, despite Geraldine's objections, I insisted on returning to Kenley Court. My flat was no longer a crime scene and the forensic team had now finished their search for evidence. Although, as Claire observed sardonically during a visit to me at Geraldine's flat, there are not many criminals who buy groceries, cook and clean. The SOCO team had removed the clothes and shoes that Robbie left behind and taken photographs, including one of the blood stains from my facial injuries.

Before heading home, I went back to Bromley Police Station to give a more detailed statement to officers from CID, and was supplied with a police response alarm. I was aware that those close to me thought returning to Kenley Court was a strange choice after what had happened, but to me it felt right. And Leo was there, on the ground floor. That made me feel a little safer. I had been signed off work, but fully intended to be at St Anselm's the following Monday, bruises or no bruises.

On Thursday morning, my doorbell buzzed.

'Courier,' the voice crackled over the intercom. 'Delivery for Pearson.'

I hesitated a few seconds then pressed the street door release button. There were heavy footsteps on the stairs, and a firm rap on my front door. My breathing quickening, I attached the security chain and pulled it open a couple of inches. A tall figure in bike leathers stood there, his face obscured by a motorbike helmet. He thrust a large padded envelope into my hand and strode off.

Once I'd replaced the chain I turned the package over in my hands. The courier company had attached a printed label with my name and address on it, but there was no clue as to the contents. It was quite heavy and felt lumpy. Instinct told me not to open it. Instead I messaged Leo.

*Are you at work?*

*Yes, but can come over if you need me*

I hesitated a few seconds, then typed a second message.

*No, I'll come to you. Meet me in the canteen in ten?*

It would be good for me, I reasoned, to normalise being back at St Anselm's ahead of my return to work. As I sat down at a table I attracted some curious glances, a few nervous waves, and mouthings of 'hi'. Andreas Koros did a dramatic double take, which I pointedly ignored. People would quickly forget, I reminded myself. The gossip about me would die down, just as the bruises on my face would fade.

Leo bought himself a coffee and carried it over to the table. 'What's up?'

I held up the package. 'This arrived. And... I know it sounds weird, but I didn't want to open it on my own.'

'You did right.' His voice calmed me, that radio presenter's baritone that had been one of the first things I noticed about him. 'Want me to do it?'

He took the envelope from me, opened it and slid out a lightweight laptop and two phones: one a smartphone, the other a cheap SIM-free burner phone. Reaching back in, he pulled out a handwritten note, which he handed to me.

*Here you are, Bryony: here's all the evidence against you. What you decide to do with it I will leave up to you. Til we meet again. xxx*

There they were like cold fingers reaching out from the past: the three kisses. I felt my stomach drop.

'Is it from him? From that guy who was in your flat?'

I nodded and gave Leo the note to read.

He frowned. 'What does he mean – the evidence against you?'

I pressed my fingers against my temples. 'He'd been hacking into my phone for ages... including reading my online journal. I presume he means the evidence that it was me that was driving the car that killed Reece Parker.'

Leo slid the devices and the note back into the envelope. 'You need to give these straight to the police,' he said firmly. 'No talking yourself out of it like before. Do you have a contact for the officer on the case?'

I nodded and pulled out a business card that I had been keeping in my wallet. 'She's DS Caitlin Warner. She gave me her mobile number.'

'Call her now,' Leo instructed me. 'I'll wait here while you do it. I'll even come down to the station with you if you like.'

The phone was answered after a few rings. 'Ah, Ms Pearson,' DS Warner said when I explained who I was and what I wanted. 'Actually, I was about to come over to see you anyway; we need to speak to you. Are you at home now?'

I told her that I wasn't but that I could be there in a few minutes.

'I'll come with you,' Leo said firmly. 'I won't come up to the flat, but let me walk you home, just in case you're being followed. This...' he indicated the envelope '... is proof your stalker is still very much out there.'

The doorbell rang fifteen minutes after I was back in my flat and I buzzed in two detectives: DS Warner and her colleague DC Templeton. Warner was a short, square woman with scraped-back hair and a mannish dark trouser suit. Minimal jewellery, minimal make-up. Templeton was a slight young man with a heavily freckled face.

'It might be an idea for you to sit down,' Warner said, indicating the sofa that I had slept on so recently. 'We have some news for you.'

I sat, and she sat next to me, adopting an expression of professional concern. Templeton hovered awkwardly behind the sofa.

'I'm afraid the body has been found, of a man who threw himself into the Thames from Southwark Bridge and unfortunately drowned. We're awaiting formal identification, but we have reason to believe it's that of Robert Makepeace.'

## FIFTY-THREE

### BRYONY

Now

Robbie's death changed nothing, yet at the same time changed everything.

He had intended me to make the choice. I realised this after I made cups of tea for the detectives and they subsequently left my flat: without Robbie's devices.

'You said you had something you wanted to talk about?' DS Warner had asked me as we waited for the kettle to boil.

'I'd just been wondering if there was any news of Robbie's whereabouts,' I replied. This was not an outright lie. I had, naturally, been wondering.

And so the police officers had no knowledge that Robbie's last act was to arrange for his laptop and phones to be delivered to me. In handing back the data he had stolen from me before he took his own life, Robbie was offering me the chance to take control of the narrative. In whichever way I chose. I could destroy the laptop and phones and say nothing, or I could hand them over to the police for them to be analysed and for the truth about that night in June nearly six years ago to become public knowledge. It was up to me.

Once the shock of this new state of affairs had subsided, I desperately wanted to speak to Leo. As soon as it was late enough for him to be back from work, I ran down the stairs and knocked on his door.

Ingrid opened the door. Ingrid, his sick sibling who I had mistakenly taken for his wife when I first moved in. She was wearing a thin cotton robe and the usual Birkenstock clogs on her feet. Her skin was the colour of a wax candle.

'He's not in,' she said flatly. 'He's out with Martine.'

The dietician girlfriend. I'd all but forgotten about her.

'Would you like some tea? I hear you had a bit of trouble... in your flat.'

This was the longest sentence I'd ever heard Ingrid utter, and the only social overture she'd ever made.

'No, you're all right.' I smiled. 'Thanks though.'

She gave me a brief smile in return and closed the door again. I returned to my own flat, feeling deflated and still unsure how to process the news of Robbie's death. I didn't want to do so in the very flat where he had kept me imprisoned, but if I went to visit a friend like Claire or Rochelle, I would be forced to talk about it, and I did not want to do that either. So I left Kenley Court and walked to the Odeon on the high street, where I bought a ticket to watch a film alone. I chose a romcom. It seemed fitting.


I had only been back from the cinema thirty minutes when there was a tentative tap on my front door.

After first fetching my police alarm and using the security chain to check the identity of my visitor, I opened the door to admit Leo.

'Ingrid said you were looking for me earlier, so I thought I'd better check up on you.'

'She said you were out with Martine...' I set the kettle to boil to avoid making eye contact as I asked, 'She's your girlfriend, right?'

He shrugged. 'It's just casual. Nothing serious.'

I made us both tea and relayed the day's events once we had sat down.

'But...' Leo looked confused, frustrated even. 'You didn't hand over Robbie's devices? Even though they've just found his body.'

'It hasn't been identified yet. And I just thought... what if he's not actually dead?'

'Bryony...' Leo set down his mug and buried his face in his hands. 'The police must be sure or they wouldn't have told you.'

'We thought Kyle Kirkwood was dead, and he isn't,' I pointed out.

'Exactly. Kirkwood is still out there and he knows that you were the person driving the car that killed his cousin. So all the more reason to get all the facts out there. So he no longer has a hold over you.'

Leo was right, and I knew it, yet some perverse instinct in me wanted to keep the truth buried. Part of me wanted to steal out in the night and throw the laptop and phones into the waters of the Thames, into Robbie's own intended grave.

I admitted as much to Leo. 'I was thinking I'd just chuck the laptop and phones in the river.'

He shook his head, not quite able to suppress a smile. 'Bryony, I think you know deep down that's not the answer. And listen, anyone of us is only a second's inattention away from an accident when we're driving. Parker's death was awful, but there but for the grace of God go any one of us who get behind the wheel.'

I flung my head back, closed my eyes and let out a deep sigh.

'Tell you what, I'll put you in touch with my mate Steve Adkins. Remember I told you about him? It's high time we stopped acting like a pair of vigilantes and brought in the professionals.'

I went to my father and stepmother's house in Sussex that weekend and returned to work on Monday.

On Tuesday evening, I bumped into Leo as I was leaving the hospital.

'How are you doing?' he asked, his eyes going automatically to the fading bruises on my face.

'Not too bad,' I told him, managing a smile. 'Listen, I wanted to ask you over for supper as a thank you for all you've done. I was going to do it anyway, before...' I flapped a hand in the direction of the bruises. 'Before this happened.'

'Are you sure?'

'Yes, I'm sure.'

'Look, it's a lovely idea, but maybe your flat is not the ideal venue. Not at the moment.'

There was a silence during which we must both have been thinking that the last time he was there, I had been tied up and he had been helping to break the door down.

'How about grabbing a meal at a pub,' he suggested quickly. 'The Bricklayers Arms?'

I shook my head; it reminded me of my early dates with Robbie.

'The Bunch of Grapes?'

I thought of Andreas. 'Too many people from work.'

In the end we wound up eating scampi and chips at a place called the Ten Bells, on the outskirts of Sydenham, but the events of the past three months came with us, too, and sat there between us like the proverbial elephant. Both of us tried to keep the conversation light, but still it was awkward. Our mutual interests and the things we had in common did not really have a chance to surface from beneath the weight of what we had both witnessed. In relationships – even in friendships – it seemed that timing was everything.

Later that week, Steve Adkins officially became my legal counsel. Together he and I took Robbie's phones and laptop to Bromley Police Station, and I gave DS Warner a lengthy prepared statement covering my involvement in the crash that killed Reece Parker and admitting that I had been the driver. By that time dental records had formally identified the body in the Thames as Robbie Makepeace.

I endured a stressful couple of weeks before Steve's name flashed up on my mobile while I was working in the MRI unit. I excused myself from the control room and went into the corridor to take the call.

'Bryony... Steve Adkins. I've got some news for you. Are you okay to speak now?'

My heart thudded against my sternum. 'Yes.'

'I've had a call from one of the lawyers at the CPS, and they've decided it's not in the public interest for them to proceed with either the death by dangerous driving charge or one for perverting the course of justice.'

I let out my breath in a huge exhalation. Steve waited a few seconds for me to collect myself before continuing. He stuck to the stiff, slightly formal jargon beloved of those working in the criminal justice system, but the gist of the message was clear enough.

'They take into consideration the false imprisonment by Makepeace, obviously, and analysing the content on his devices helped with filling out the picture. And then there were the mitigating factors from your revised statement: the fact that you had initially taken the wheel to try to prevent someone intoxicated from driving, and that Makepeace had initiated unwanted sexual contact while you were in control of the vehicle, preventing you from paying proper attention to the road.'

'So... is that it?' I asked, my voice barely above a whisper. I was leaning against the wall now.

'That's it, Bryony. The case against you has been closed.'

With the phone still in my hand, I slid further down the wall until I was on my knees. It was over; this reckoning that I had been running from for years. There was no need to keep running anymore.

# FIFTY-FOUR
## AFTERMATH

The months that followed were eventful, as spring arrived and slipped into summer.

I did not attend Robbie Makepeace's cremation. According to DS Warner, a few of his friends later took his ashes back to Scotland and scattered them there. Instead, very early one morning I took a bunch of pink roses to Southwark Bridge and dropped them into the water, waiting until they had drifted out of sight. By then I felt nothing but pity for Robbie, but I did this for myself as much as for him; to mark an ending.

Claire's son, Ronan Patrick Byrne, was born safely in early June, and I was named as one of his godparents, as was Shane Quinn, who had just started training as a chef. Shane and Kayla became engaged, and Shane was able to bring his influence to bear on his future father-in-law, Calvin Jevons. Jevons's word was enough to ensure that Kyle Kirkwood stayed well away from me. I never set eyes on him again.

As for Leo and I: after our evening at the Ten Bells we maintained a friendly but slightly awkward distance. Ingrid Salvesen's illness went into remission and she moved out of his flat. I thought that Martine might move in, but it turned out that she and Leo had quietly broken up. Leo, finally, was single. At one time this might have presented an interesting possibility, but the reality was that too much had happened; too many dark and frightening things that we had witnessed together. It would be impossible to capture the carefree mood that ought to accompany the start of a romantic relationship.

Besides, after a couple of months it had become clear to me that I needed to put some distance between myself and Kenley Court. My flat had been my haven, then became my prison. Much as I tried, it was impossible to feel the same way about the place. But one day in the future perhaps, when neither Leo or I were still living in that building, could something happen between us? Deep down, I knew I had not ruled it out.

For the time being I was focussed on creating some distance. I was thinking about joining Flora in New Zealand – not forever but perhaps for a six-month sabbatical – and had started looking at radiography jobs in Christchurch. I wasn't yet sure whether I was going to sell my flat or rent it out, but one oppressively humid day in July I called into the local estate agent to make some initial enquiries.

As I was emerging from their offices into the glaring heat of the street, distracted by the possibilities ahead, I ran straight into a tall figure, almost treading on his feet.

'Oh, I'm sorry!' I looked up at a familiar set of dimples.

'It's Bryony, isn't it? Tom. Tom Burridge... don't tell me you're selling the flat already?'

'Thinking about it. But more likely renting it out as an investment.'

He turned down the corners of his mouth. 'That's a shame.'

'Long story. Very long story.'

He took in my face, held eye contact.

'Here's an idea,' I said, 'why don't I tell it to you over a drink. Preferably a long cold one.'

'Do you mean right now?'

*Timing is everything*, I reminded myself. Of all the many things I had learned in recent months, this was now uppermost in my mind.

'Yes, right now.'

He looked slightly fazed by my spontaneity, shooting his cuffs so that he could check his watch. 'Um, let's see... I've got an hour before my next viewing. I suppose it could be right now.'

'Only I'm never having a drink with a man again unless we arrive there together. Just in case I'm stood up. Or he turns out to be someone else.'

Tom raised his eyebrows. 'Wow. Is that part of the story?'

'It is.'

'In that case, let's go right now...' He gestured to his right, indicating that we should start walking along the street in the direction of the nearest pub. 'Because I want to hear your story, Bryony Pearson. All of it.'

## A LETTER FROM ALISON

Dear reader,

Thank you so much for choosing to read *The Good Neighbour*. If you enjoyed it and want to keep up to date with all my latest releases, just sign up at the following link. Your email address will never be shared and you can unsubscribe at any time.

*www.bookouture.com/alison-james*

All thriller writers have to be amateur students of human behaviour. At the heart of constructing a plot there is always the same question waiting to be answered: why do the characters make the decisions they do, and how do they deal with the consequences? Bryony Pearson makes a fatal error and gets away with it, but discovers that she still can't escape the fallout from her actions.

I hope you enjoyed reading *The Good Neighbour*, and that if you did you would consider writing a review. It's always good to hear what you think, and it makes such a difference helping new readers to discover one of my books for the first time.

I also love hearing from my readers – you can get in touch through my social media.

Thanks,

Alison James

# KEEP IN TOUCH WITH ALISON

facebook.com/Alison-James-books-1882183775425985
tiktok.com/@allyjay855
x.com/AlisonJbooks

# PUBLISHING TEAM

Turning a manuscript into a book requires the efforts of many people. The publishing team at Bookouture would like to acknowledge everyone who contributed to this publication.

### Audio
Alba Proko
Melissa Tran
Sinead O'Connor

### Commercial
Lauren Morrissette
Hannah Richmond
Imogen Allport

### Cover design
Eileen Carey

### Data and analysis
Mark Alder
Mohamed Bussuri

### Editorial
Natasha Harding
Melissa Tran

**Copyeditor**
Donna Hillyer

**Proofreader**
John Romans

**Marketing**
Alex Crow
Melanie Price
Occy Carr
Cíara Rosney
Martyna Młynarska

**Operations and distribution**
Marina Valles
Stephanie Straub
Joe Morris

**Production**
Hannah Snetsinger
Mandy Kullar
Ria Clare
Nadia Michael

**Publicity**
Kim Nash
Noelle Holten
Jess Readett
Sarah Hardy

**Rights and contracts**
Peta Nightingale
Richard King
Saidah Graham

Made in the USA
Columbia, SC
02 October 2025